Loose Ends/ Mind Tricks

SAUL WARSHAW

Full Moon Publishing, LLC

Glade Spring, VA

Website http://www.fullmoonpublishingllc.com

Cover Designer Danielle Stamper

ISBN: 1946232424
ISBN-13: 978-1946232427

CONTENTS

LOOSE ENDS

SAUL WARSHAW

CHAPTER 1

THE YEAR 2004

Rose Shapiro, my secretary-receptionist-bookkeeper-Jewish mother-everything called on the intercom.

"A Mr. Martin Gershon is on the line. He says he is a lawyer, and he needs to talk to you."

The "you" in this case – is me.

I'm Will Jonas, and for the last nine years, I've been running a private investigations agency, which I started after I retired from the Los Angeles Police Department, where I'd put in 30 years, most of them as a homicide detective.

I didn't recognize Gershon's name – but when a lawyer calls, it's usually because he has some investigative work for me to do.

So of course, I picked up my phone. Hey, I always can use new clients.

"Mr. Gershon," I said, "What can I do for you?"

"Mr. Jonas, you can listen to what I have to say – and then I hope you'll agree to go with me to the State prison in Lancaster, to talk with my client."

"Whoa, let me interrupt you right there. I have to tell you that if I had a nickel for every inmate who sends me letters claiming his innocence – if only I could help – well, I'd be retired and working on my golf game."

"This is different," Gershon came back at me. "My client is not the subject here. It's his cellmate. My client believes the guy has been railroaded into prison for up to 11 years, for a crime he did not commit. Even though he did plead guilty. But my client says there are – what he calls 'very odd circumstances' that make the whole conviction suspect."

"Look, Mr. Gershon…"

"Call me Marty."

"Okay, Marty. What you're telling me *is* a little different, since it's not your client who's claiming he was wrongly convicted. I see that. But what makes your client capable of deciding that his cellmate is innocent? Is your client one of those jailhouse lawyer types?"

"No, he's not. Let me explain. First off, my client is now a third of a way through a 20-year sentence for murder. That charge is not going to change, and his sentence is not going to be reduced. In other words, he's not getting any sort of a deal here.

"But before he was convicted, my client had a doctorate in psychology, and a successful practice. And since he's been in prison, he's kept at it. Informally, of course. And over the years, he's helped many prisoners deal with their rougher mental health problems.

"And what he's telling me is that this cellmate of his—and he's only been his cellmate for several weeks – is not guilty. He is convinced that the man did not commit the murder for which he's been convicted."

"Still, Marty," I came back at Gershon, "What you're telling me is a lot of subjective stuff. Nothing factual. And I just don't see how I can help."

"Will, when my friend in prison asked me to help, I knew I'd need a top flight investigator with a background in homicide. I did a computer search. Saw your name, among others. And then I Googled you. Interesting stuff. You and your partner, Charlie Black, solved a lot of high visibility homicides. Got a lot of press coverage.

"And as I read through those clippings, there was something you said, that convinced me you were the investigator I wanted.

"You were talking about the need to make sure policing and justice were not just for the privileged. They were for everyone. And sometimes, in order to bring justice to the underprivileged, you and your partner would bend the rule book.

"Will, do you remember saying that?"

"Yes…but…"

"No 'buts' Will. You said it. And here's an opportunity for you to live up to what you said. You'll be compensated for your work of course. My firm will put you on retainer, as soon as you agree. Come on, Will. Let's bring some justice to someone who just might be innocent."

Marty went silent. Like any good lawyer, he knew when to end his argument – his summation – on a high note.

"Okay, Marty," I gave in. "You win."

CHAPTER 2

Which is why, the next day, I'm sitting in Marty Gershon's Lexus, on State Highway 14 North, riding up to the California State Prison, Los Angeles County, in the city of Lancaster.

Lancaster is in the northern part of the County, in the Antelope Valley. This is in the Western Mojave Desert, a little over an hour's ride north, from the San Fernando Valley, and my office in Woodland Hills.

With a population of about 168,000 people, Lancaster is California's 31st largest city and it has a lot more going for it, economically and culturally, than the state prison. Back in 1992, there was some initial opposition to the prison, but that quieted down, with the dropping of the description of the place as "Lancaster State Prison."

I'd used the time on the trip to Lancaster, to learn more about the persistent, and persuasive, Marty Gershon.

"I'm a partner in a law firm in Encino," he told me. "We specialize in real estate law. Shopping centers, multi-story office and residential buildings, major long term commercial tenant negotiations."

"So why are you representing an ex-psychologist, who's been convicted of murder?"

"Jack Lewis and I became friends in the first grade, in Van Nuys," Marty answered. "And we've remained friends. All the way up to, and including today. And before you ask, let me say that I know Jack did commit the murder. He admitted it. Openly. After his conviction and sentencing."

Marty waved his hand at me.

"Any more questions about Jack – I'd like you to ask him yourself. I need you to be convinced, both of his sincerity, and the truth of what he is claiming about his cellmate."

I asked, "Same reason you won't tell me anything more about the cellmate? Because you want me to hear the deal firsthand, as Jack sees it."

"Yes. If you're going to take this on, I feel you need to listen to Jack first. And then do your own investigating."

"Okay, so I'm doing that," I pointed out, "although it's kind of bassakwards."

Marty looked over at me and grinned.

"Hey, Will, I'm a lawyer. You know lawyers can't do anything in a straightforward way."

"Yeah, I know. Convoluting is built into your DNA."

....

I'd been to the prison a few times, but this would be my first as a private investigator. And given that fact, I decided I'd leave my weapon at home. I usually carry a Glock 22, but it was sitting in my desk drawer, safety on.

As Jack Lewis's attorney, Marty did not need to follow the visitor day rules. Instead, he had to arrange a client-lawyer appointment, which he'd done, listing me as his investigator. After the necessary sign in procedures, we were put in a small client/attorney meeting room, which was furnished with a table and two chairs on one side and one chair on the other side.

Marty and I sat down, and a moment later, a guard brought Jack Lewis in, guided him to the chair opposite us, and connected Lewis to the table with a heavy metal chain.

"I'll be right outside the door," the guard told us.

He gave Lewis a silent warning, then he left, and we were ready to go.

Lewis was Marty's age, of course, but prison had imprinted him. His skin was pale. He was a bit hunched over. And his eyes kept moving, as if he were checking to see what dangers might threaten him.

But once he started to talk, Lewis looked more confident, almost like this was a doctor/patient meeting.

"I want to thank you, Mr. Jonas, for agreeing to come here today."

"Thank Marty," I replied. "He ought to be a lawyer," I joked. "Very convincing guy."

"Well, I hope you're open to more convincing?"

"Always open.   But I'm a long way from that stage, as it concerns your cellmate."

"Fair enough. I'll tell you about him in a moment, but first, I want to clear the record as it relates to me.

"Yes, I am a convicted murderer. Of my wife's lover. A killing that I have wished I'd not done, oh so many millions of times."

Lewis shook his head.

"But I have no excuses. I did do it. And…whatever happens to Carl Hannaford, as a result of our efforts here today – well, it won't affect even one iota of the remaining portion of my sentence. Are we clear on that?"

I nodded. "Yes. And is this Hannaford your cellmate?"

"Yes, he is."

Lewis settled into his chair and continued.

"During my years in prison, whenever inmates learn that I was a psychologist on the outside, some of them come to me, asking if I can help them through whatever emotional difficulties they're having.

"Sure, some of them are phony in their approaches –you know –a misguided belief that maybe something I find in them, will help them get reduced sentences. Those, I can spot easily, and I never pay them any further attention.

"But sometimes, I am able to help some inmates better understand their anxieties, and how to deal with them."

"Has Carl Hannaford come to you for help?" I asked.

Lewis shook his head.

"No. He has never asked me for any help."

"So what makes you think he may be innocent?"

"It's a mixture of things. My observations of his behavior. And if you will allow me to still use the term, my professional training as a doctor of psychology, with nine years of clinical experience."

"Tell me more."

"It started the first night Carl was assigned to the cell. That's about six weeks ago. That night, and most nights thereafter, when Carl falls asleep, he exhibits signs of severe disturbance in his dreams. I don't want to call them nightmares, because I've not had an opportunity to discuss them with Carl.

"And there also are things Carl says – regularly -- in his sleep state. And which he often mumbles, when he is awake. And these are very disturbing to me.

"One phrase that he frequently says is… 'He says I killed the man. Don't remember. But he says I killed the man.'"

"Have you ever questioned him about this?" I asked.

"Yes, I have. But all I get back from Carl is…a confused look. And then, he sort of mumbles that phrase again – 'He says I killed the man. Don't remember. But he says I killed the man.'

"What really bothers me about this is – here we have a guy who confessed to the police right from the start that he was guilty. Never any doubt. But now, he evidently has all sorts of doubts.

And put this together with that phrase he keeps using – 'He says I killed the man' – and I get the feeling that there is something not right about his confession. Like he was pushed into saying he did it."

"Whoa," I interrupted, "That's a pretty big leap you're making."

"Not such a big leap, Will, when we take into account the kind of mind this fellow has."

"Meaning?"

"He is at the bottom of the intelligence curve. I'm not able to do any testing on him, but I'd be surprised if his IQ is any higher than about 65.

"Someone with such a low IQ can easily be led, convinced, pressured into doing things they don't want to do.

"At the same time, though, they can have – and I believe Carl does have – a sense of what is right and what is wrong.

"Put this all together, and I think there is a good chance that Carl either may not have committed this murder. Or if he did it, then he was pressured into it, by another party."

I pointed out, "Except that he did confess to the killing. So maybe all he's exhibiting now, is a sense of regret. Because he knows he did something wrong."

"I don't see it that way," Jack answered. "I believe that someone convinced him that he *did do the killing*. That would explain that phrase he keeps repeating – 'He says I killed the man. I don't remember. But he says I killed the man.'

Jack sat up straight in his chair. He looked at Marty and then he looked at me. He took a deep breath and then spoke – slowly and with conviction.

"Will, Marty – I do not think Carl Hannaford committed any murder. I think he was talked into believing he did. But the functioning part of his brain, despite its low level of intelligence, knows he did not commit that crime. Someone else did that killing, and somehow has managed to frame Carl for it."

For a while, after Jack finished, Marty and I were quiet. Each of us reviewing what Jack had said. I broke the silence.

"Well, I think we're dealing with a real long shot here." I nodded at Jack. "You've laid out a nice case. It may be true. Or it may not be."

"So, where does this leave us?" Jack asked.

I turned to Marty.

"I don't know about you, but I'm willing to do some more investigating. How about you?"

"I believe Jack has it right," Marty said. "So count me in."

"Great!" Jack said. "So, what's next?"

"What's next depends on you," I answered. "You need to get Hannaford to agree to talk with Marty and to appoint Marty as his lawyer.

"Explain," I said to Marty.

Marty said to Jack, "Being Carl's lawyer is key here. Because once I'm his attorney of record. I can request and get, all of the paperwork on this case. Carl's arrest, his confession, the police reports, the coroner's report, all witness testimony, the arraignment, the judge's sentencing. In other words, everything connected with the case.

CHAPTER 3

"And that's when my work starts," I said to my wife, Lu, and to Charlie Black and his wife, Sheila, over dinner that night at our condo in Tarzana.

"I need to go through everything Marty gets. See if all the pieces fit. If the investigation was done right. See if I've got anything to question or examine."

"Decide if this Jack Lewis is one smart guy," Charlie offered his opinion, "Or just another jail house lawyer with a psychologist's training."

"And while you two are figuring that out," Sheila said, "I think the most important thing here right now, is that we all agree that Lu has officially earned her chef's degree. Or cap. Or whatever it is they award master chefs. Dinner was great. Just great."

"Thank you," Lu said, the big grin on her gorgeous face showing her appreciation for Sheila's words.

Time for a bit of background here.

About a year ago, when Lu and I had been married for three years, she announced that we were eating out too much.

"Costs too much, and not good for our health. So, I'm going to learn to cook."

"Lu," I pointed out, "about all you can cook is a hardboiled egg."

But Lu – being the determined, goal oriented person she is – well, off she went to chef's school at night. Couldn't go during the day because of her job as chief computer programmer at one of the larger, multi-branch banks in California. And within six months, we were eating regularly at home. And I don't mean hamburgers and hot dogs.

As for Sheila, she and my first wife, Vera, who'd died of cancer six years ago, had been close friends. And Charlie and I were partners – and friends – as homicide detectives, for a good twenty of the thirty years I'd been on the job with the LAPD.

As couples, we'd also been close.

So when Lu and I married, Sheila and Charlie made an effort to become friends. Luckily, the women did hit it off—and we'd have dinner together every week or so.

And just to complete the picture, I bet Lu is the best looking chef you've ever seen. Sheila McCelland is 45 – and thanks to regular exercise and good eating, she looks a good ten years younger. She's got deep red hair – hey, what would you expect from someone with a last name like McClelland – along with about 136 pounds, nicely distributed over a five feet nine inches frame –

all topped by an angular face with a model's high cheek bones and a perfect nose. I'm a lucky guy.

"Where did the murder take place?" Lu asked. "In Lancaster? Where the prison is?"

"No," I answered. "It was in Junction City."

Lu shook her head.

"Junction City? Never heard of it. Somewhere up North?"

Charlie answered Lu.

"Nope. Right here. In Los Angeles County. One of those small cities out near the 110. Not much there. Mainly warehouses and now, they're starting to build those distribution centers, for getting orders out to people who buy on the internet."

"How'd you know that, Charlie?" Sheila asked. "Just some more of that general information your brain keeps storing? Getting you ready for your shot at Jeopardy?"

"Well, you know me," Charlie said. "I like information. So, I was looking at a book that discussed the smaller cities of Los Angeles County. And there was this write up on Junction City. So…"

That's my former partner. Always coming up with little facts. Like the info on Junction City. Charlie is one of the smartest people I know. Definitely a brainiac. And just as definitely not someone hot on physical fitness. He was about 5 feet nine inches tall, and he weighed a well-rounded – and I do mean, well-rounded – 195 pounds.

When we were working together, Charlie was always the

"good cop" and I was the "bad cop." Made sense. Against his five nine frame, I was 6 feet 4 inches, and thanks to being a nut about physical fitness, I kept my weight at 210 pounds and was in generally good shape.

I say – generally good shape – because I'm now starting to meet up with some new aches and pains – especially in the morning and on damp days. Understandable, I keep telling myself. After all, a few months ago, I turned 62. Kind of a depressing fact – and one I try not to think about too much.

Now, I continued on with my description of Junction City.

"Got a population of about twenty thousand. Mainly poor. Plenty of minorities. Some beat up private housing. Several trailer parks."

"I see you've already started your research on this one," Charlie said.

"Well, I had a little time, so I printed out some stuff on the computer," I said.

"Oh my!" Lou said. "You? Doing a Google search? You're joining the 21st century! Now *that* is an accomplishment."

CHAPTER 4

"You? On your computer?" Rose said, the next morning in my office, echoing Lu's comment.

She continued, "I better tell the cleaning service to be sure and dust off your keyboard. Wouldn't want you to work on a dirty one."

"There you go," I said, with mock (or maybe it wasn't so mock) exasperation. "Everyone is making fun of my accomplishments, on the computer. I don't see why. I knew *I* was going to start to use it, whenever *I* decided *I* was ready."

"Well," Rose said, "I better start thinking about retiring. You are not going to need me anymore."

"Not so," I said, no more joking in my tone.

And I meant it. Ever since Rose joined me, eight years ago, she's been the reason our two-person office runs as well as it does.

Rose Shapiro, my now-70-plus, gray-hair-tied-in-back, short and round lady, who, as I told you before, functions as my secretary-receptionist-bookkeeper-Jewish mother-everything helper.

I still remember when Rose joined me. It was the end of a frustrating day. I'd interviewed a half dozen ladies, sent over by the employment agency, for the job opening I had for an all-around -the-office-person.

No one came even close to what I was looking for.

And then, in marched Rose. Yes. Marched. Rose never walks. In those black, lace-up, flat heeled shoes, she marches. And nothing gets in her way.

In Rose marched. She took one look at me.

"Sit down," she ordered.

I obeyed.

And Rose then made me the best cup of coffee I'd had, since my wife, Vera had died four years earlier.

Hired her on the spot.

Although, in truth, I think Rose hired herself.

But whatever, things had turned out great.

Now, Rose asked, "Is there anything you need me to do on this case, yet?"

"Nah. I got the background I need on the place. Now, I have to wait, until Marty Gershon's friend, Jack, gets his cellmate to agree to see us."

"Good," Rose said, handing me a pile of papers. "Then you have the time to go through these files and sign off on them, so I can bill the clients."

I hate paperwork.

"Do I have to?"

"Do you like to eat?"

I didn't have any answer for that, so I took the files from Rose, sat down behind my desk, and started doing the executive thing. It took about an hour, until I finished the paperwork. And then I was rewarded, as Rose buzzed me on the intercom.

"It's the call you've been waiting for," she said. "Marty Gershon."

He told me, "Just got a call from Jack. Carl Hannaford has agreed to meet with us. I'm working now on scheduling that meeting."

CHAPTER 5

It took some time, but two days after Marty called, here we were again — he and I – on State Highway 14, approaching Lancaster.

On the way up, we'd discussed what we wanted from the meeting with Carl Hannaford.

Marty said, "I need to get Carl to name me as his attorney of record." He tapped the envelope lying on the middle console between the two front seats. "I've kept the agreement very simple. It just states that Carl is appointing me as his lawyer. If he signs, it'll hold up to any challenge."

Then, there was what I wanted to get out of the meeting.

I told Marty, "I want to see if I agree with Jack Lewis's evaluation. That Hannaford did not commit the murder. That he was somehow talked into confessing to something he didn't do. And also, I want to see about Hannaford's mental state. And his intelligence level."

"Good luck on that stuff," Marty said. "You're not dealing

with facts, there. Just your impressions."

"Yeah, I know. But as a homicide detective for thirty years, that's how I started most investigations. With my impressions. So, no problem operating that way."

We arrived at the prison, parked and went into the main entrance. But instead of getting in line with the other folks waiting to see inmates, we went to a different, closed window.

Marty tapped on the glass, and when it was opened by a middle aged clerk, he told her we had an attorney-client meeting scheduled with Carl Hannaford.

The clerk looked at a printed list and then nodded at an entryway with a metal scanner at the end of the room.

"I believe you know the way, Counselor?"

"Certainly do. Thank you."

Marty walked toward the entryway, nodded at the attendant and then went through the scanner. I followed. We then went to the nearest door on the right, opened it and stepped inside, where we were met by a prison guard, who looked familiar to me. I tried to remember his name.

And while I was doing so, I think the guard was trying to tap in to his own memory bank, because it took him a few seconds to remember my name.

"Nice to see you, Will," he said.

"Hello, Ed," I said, as I remembered Ed Chomsky. Long time guard here at the prison.

Chomsky led us down a short corridor and into a small

conference room, just like the one in which we had met with Jack Lewis. A table, two chairs on one side, one chair on the other.

He waited until we were seated, then he went to get Hannaford, who must have been right outside the room, judging by how quickly Chomsky brought him in.

Then the usual securing-the-prisoner-to-the-table ballet we'd seen with Lewis, and now, we were alone with Hannaford.

I gave him a once-over.

Judging by how he stacked up next to Chomsky, Hannaford seemed to be about six feet tall.

He looked younger than his age, 22. Dark hair, cut prison-short. A round face. Eyes that looked mainly downward. A slightly receding chin that supported a thin set of lips. A nose on the long side and slightly bent, maybe the result of having been broken?

As we had agreed, Marty spoke first.

"Hello, Carl. We're the people Jack Lewis told you about. I'm Marty Gershon, and I'm a lawyer."

He pointed at me.

"And this is Will Jonas. He works with me, as an investigator."

Hannaford looked at Marty, then at me. And in that look, I could see that Jack Lewis had been right about one thing. Carl Hannaford wasn't playing with a full deck.

It took Hannaford a while to process who we were. And then he remembered.

"Jack Lewis said I should see you. I have these bad dreams. Can you help me with them?"

I jumped in.

"What kind of bad dreams, Carl?"

Carl didn't answer right away. It seemed to me, he was having a hard time focusing on what he wanted to say. Then, he did speak.

"Bad dreams. About killing a man. I...I killed the man. He says I killed the man. Don't remember. But he says I killed the man."

"Who says you killed the man, Carl?" I asked softly, gently. "Who says you killed the man?"

Carl took some more time before he answered.

"My Dad. He told me. I killed the man. I don't remember. But that's what he told me. That's what he said."

Marty asked, "Carl, do you know who Manny Estevez is?"

This was the name of the homicide victim.

Carl's look was blank.

Marty asked again.

"Do you know who Manny Estevez is?"

Again, no reaction from Carl. No indication that the name meant anything to him.

"Carl," I said, drawing his attention back to me, "Do you remember a fight you had with Manny Estevez? That night? Behind the UnaMas Bar? In Junction City?"

On purpose, I had mentioned the name of the bar, behind

which, Estevez was knifed to death.

Carl said, "I like UnaMas."

"Do you know what happened there?" I asked.

Carl thought for a moment, then responded.

"He says I killed the man. Don't remember. But he says I killed the man."

"How did you kill him, Carl?" I asked.

"With the knife my father showed me," Carl said.

"When did he show you the knife?"

"When we went back there, to look at what I'd done. My Dad said we had to go back. To confess."

I switched gears.

"Tell me about your family, Carl. Who is in it? Your father? Your mother? Your sister?

I'd read up on the family before the meeting, but I wanted to see what he would say.

"Yes," he answered. "There's my father. And my mother. And my sister." He smiled. "I miss my sister a lot. I love her very much."

I'd read that Carl's sister –Melanie — was 12 years old.

"What's your sister's name?"

Carl didn't answer at once. Then he did.

"Melanie. That's my sister," he told me.

I'd heard enough to get me started.

"Thank you, Carl," I said, and I nodded at Marty.

"Carl," Marty said, "We are here to help you. Jack Lewis

thinks we can help you."

Carl smiled.

"I like Jack. He helps me sometimes. When things are…sort of…mixed up."

"Well, Jack thinks things may be a bit mixed up for you, now. So, we want to help you."

Carl picked up the envelope he'd carried in, opened it, and took out the single sheet.

"But in order for us to help you, you need to agree that I can be your lawyer."

"I had a lawyer before…" Carl said vaguely.

"But now *I* need to be your lawyer," Marty explained.

"So we can help you," I tossed in.

Marty turned the paper so it was facing Carl. He took his pen and held it out to Carl.

"All you have to do, Carl, is to sign this. And I'll be your lawyer."

Carl looked at the paper. I could see he was reading it. Slowly. But he was reading it. Then he looked up.

"So you can help me?" he asked. "With my bad dreams?"

Marty and I both nodded.

"Yes," Marty said softly. "That's what we want to do."

CHAPTER 6

"Getting Carl to sign me on as his lawyer, was like taking candy from that proverbial baby," Marty said, as we headed south on State 14, leaving Lancaster and driving back toward Los Angeles.

"I know what you mean," I agreed. "But at least we can hope that we're doing it for Carl's own good. We need that agreement in order to move ahead."

Marty nodded.

"Yeah, I know."

He switched topics, and asked, "What's your assessment as to Carl's mental capacity?"

"I think Jack Lewis is right on...about Carl's level of smarts. There's not much there."

"I agree," Marty said. "And it raises the question -- did Carl's defense lawyer bring Carl's competence into discussion at the trial?"

"And," I added, "was Carl tested, to see if he was mentally

competent to stand trial?"

"Something worth checking out," Marty said.

"There's a lot worth checking out," I answered.

Marty looked over at me and smiled.

"Hey, it sounds as if you're starting to be convinced that Jack is right, when he says he thinks that Carl did not kill anyone, and that he was framed."

"Not ready to go that far, yet," I answered. "But there is plenty for me check out, once you get all the paperwork on the case."

"I'll be filing for it tomorrow," Marty said.

"Okay."

I hit the lever that pushed my seat down as much as possible.

"So, wake me, James, when we arrive at my office."

"Wake you, James? My ass!" Marty said. "I'm a lawyer. Not your chauffeur."

"There are some who would argue that the difference between the two is miniscule."

"Hah!" Marty came back at me. "I bet you don't even know what 'miniscule' means."

I decided not to answer Marty. Arguing with the hired help can be so tiring...

.

CHAPTER 7

"We may have a problem," Junction City Chief of Police, Eli Russell, told Mayor Anthony Crane, on the phone.

"And what would that be, Eli my friend?" the Mayor asked. He was feeling good this morning. An early hours screwing session with his wife, Ellen, had set the tone for the day. And not for the first time, did Anthony pat himself on the back for having divorced his first wife and replaced her with the fifteen years younger, Ellen. Much more, and better, morning action!

"Carl Hannaford has a new lawyer," Russell told Crane. "A partner in one of the larger firms in the San Fernando Valley. In Encino."

"What? How'd that happen?" The Mayor shouted, the good time with Ellen now a fast fading memory.

"Here's what I know, from my contacts in the prison," Chief Russell said. "A while back, Hannaford was moved in with a Jack Lewis, because there was an empty bunk in Lewis's cell. Lewis – he's in for murder – is one smart guy. Was a practicing psychologist on the outside. And he's been helping Carl with – what Lewis calls 'confusing memories' – that he says Carl has been experiencing."

"What does Lewis mean by confusing memories?"

"Well, according to my informer, Carl keeps walking around saying something like" – Russell looked at the note on the piece of paper on his desk – "He says I killed the man. Don't remember. But he says I killed the man."

"Shit!" Crane muttered. "Sounds like Carl is beginning to question what we've been having his father drill into him. And that's not good."

"No it isn't," the Sheriff agreed. "And I also found out that it's Lewis who pushed Carl to get a new lawyer. So, yesterday, this Encino lawyer came up, along with his investigator, a retired L.A. Police Department homicide detective. A real hotshot back in the day, from what I read about him. They met with Carl, and he signed up with the lawyer, as his counsel."

"Can Carl do that?" the Mayor asked. "I mean, Carl isn't the brightest bulb in the lamp. Can he do that on his own? Get a new lawyer?"

"Of course he can, Anthony. Don't you remember? When this whole deal started, how we pushed the point that Carl was mentally competent, and therefore qualified to stand trial? No way can we go back on that now."

The Mayor thought for a moment.

"We need to get Carl transferred out of that psychologist's

cell. ASAP. As long as Carl is there, this doctor is going to keep discussing things with him. And that isn't good."

"I'm already working on the transfer," the Chief said. "It'll cost us a few bucks, but he'll be out of there."

"And," the Mayor continued, "What about Carl's father, Gordy? Is he talking with Carl on a regular basis? To make sure Carl keeps thinking the way he's supposed to?"

"Well, yes…"

Crane heard the hesitation in Eli's answer.

"So," he asked, "Has he been doing that? Gordy was supposed to visit Carl at least once a week. Has he been doing that?"

"I …don't know," Eli admitted.

"Damn it, Eli, I don't want to hear that kind of an answer. You better get this straightened out with Gordy."

"I will," Eli promised. "I'll get Gordy to make the visits. If I can keep him sober enough."

"I don't want to hear any excuses!" the Mayor said. "For what Gordy is getting out of all this, he'd better watch his drinking and he better make those visits."

There was a pause in the conversation, and then Anthony spoke again, his voice now softer and friendlier.

"Sorry, Eli. Didn't mean to land on you so hard. I know you realize how important all this is. Everything's tied into everything. So we have to make sure about all parts."

"I hear you, Anthony," Eli assured the Mayor.

He switched subjects, and asked Anthony, "What about Gus?

You going to tell him what's going on?"

Crane sighed.

"I better. Seeing how this will affect him, if things start going bad."

"Hell! If thing start going bad, we're all going to be in the shithouse," Chief Russell said.

CHAPTER 8

Marty had told me, on the drive back from Lancaster, that he'd ask for the case files the next day. This would include the Junction City Police Department files detailing the initial investigation, Carl's confession, his arrest and arraignment, the district attorney's report, the public defender's report, the coroner's report, witness statements, the probation department report, the court sessions, sentencing recommendations, the Judge's sentencing report -- In other words, anything and everything about the case, start to finish.

I figured it would be a few days until the files started coming in, so the day after our meeting with Carl, I was concentrating on a personnel report for another client, when Rose buzzed me on the intercom.

"There is a Chief of Police, Eli Russell, of Junction City, on line 1. He wants to talk with you."

Was I surprised? Not really. I'd figured that once Marty's request for the Hannaford file went in, the police department would be one of the first to react. Sort of a "my balls are bigger than your balls" move. Maybe along with a smooth offer to be as helpful as possible – professional courtesy and all that.

Well, might as well see how this chief was going to play it.

I picked up the phone.

"Good morning, Chief Russell. Good to hear from you."

"Good morning, Will," the Chief said. "Okay if I call you, Will? Or would you prefer Detective? You were one for so long – 30 years with LAPD –so maybe you'd prefer that title?"

Obviously, Russell wanted me to know that he'd checked my background. So what? It was okay with me.

"Just call me Will," I said. "What can I do for you, Chief?"

"Well, I'll get right to it. Frankly, I'm wondering why I'm sitting here, with a request from a lawyer – Martin Gershon -- for our records pertaining to the arrest and conviction of Carl Hannaford, for the killing of Manny Estevez, just about a year ago; this was a clear case of voluntary manslaughter. The perp – Carl Hannaford – confessed to the crime, he received a fair sentencing of six years –he could have gotten as much as eleven – he's been incarcerated in the state prison at Lancaster, to make it geographically fairly easy for his family to visit – so, what's the problem? Why are you and this Gershon interested?"

"Evidently," I answered, "There is some concern as to how Hannaford was processed through the system on this one. If you listen to him, he sure does sound like he doesn't quite understand how he got where he is. Might be a mental competence thing involved here."

"Will, it sounds like you're getting your information from Hannaford's cellmate – Jack Lewis. And if so – frankly – I'm surprised. You've been around long enough to know about jail house lawyers. And that's all that Lewis is."

"It may be a little different this time," I answered. "Lewis is also a trained psychologist."

"And a convicted murderer," Russell interrupted.

"Which he is the first to admit," I came back at him. "But I've seen Hannaford up close, myself. And I'm wondering about how he's been handled."

"If you're saying that…" the Sheriff cut in…

"I'm not saying anything about how your department handled this, Chief. I'm just letting you know my first impressions, since you've been good enough to call me. But I don't think I want to say anything more now, until I've had a chance to review the files."

The Chief was silent for a few seconds, as he wondered whether to keep the conversation going. Then he decided he'd probably not get anything more.

"Well, all right then," he said. "We'll be getting the package out to Gershon soon. And I sure hope you'll come to see me, when you're next in Junction City."

"Of course, Chief. Will do."

CHAPTER 9

"They're starting to get worried in Junction City," I said to Marty Gershon a few minutes later, when my call to him went through to his line.

I explained, "I got a call from the Chief of Police, Eli Russell. Supposedly just to let me know the files were on the way. But of course, he was probing, to see what we knew and what we were planning."

"And of course, you left him clueless," Marty said.

"Just said enough to maybe raise his blood pressure a bit."

"No 'maybe' at my end," Marty said. "I *know* their blood pressure is going up."

"And you know this because…?"

"Because Jack Lewis called. He told me that, earlier today, Carl Hannaford was moved out of his cell."

"Looks like they're worried Jack might learn something more from his discussions with Carl," I said.

"That's what Jack figures."

"Any idea where they're moving Carl?"

"Jack asked, but the guards making the transfer didn't tell him anything."

Marty changed subjects.

"What's your next move, Will?"

"I need to review the files. In detail. I want to see how they processed everything. Make sure it all was done right, procedurally. Or not. Once I have some clear facts there, then I want to start talking to the key players. And of course, the main thing I'm interested in, is figuring out why Carl keeps saying that phrase he uses… 'He says I killed the man. Don't remember. But he says I killed the man.'"

CHAPTER 10

Chief Russell steered his patrol car to the curb in front of Gordy Hannaford's beat up house in Junction City.

Looking up and down the block, the Chief saw several old, small homes. Probably 12 to 13 hundred square feet each. A few looked like the owners were trying to keep them in decent shape. But the majority had cars parked on what had been front yards, and things went downhill from there.

The Hannaford house was among those on the eyesore side of things. It was badly in need of painting. A couple of vertical porch posts were a shade of light gray, and were not a match for the peeling white paint that covered the four other posts. The front yard was one big dustbowl of brown, dry earth which looked like it hadn't seen a blade of grass in years.

"What a shithole," the Chief said aloud. Then he thought, "With the dough Gus Zeterenk is giving him, you'd think Gordy would fix the place up a little."

Chief Russell shook his head.

Gordy Hannaford worried him, now that the lawyer and his investigator were checking things out. Gordy was weak. And stupid. And an alcoholic. That's a lousy combination to be found in someone who knew as much as Gordy knew.

Not for the first time, the Chief worried about what might happen if Gordy didn't stay at least relatively sober – especially around that investigator, Jonas.

"Okay," Russell said aloud to himself, "Time to stiffen up Gordy for the next round."

The Chief got out of his car, locked it and walked up to the house. He climbed the two steps on to the porch, and looked for a bell. When he didn't find one, he rapped hard on the front door.

After a pause, with no response, Russell raised his hand to hit the door again – but he didn't have to, as it was opened by Gordy.

"Hello, Gordy," the Chief said, smiling. "Got a few minutes to talk? We need to go over some stuff. Important stuff."

Gordy looked worried.

"Sure. Sure. For you, Chief? Sure."

Gordy stepped aside, and Russell walked in, to a small living room.

The Sheriff saw Gordy's wife in the adjacent kitchen.

"Hello, Hazel," he called out.

Hazel shot a frightened look at both Gordy and the Chief, and then retreated into that part of the kitchen furthest from the living room. It was clear that she didn't want to have anything to do with any discussion Chief Russell and her husband were going to have.

Hazel's actions didn't surprise the Sheriff. It was typical of her behavior. To get as far away as possible from the focus of any attention. And not for the first time, Eli wondered how badly Gordy might be abusing his wife. And whether he should have a family services person look into the situation.

Gordy's twelve-year-old daughter, Melanie, was standing in the doorway that led to the central hall of the house. Gordy looked at her and jerked his head to the side, indicating that she should go.

Melanie looked back at Gordy. No fear in her. Unlike her mother, she did not exhibit any willingness to melt into a silent corner somewhere. She did take a step backward, though, so that she no longer occupied the doorway. She could not be seen from the living room, but she was able to clearly hear both the chief and her father.

Eli sat down on the couch, and looked up at the still-standing Gordy.

"How's it going, Gordy?" the Chief asked. "The job working out?"

Gordy was a maintenance man at one of the large warehouses that covered most parts of Junction City. It was the job Gus Zeterenk had promised, and delivered on, ever since Carl's conviction and incarceration.

Gordy was nervous. People like the Chief always made him nervous. People who had the power to screw him.

"It's fine," Gordy assured the Chief, with as much enthusiasm as he could generate, which wasn't much. God, what he'd give right now for one of those cool Buds stacked in the kitchen refrigerator.

"Been to see Carl lately?" Russell asked.

Gordy flinched at the question. He was supposed to visit Carl once a week. That's what the Chief and the Mayor had told him to do, as part of the deal.

"You need to make sure," the Mayor had explained, "that Carl keeps remembering what he needs to remember. What you told him. That he killed that Mexican, in that fight he had with the guy, behind the UnaMas Bar."

"So," Chief Russell asked, "when was the last time you went to see Carl?"

Gordy had to think! He had to remember! When did he see Carl?

And he knew.

He knew it wasn't last week. Or the week before.

"I...it was a month ago..." he admitted.

Chief Russell slammed his fist into the seat cushion of the couch, producing a cloud of dust.

"A fucking month ago? A fucking month ago?"

"I...wasn't feeling so good. I think I had the flu or something..."

"Bullshit! Bullshit! Bullshit!" Russell shouted.

He stood up, and jabbing Gordy repeatedly in the chest, he shouted at him.

"Listen, you! From now on, you make sure you see Carl

EVERY week! Every week! You understand?"

"Y...yes."

"And what do you do every time you see him? What do you tell him?"

"I...I tell him that he killed that man. That he killed that Mexican."

"And if he doesn't sound sure? What do you do?"

"I remind him. Of his confession. How he and me went to see you. At UnaMas. And Carl confessed to you."

"And you keep reminding him, right? Every time you see him, right?"

"Yes...every...every time I see him."

"And how often is that?"

"Every week. I need to see Carl every week."

CHAPTER 11

Whenever I start a new investigation, I like to have as much background knowledge as I can. And I sure didn't have that kind of information about Junction City and the key players.

So, it was time to meet with Louis The Fisherman.

To explain, when I was still with the LAPD, Louis became one of my snitches. An informer. I had arrested him on a case with a potential charge of grand theft, and the probability of a multi-year sentence. At that point, Louis told me he was ready to trade: his information, for the dropping of the charges.

His information had turned out to be well worth the trade.

And thus was born my ongoing association with Louis.

Unlike most snitches, Louis was one very intelligent guy. He definitely did not fit the usual pattern of a snitch. You know how some people are destined for great things in whatever career path they take? Well, snitching is what Louis was born to do. A real American success story. So much so, that he earned the nickname, "Louis The Fisherman."

Louis would cast his nets out, trawl around, and come up with all kinds of information to sell to the police, or to private parties like me.

Of necessity, because too many people would be happy if he were dead, Louis became a master at being – nowhere. You couldn't find Louis, if you didn't know how. If you didn't have one or more of his ever-changing telephone numbers. That was the only way to contact Louis. Call him on one of his phones, leave a message, he'd call you back, set the place for the meet.

Notice, he set the place. And the time. And the conditions. That was how Louis managed to stay alive – a real accomplishment, because longevity wasn't the usual destiny of an active snitch.

After the usual back and forth of telephone contacts, Louis told me to meet him in the first row of the parking lot fronting Vons Pavilion supermarket in the shopping center at Victory and Platt, in Woodland Hills.

I was to park in that row at 8:45 PM tonight, and Louis would join me.

So, here I was, in the front row, five minutes before the appointed time. And so it was, that at 8:45 precisely, Louis climbed into the front passenger seat of my car.

"Out of the parking lot, please, Will, and proceed south on Platt" were his opening words.

"And hello to you, too, Louis," I said. "Still playing it close to the vest."

"Always, Will. And to answer your question, I'm fine. You

the same?"

"The same."

"So, what do you need, Will?"

As you can see, social chit-chat is not to Louis's liking.

I handed him an envelope.

"I need to know more about a small L.A. County city – name of Junction City – down near the LA Harbor area. And about some people in it."

"Active little city," Louis said, "With some interesting business and municipal practices."

"You know the place?"

"Of course."

And yeah, you wouldn't think they were supposed to have such feelings, but Louis's pride obviously had been pricked when I asked if he knew about Junction City.

Well, the man takes pride in his work!

And he's also a businessman.

"Costs have gone up, since that last job I did for you, Will."

"So, what's this going to cost me?"

"I assume you want a solid report, right? Not just a top-skimmer?"

"Solid…yes."

"Okay. That will be $1,500.00. And of course, payable in advance…in cash, please."

I'd figured the price would be about that amount, so I had the money with me.

"Okay, I'll give it to you, as soon as we stop. Now, how about delivery?"

"A few days. Maybe four or five, at the outside."

Louis waved in the direction of the curb.

"Please pull over here, Will."

I did, and then I gave Louis the $1,500.00

We had stopped a few blocks north of Ventura Boulevard, a heavily trafficked street, where Louis could easily lose any car following him.

But what car did he have for himself?

Not to worry.

I looked in my rear view mirror, and saw a car pull into the curb, right behind us.

"There's your trail car, Louis."

Louis smiled.

"Hey, Will. Glad to see you're still sharp. What? Been nine years since you left the job? And you're 62? Good to see you still got it."

And then he was gone.

And I was left – again – with thinking about growing old. Lousy thought!

CHAPTER 12

Gus Zeterenk looked at Mayor Anthony Crane and Chief of Police Eli Russell. They were meeting in Zeterenk's office, at his building construction company, Star Development, in Century City in Los Angeles.

Crane and Russell had just briefed Zeterenk on what had been happening with Carl Hannaford, and Zeterenk was not happy.

"Jesus Christ Almighty." Zeterenk shouted. "This unraveling can't go any farther! There's too much involved here."

"We know, Gus," Mayor Crane said calmly. "And we've taken the necessary steps to make sure nothing more happens."

"Like we said," Chief Russell pointed out, "Carl's been moved out of that psychologist's cell. And Gordy Hannaford knows he has to visit Carl every week, to reinforce Carl's belief in what happened."

"Carl has to be kept focused on that," Zeterenk said.

"We understand," Mayor Crane assured him.

Gus looked at the Mayor and the Chief.

"Look," he said, "we're getting a really good deal out of our...activities...in Junction City. And those can go on for a long time." He shook his head. "But its Carl's conviction that's the most important thing here. It's got to stick. To protect Donald."

"We understand your point, Gus," Crane said.

Gus focused on Crane, then on Russell, and then on both of them.

"Please! Keep it top-of-mind."

Zeterenk continued to stare at the two men, until they nodded their heads in agreement.

CHAPTER 13

The files from Junction City arrived at Marty's office the next day. And after he had copies made for himself, Marty messengered the package over to me.

I wanted to get a head start on going through them, so I lugged the file home, had dinner with Lu, and then told her that I was going into my small home office to start reviewing the files, and not to wait up for me.

My first objective was to see if every step in the prosecution process had been carried out properly, as Carl Hannaford transformed from a confessed-killer-at-the-scene, to a convicted felon, to a California state prisoner.

Why was this important?

Because if Jack Lewis's hunch was correct, that Carl Hannaford did not kill Manny Estevez, then Carl of course did not belong in prison.

And if this really was the situation, then I suspect that somewhere within the processing of this case – from crime scene to sentencing – something was done incorrectly. And it was on that "something" that I'd have to concentrate, if we were to get Carl out of prison.

Okay, time to start reading and reviewing.

First thing I saw was that Chief Russell was the arresting officer. A little unusual, but with such a small force – the department had only 10 officers including Russell – I could see how the Chief could have ended up as the arresting cop.

According to the report he wrote up, Russell got to the crime scene – the alley next to, and behind, the UnaMas Bar -- at 3:08 AM. Sunday morning, June 22nd of last year, 2003. The Chief was alerted to the crime scene by an anonymous call to the stationhouse, at 2:35 AM.

Once at the crime scene, Russell found the victim—later identified as Manny Estevez, lying on the ground. He appeared to be deceased. There was a large gash across his throat, apparently severing the carotid artery.

Russell immediately called for an ambulance from the Los Angeles County Fire Department. Like many of the small cities in the area, Junction City had a contract with the County for ambulance services.

The ambulance arrived at 3:25 AM. The medics examined the victim and confirmed Russell's belief that he was dead. No need to transport the body to the hospital, for medical care.

Russell, at 3:35 AM, called Dr. Gary Webstein, a Junction City general practitioner, who served as the volunteer coroner for the city. Webstein arrived at 3:55 AM and made the official pronouncement as to the victim's death.

Upon request from Chief Russell, Webstein gave the Chief an estimated time of death, as being between 11:00 PM Saturday night and 2:00 AM Sunday morning.

According to Chief Russell's report, when he had first arrived at the crime scene, Gordy and Carl Hannaford were there. Now, when the Chief had completed his work with the medics and with Dr. Webstein, Gordy approached Russell. He told the Chief that Carl had confessed to him that he had accidentally killed the victim. That this had happened during an argument they had, which started in the UnaMas Bar.

Gordy then unwrapped a small towel he was carrying, and showed Chief Russell a large knife. He told the Chief that Carl had this knife and had given it to him. Carl told the Chief that in a "stupid move" he decided to see if he could help Carl by destroying the evidence linking Carl to the killing. So, he had washed off the knife. He'd also had Carl take off his clothes, which had blood on them, and he had burned them.

"I was a stupid father," he said to the Chief, "wanting to help Carl. But I realized this was wrong. So, then we came back here."

Chief Russell, according to his report, went to Carl. He read Carl his Miranda Rights – the shortened version – which Russell wrote in his report as being as follows:

"You have the right to remain silent. Anything you say can and will be used against you in a court of law. You have the right to speak to an attorney, and have an attorney present during any questioning."

Chief Russell then asked Carl if he understood what he had just read him.

Carl replied by saying, "I killed the man. Don't remember. But he says I killed the man."

Chief Russell asked Carl – who told him he had killed the man?

Carl said, "My Dad. He says I killed the man."

At this point, two Junction City policemen had arrived and Chief Russell ordered them to handcuff Carl, place him in their cruiser, and transport him to the Junction City jail, to be held there, until later in the morning, when he would be transferred to the Los Angeles County Sheriff's Department and the LA County Jail.

This was the end of the Chief's scene-of-the-crime-and-arrest report. It seemed to cover all the necessary bases, but there was a lot of additional information that I wanted. From the Chief. And from Carl. And Gordy. Questions about possible witnesses. About the victim. About the details of the argument itself. Also, did Carl and the victim know each other, before their fight? And whose knife was it – Carl's or the victim's? And how did Carl and Gordy get together after the killing? And where? And what was the argument about, in the UnaMas? You get the idea?

For the next hour, I skimmed through the rest of the files which covered:

...Carl's transfer from the Junction City jail to the Los Angeles County jail in the

Old Courts Building in Lancaster.

...His meetings with a public defender.

...The processing of the arraignment papers by a deputy LA district attorney.

...Carl's arraignment before a County Judge, where he pleaded guilty.

...The Probation Department's case review and sentencing recommendation.

...The final hearing before the Judge and the Judge's sentencing of Carl

All of these papers seemed to be in order, although I did have some questions I wanted to ask the public defender and the deputy district attorney. And there were some questions I wanted to ask the coroner for Junction City, Dr. Webstein.

CHAPTER 14

But before I started any of those interviews, I wanted to discuss everything with Marty Gershon and Charlie Black. Charlie couldn't get officially involved, of course. Junction City, geographically, was way out of his area of responsibility. But I wanted to tap him for any knowledge he had about the Junction City PD, and Chief Russell.

The next day, the three of us sat down in one of the small conference rooms at Marty's law firm in Encino.

Marty, in answer to my opening question, said, "Yeah, I've gone through the files Chief Russell sent over. But I didn't spot anything that troubled me. Now, Will, you're the expert here on this paperwork. You've seen – what? – hundreds of similar files? How does this one strike you? Anything not kosher? Something that we can grab on to?"

"I don't see anything that stands out as being wrong," I answered. "What l do see, though, is a thin file. Very little detail. I want to know more about any witnesses. Was there an autopsy? I don't see any report from the coroner. And what about the district attorney's office? And the public defender?

I turned to Charlie. I'd given him a copy of the file to review.

"Charlie, what's your reaction?"

"Same as yours," Charlie answered. "All the necessary steps are followed, from arrest right through to conviction, sentencing and incarceration. But it's thin on detail."

"So," Marty said, "We have no clue about the big question: who is the real killer? Because if Jack Lewis is right, it is *not* Carl Hannaford."

"Well," I offered. "I'm going to be doing some interviews, starting tomorrow. Let's see if they lead us in the right direction."

"Who are you seeing?" Marty asked.

"First, Chief Russell. Tomorrow morning. Who wasn't too happy to hear from me. Then, I'm going to try and see Gordy Hannaford."

I asked Charlie... "What can you tell me about Chief Russell and his department?"

"I don't know the guy personally. But I did talk to a few of the cops I know, out in that part of the County, and the word I get is that Russell is a hardliner. And territorial. Even more so than usual. He's used to running things his way. And as far as Junction City is concerned, he's also in tight with the Mayor. And there's a Los Angeles developer with whom they're both close to, on projects developed, or being developed, in Junction City. Name of...Gus Zeterenk. His company is called Star Development, and it's headquartered in Century City."

"We know anything about him? Or his company?" Marty asked

I looked at Charlie. Charlie looked at me.

"Don't know anything," I said. "But if he's a player, I bet the Fisherman will give me some information in his report. In the meantime, I'll have Rose do a search on him."

"The Fisherman?" Marty asked.

"Will's got a guy," Charlie said, "I'd call him a snitch, only Louis The Fisherman goes way beyond that job description. Anyway, Louis can turn up every speck of dirt on anyone and everyone."

"I should have his report in another day or so, and I'll let you know," I said.

CHAPTER 15

Right on the dot – at 10:00 the next morning, I was shown into Chief Russell's office in Junction City.

Actually, I'd arrived at 9:45 – lighter than expected traffic on the southbound 405 and 110 freeways, but Russell decided that the home dog's clock would be the one to play by. So I'd done a little humble-sitting in the station's reception area, fronting the desk sergeant's stand. No matter. I'd been kept waiting by heavier weights than Chief Russell. So, I just relaxed until his receptionist came, to take me to his office.

The Chief was sitting behind his large, designed-to-impress oak desk, wearing his full uniform, including his jacket with its display of look-at-all-the-citations-I've-earned medals.

Russell got up and came around the side of his desk, handshake-ready, and with a welcoming smile.

"Will Jonas," he said. "You've got a very impressive record with LAPD. It's a pleasure to meet you."

"Good to meet you, too, Chief," I returned his we're-all-friends-here smile.

"Come on, Will," Russell said, still holding my hand and guiding me toward a large couch off to the side. His brag wall was above and behind the couch. The usual grouping of state and regional notables – along with a Washington gallery of politicians and bureaucrats.

I nodded at the wall.

"Speaking of impressive…" I said.

Russell smiled.

"Well, we may be just a little city, but we like to do things right. And the recognition has followed."

I saw the opening I wanted, and as we sat down, I took advantage of it.

"On the subject of doing things right, Chief, I want to explain why I'm here today."

"That would be good," Russell said, the smile gone, and a harder surface now covering his face.

"Chief, the reason Marty Gershon is Carl Hannaford's new lawyer, and I'm his investigator, is because we're not at all sure Carl is guilty. We think he may have been wrongly convicted."

The Chief looked at me, his expression one of disbelief.

"Not guilty? Hell, this was one of the most straightforward cases I've ever handled. No doubt about it. Starting with Hannaford admitting he did it. And staying with that claim, all the way through, even though we gave him plenty of opportunities to plead not guilty."

Russell shook his head.

"Will, I respect the fact that you spent 30 years investigating and solving many more homicides in LA, than I ever will, here in Junction City. But you're wrong on this one, my friend. You're wrong on this one."

"Mind if I ask you some questions?" I asked.

"Go right ahead," Russell replied.

"Okay, here's the first one. Your report doesn't list any witnesses at the scene. Anyone describing what took place that Saturday night. A bar fight without witnesses? Not very likely. So, where are the witnesses in your report?"

"When I got to the scene," Russell answered – "and I was the first responder –there weren't any witnesses. Just a dead Mex lying in the alleyway near the back-end of UnaMas."

Russell shrugged.

"Frankly, what I suspect happened is, if there were any Mexican witnesses, and they saw the victim get stabbed and dying, they went the hell back to Mexico, that same night. If I was them, with no papers and what, I'd sure not want to get involved in something like this. No way."

"And what about Anglo witnesses? None of them?"

"Didn't see any," the Sheriff answered.

"And how about an autopsy? How come none was done?"

"My decision. I figured it would be an unnecessary hit against our budget. I just didn't see why we needed an autopsy. We knew what killed the victim. His carotid artery was sliced wide open, and he bled out. Plus, we already had a confession. And we already had the victim pronounced dead by both the medics and the coroner. I'll take responsibility for making that decision. And if I had to make it again, it'd still be the way I'd go."

I asked, "If we decided we wanted to do an autopsy, would you have any problem with our exhuming the body?"

Russell laughed.

"Would I be opposed to it? Hell no. But you better have a long shovel."

"Why's that?"

"Because the body is back in Mexico. The victim's family asked for its return. And after Hannaford was found guilty, and sentenced, I couldn't see any reason not to comply with their request, so off it went."

I switched subjects again.

"Okay, let me ask you about Carl Hannaford, and his confession."

"Damn lucky break, that one," the Chief said. "He and his Dad, Gordy. There they were. At the crime scene. With Carl all ready to confess. Hell, I had to stop him, and read him his Miranda Rights. *Then,* I took his confession."

"Chief, I heard Carl's confession, when Marty Gershon and I met with him. And I've read what you wrote in your report. What Carl says, sounds to me, like something rehearsed. Like he wasn't sure of confessing. But was just mouthing some words that someone had drilled into him."

The Chief shook his head.

"Will, when you met with Carl, I'm sure you noticed that he isn't the brightest guy. He just doesn't talk much in long sentences. Or very meaningful sentences. I'm convinced that what he said, what he confessed, is what it is. A true confession."

It was clear to me that Chief Russell had done a good job anticipating what I'd be asking. He had his answers ready and complete.

Did I have other questions I wanted to ask? Yes. But was I going to ask them? Nope. All I would get from Russell would be his canned answers. Not good enough.

Russell had done a lot of "cleaning up" around this homicide. No autopsy. Shipping off the victim's body, so no one else can do an autopsy. Having a feasible explanation as to why there were no witnesses. Get the picture?

The Chief was covering up something. I felt it. I knew it. I just couldn't figure it out yet. But I would.

CHAPTER 16

Gordy Hannaford was next on my list. I didn't know anything about him, except that he was Carl's father, and the person who seemed to have the most involvement with Carl and his confession.

I'd asked Rose to do her computer magic and get me some background on the guy, and she came up with the following:

...Hannaford was a custodian at one of the large number of warehouses that were the bread and butter of industry in Junction City. He'd had that job for about a year.

...Before that, he drifted from one low level job to the next. Much of it day work – the kind you pick up when you wait early in the AM outside Lowe's or Home Depot.

...Gordy had a history of heavy drinking. A string of arrests for drunk and disorderly. But nothing serious.

...He was married. Wife's name, Hazel. Two children. Carl, his son, was the oldest, at 22. And there was a twelve-year-old daughter, Melanie.

Rose also gave me directions to where Hannaford lived, a half a mile west of downtown Junction City. I got there about 6:30 PM, figuring Carl would be home, after work.

His house was one of a dozen rundown homes on the street. A few showed some effort at upkeep by the owners, but the chief decorative feature of most of the places was a car, up on blocks, on what used to be the front yard.

No car on Gordy's front lawn. Just dry earth, with every ounce of moisture sucked out of it many years ago.

I locked my car and walked up to the front door, which was set back on a two-step porch. Didn't see any doorbell, so I knocked on the door.

"Who the hell?" Some guy – I assumed it was Carl – grumbled out loud.

"Mr. Hannaford," I answered, "My name's Will Jonas. I'm a private investigator, and I'm working for your son's new lawyer, Marty Gershon. Can I talk to you, please?"

"Shit!" was his single word response to my question.

"Please, Mr. Hannaford," I pressed on. "We need to talk. It's important."

"I don't need to talk you. You're not a cop," he answered back.

I was puzzled by what Hannaford said. Here I was, working with the lawyer his son had just hired, and the guy didn't want to talk to me? Odd.

Hannaford sounded like he'd had a drink – or two – and I remembered what Rose's report said about his drunk and disorderly record. And I guessed – hoped, actually, — that Hannaford might be the kind of drunk who needed to be overpowered, rather than sweet talked. So I threatened.

"If I get a subpoena, then you will have to talk to me," I told him. And then, deliberately, I hardened my voice. "If you make me get a subpoena, I'll be a lot tougher on you. That…I promise. So why not do it the easy way, Mr. Hannaford? Open up, let me come in, and let's talk about how I'm here to help your son."

For a few seconds, nothing from inside. Then I heard someone walking toward the door, it opened, and there was a guy I assumed was Gordy Hannaford.

But just to make sure, I asked. "Gordy Hannaford?"

The man stood in the doorway. He swayed just a little bit, and his eyes were slightly glazed over. I revised my earlier estimate. Hannaford had downed 3 or 4 shots already, rather than just a couple.

"Yes…" Hannaford answered.

I took a step forward, crowding Hannaford in the doorway, and he stepped back into the small living room. I followed. Off to the rear and to my left, I saw a woman standing in the kitchen.

"Good evening, Mrs. Hannaford," I assumed.

No acknowledgement, however, as the woman moved out of my line of sight.

Looking in the other direction, I saw a young girl standing in the doorway that led out of the living room and to the rest of the house. This had to be the daughter, Melanie.

"Hi, Melanie," I said.

The girl didn't reply and remained standing in the doorway.

Gordy Hannaford looked at his daughter.

"You," he addressed her, "Outta here. Go to your room."

For a moment, the girl resisted. But then, still saying nothing, she left the doorway.

I figured that I'd performed the necessary social amenities. I'd introduced myself to Gordy. And I'd greeted both his wife and his daughter. Now, it was time to get down to the serious stuff.

I sat down in one of the chairs in the living room, and nodded to Gordy to sit on the couch, facing me.

He did.

"How's Carl?" I asked. "Okay in his new cell?"

"Fine," Gordy answered, his hands held tightly in his lap.

Gordy's attitude bothered me.

Here I am, an investigator for his son's new lawyer. That puts Gordy and me on the same side, right? But he's treating me like I'm the enemy. Time to see what that's all about.

"Mr. Hannaford, maybe you don't understand what I'm doing here. I work for your son's new lawyer, Marty Gershon. He's convinced that Carl did not kill Manny Estevez. And my job is try and find out if Marty is right. Because if he is, then Carl is innocent, and he should not be in prison."

Gordy looked at me.

"But Carl confessed," he said. "I was with him, when he confessed to Chief Russell."

I thought back to my notes from the first meeting Marty and I had with Carl, and I remembered Carl saying: "I killed the man. He says I killed the man. Don't remember. But he says I killed the man."

And I remembered asking Carl – who told him he killed the man? And Carl had replied, "My Dad. He told me."

"Gordy," I said, "Carl says *you* told him he had done the killing. What's that all about? What did you know, so that you could say this to your son?"

"Because of what happened," Gordy said. "Back here. Before Carl confessed to the Chief."

"What do you mean?"

Gordy took a deep breath and then spoke in a monotone, as if he was pulling out words he didn't want to say.

"I...I was home. Here. And Carl came in. He was drunk. Drunk. And he had blood all over his shirt. And some on his pants, too. When I asked him what happened, he said...he killed someone. In the alley. Behind the UnaMas Bar."

"And then...he took a knife out of his pocket. And there was blood on it."

"I got scared. Scared for him. So I made him take off his shirt and pants, and I burned them. In the backyard. And I washed and cleaned the knife."

Gordy looked at me, pleading.

"Yes, I know it was wrong. But I did it...because I wanted to help Carl. To save him. To get rid of the evidence."

Gordy shook his head.

"But then I thought…there probably were people at UnaMas who saw what happened. And so it probably would be better for Carl, if he confessed. Maybe it would go easier on him? On how long a sentence he'd get? You know? On those tv programs, they're always saying that if a killing is an accident, it…it counts for a better sentence? And I figured, this could help Carl. So, I told him he had to own up to it. That he'd killed someone. And we had to go back. And confess. And hope for the best."

When Gordy finished talking, I realized that what he had just told me, knocked the hell out of our theory that Carl was innocent. I mean, here is Carl's father, telling me that Carl had told him that he killed someone. And the only dead someone back there in the alley was Estevez. The very person Carl had been convicted of killing!

Case closed, huh?

Maybe with Chief Russell.

And maybe with Gordy Hannaford.

And maybe even with you.

But not with me. Definitely not with me.

Look. I was a homicide detective with LAPD for most of my 30 years on the Job. Murders are messes. Homicides got a million details to them – any one of which can lean toward guilt – or innocence.

But here – here with Carl Hanneford's killing of Manny Estevez – well – both Chief Russell's answers and Gordy

Hannaford's answers were – too damn clean. Too perfect.

And murder is never perfect. Murder is messy. And there are loose ends. And not everything is explained and clear.

I looked at Gordy Hannaford. After his speech – and that was what it was sounding more and more like to me –a rehearsed speech – he was sitting as small as he could. Looking like he was trying to disappear.

I took out one of my business cards and put it on the small table in front of the couch.

"Gordy, I've got more questions, but not today. I'll be getting back to you. But if, in the meantime, you want to reach me, I'm leaving my card, right here, on the table. Call me any time."

I didn't really expect Gordy to call. No matter. I knew I was going to come back at him, again.

But first, I wanted to look for all of those loose ends that I knew were out there. Need to find them. Need to tie them together.

CHAPTER 17

After I finished with Gordy Hannaford, I drove back to the few streets that made up downtown Junction City. My destination: the UnaMas Bar. I wanted to talk to the bartender. See what he knew about the homicide.

UnaMas was about three blocks south of police headquarters, where I'd met Chief Russell. Typical neighborhood bar. Couple of windows, with neon signs promoting Pabst Blue Ribbon, Miller and Budweiser beers.

Inside, the place was quiet. The lighting was dim. I checked my watch. Just 7:30. A little early for a busy bar., although there were a few drinkers in the house. Two men, sitting several stools apart at the bar. And two more sitting at individual tables. All looked like serious drinkers, on the way toward their own blurred nights.

One bartender, who looked like he was in his mid-fifties. Neat in his full apron, covering his white, open necked, long sleeved shirt. Dark pants. A name tag on his apron told me he was Fred.

Fred was polishing a glass when I sat down at the bar. He gave the glass one last swipe, stacked it, and gave me a bartender smile.

"What can I get you?"

I shook my head.

"Just club soda. I'm a friend of Bill's."

His smile was warmer.

"Good for you," he said. He poured the glass of club soda and set it down in front of me.

"On the House."

"Thanks."

"So, Friend of Bill's, what're you doing in here?" he asked.

"Looking for information."

I handed him one of my cards. There was a twenty wrapped around it.

Fred separated the twenty from the card, put the money into the left breast pocket of his shirt.

"Thank you for the advance payment."

He read the card.

"Will Jonas, Private Investigations. Woodland Hills. That's up in the San Fernando Valley. Part of Los Angeles, right?"

"Right."

"Long way off. What can you be looking for down here, that would be of interest in the San Fernando Valley?"

"Anything you can tell me about that killing a little over a year ago, out in your back alley."

"You mean, when Carl Hannaford killed that Mexican fellow."

"You remember it?"

"Sure do. I own the place, now. After that killing? Business went down. That hurt the owner. So I was able to get a good deal when I bought it from him."

He looked around.

"Got some plans for this place. Add a nice kitchen. But all that depends on this being the sort of place where young families will be willing to come. So, no more murders, here, thank you."

Fred smiled.

"Sorry. Didn't mean to go off like that. But I'm beginning to make some changes here, and I'm hoping they work out okay."

"I understand," I assured him. "And good luck."

I took a sip of my club soda.

"I'd like to ask you some questions about what happened that night. Okay?"

"Okay."

"To refresh your memory, it was Sunday, June 22nd. According to the police report, an anonymous call came in to the police station at 2:35 AM, saying there was a body, back in the alley, next to UnaMas. Then, Chief Russell arrived and found the body at 3:08 AM."

"Sure took them long enough," Fred interrupted.

"What do you mean?"

"I mean, I called it in, over 5 hours earlier. About 9:00 PM, Saturday night."

"To 911?"

"Nope. Direct to the Junction City Police. To whoever was on duty at the Desk. Being only a few blocks away, I figured they could get here a lot faster than anyone at the 911 end of things. Well, I guess I was wrong, huh?"

I didn't answer him. I had some questions of my own, on this timing point that I wanted to think about.

Instead, I went on to another subject – the argument that Carl and the victim had, according to Chief Russell's report.

"Fred, I understand there was an argument between Carl and the homicide victim, right?"

"Wrong."

"Wrong? There wasn't any argument?"

"Yeah, there was an argument. But Carl wasn't involved. At least, not while the argument was going on in here. What happened out in the alley? I can't tell you anything about that."

"So, what about in here?"

"It started about 8 o'clock. Between a Mexican guy and a white guy. Got pretty heated, the more they drank. So I cut them both off, about 8:30, when I told them to take it outside."

"A white guy and a Mexican guy, you say? Do you know who they were?"

"I'd seen the Mexican guy in here a few times. Don't know his name. He's the one who ended up dead."

"What about the white guy?"

"Never saw him before."

"What'd he look like?"

"Average looking."

"Tall? Short? Fat? Thin?"

"About my height, I think. I'm five-ten. He was thin. Well put together."

"Any idea how old?

"Maybe…early twenties."

"Okay, what happened?"

"As I said, I told them to take their argument outside. And they did. Followed by some Mexicans, who looked like they weren't involved – they just wanted to watch the action."

"Did Carl Hannaford go out with them?"

Fred nodded.

"I tried to stop him. Told him not to go outside."

"He didn't listen?"

"Have you met Carl?"

"Yes."

"Not too smart, right? In fact, just plain dumb. Nice kid, but truly dumb. Plus, that night, he'd had too much to drink."

Fred sighed.

"He's legally old enough to drink, of course. But between not being able to hold his liquor, and his not being very bright – well, whenever he's in here, I try to keep an eye on him. But not this time, though. He had gotten pretty soused. And he went outside, with the crowd."

Fred shook his head.

"I guess somehow, once everyone was outside, Carl must have

gotten into it, with that Mexican. And he killed the guy. I'm sure he didn't mean to. But dead is dead, right?"

"Right."

Fred had to stop and take an order from one of the tables. Then he came back and continued.

"Okay, by about 8:45, no one had come back into the bar – from the fight. So I went outside to check.

"I went into the alley. All the way back. And that's when I saw the guy on the ground. He was lying still. Big pool of blood around his neck. I did two tours in Iraq. Saw plenty of dead soldiers with their carotids blown open and then they bled out and died. This guy was dead."

"That's when I came back inside and called the local stationhouse."

"And you say you called it in about 9 PM?"

"Yup."

"And did you identify yourself?"

"Sure did."

"When you went out to the alley, was anyone there? Was Carl there?"

"No, to both your questions. No one was there. Just the dead guy."

Fred didn't have anything more to tell me, so I left.

On the way out, I went over what he'd said.

Here, we have Fred, calling things in about 9 PM. And identifying himself.

And here, we have the Chief, in his report, saying that he got the first word from the stationhouse at about 2:35 AM, after they received an anonymous call.

Big difference of five and a half hours. Plus different IDs for the call-in.

Conclusion?

Either someone has a very poor sense of timing.

Or more likely, someone is lying.

And so we have…more loose ends.

CHAPTER 18

ONE YEAR EARLIER

SATURDAY NIGHT, JUNE 21ST...YEAR 2003...8:35 PM

Gus Zeterenk felt his cell phone vibrate. He looked at it, and saw that his son, Donald, was calling him.

Gus spoke to Mayor Anthony Crane and Chief of Police Eli Russell, with whom he was meeting, in the Mayor's office in Junction City.

"Let me take this, Guys," he said. "My son's calling."

Gus punched in the receive button.

"Donald? What's up?"

Gus listened, and within seconds, looked shocked.

"What? What the hell are you saying?" he demanded.

He listened again, and in his agitation, he stood, and started pacing around the office.

"You killed the guy?" he shouted. "You say you killed some Mexican?"

Gus worked to control himself. He took several deep breaths and then he spoke.

"You...sure about this, Donald? You sure you killed him?"

He waited until Donald had answered, and then he spoke again.

"Where are you now? In your car? Not...not where this happened? Good."

Gus paced and thought.

"Okay, here's what I want you to do."

"First, calm down, Donald. Calm down. We're going to handle this. Everything is going to be okay. Believe me. You believe me? You believe me, Donald?"

Zeterenk waited while his son answered him. Then he spoke.

"Donald...was there anyone there, when this happened? Any witnesses?"

Again, Gus waited while his son answered him.

"And what about when you left...when you left the alley at what...that UnaMas place? Anyone there?"

He waited while Donald answered him.

"Okay, Donald," Gus said, "Here's what I want you to do. I want you to drive straight home. And Donald. Drive carefully. Don't go over the speed limit, for God's sake. The last thing in the world that you want, is to be stopped by the California Highway Patrol. Now, when you get home, don't call anyone. Don't answer any telephone calls. Except if you see that I'm calling. Then do pick up. You understand? You only answer if I'm calling."

Gus listened to Donald, then responded.

"I'll get home as soon as I can," he said.

He paused, and then he said, "And Donald...don't worry. I'll take care of this. Everything is going to be alright. Okay, Donald....get going, now. Now."

"Gus disconnected and took a deep breath?"

Mayor Crane asked, "Gus, what's going on?"

Gus looked at Mayor Crane and Chief Russell.

"My son's in trouble. And I need your help to get him out of it."

CHAPTER 19

BACK TO THE PRESENT

It had been a full day, and I was hungry. And as I crawled in traffic up the 405, back toward Woodland Hills, I was hoping that Lu might have made some dinner for me. Something great, waiting in the refrigerator, ready to heat up in the microwave.

Great food at home was something that had only been possible in the last year or so. That was when Lu decided to become a sensation in the kitchen.

But when I opened the door to our condo at a quarter to ten, there was no welcoming Lu, who usually met me in the hall with a fresh glass of club soda. And I didn't smell anything "food like."

I looked for Lu, and found her in the living room. She was sitting on the couch, shelling and eating peanuts. The pile of broken shells outsized the unshelled pile. Lu obviously had been on this comfort food binge for some time.

I walked over to her, bent and kissed her on the forehead. Couldn't go for the lips. They were working on taking in a peanut.

"What's wrong?" I asked.

"My job may be ending," she answered.

This was a surprise. Lu was the number one computer programmer for a multi-branch California bank, headquartered in Glendale. Last I knew, she was, as they say, a star in that management setup.

"What do you mean? What's happened?"

"We may be acquired by General National Bank. Ever hear of it?"

"I know it's one of the biggest banks in the country."

"Exactly. And if they acquire us – well – what these outfits usually do, is consolidate their staffs. And guess who loses out? It's the staffers of the company being acquired. They're the ones who are let go."

"But you're the top dog in your department," I pointed out.

"Yes I am. As the department is presently set up."

Lu shook her head.

"But to General National, I'm just another body to be looked at. And a decision to be made, as to whether they can eliminate my position and save some money. Because, after all, that's one of the main reasons for the acquisition. To see if they can do more, with less overhead. In other words, with less staff."

"Hey, Lu," I said encouragingly, "So if it happens to you, there'll be a nice severance package, right? And then you can hook up with one of the other banks. You're well known in your field."

Lu shook her head.

"Just one thing wrong with that scenario, Will."

"What's that?"

"Age. My age. I'm 44 years old. Almost 45. And any company hiring in Information Technology is looking for younger people. Supposedly, they've got a fresher perspective on things. Which is a fancy way of saying, that they can do my job, at less cost."

She shelled another peanut and shoved it into her mouth.

Lu talking about her age didn't sit too well with me. When was it? Just a few days ago, when I was thinking about the fact that I was 62? Maybe on the down side of the mountain? And about the new aches and pains that I was discovering?

But, hey, you have to be positive, right?

So, I pushed the bowl of peanuts out of Lu's reach.

"Listen," I said, "Here are our choices. We can sit around and eat up all those peanuts, and feel sorry for ourselves."

I put my arms around Lu, and kissed her.

"Or we can show the world that we still have some life left in us. What do you say? Let's go into the bedroom."

Lu shook her head.

"Ah, Will. What is it with you guys? You think sex is the answer to everything?"

"Well, certainly not everything. But a pretty good part of

everything, wouldn't you agree?"

"Right now," Lu answered, "I disagree. What I want right now, is dinner. Pasta. Let's go to Fabrocini."

I know when not to argue.

"Fab's it is," I agreed, while making a mental note to avoid the meat sauce, great as it tastes. Sometimes, I've noticed lately, meat sauce leaves me a bit uncomfortable the next morning.

I shook my head.

"Ah Will," I yelled at myself, "enough already. No more health problems!"

CHAPTER 20

A couple of days after I met with Chief Russell, I was in my office, working on one of my other clients, when Rose buzzed me.

"There is a man on line1. He says he will identify himself, if you will talk to him. And he wants me to tell you that it is about Junction City."

"What's to lose?" I said. "Put him through."

And she did.

"This is Will Jonas. Who's calling me, please?"

"Hello, Mr. Jonas. I'll give you my name, but I need to ask you some questions, first. Okay?"

"Actually, not really okay. But go ahead."

"Thank you."

"First off, I know you're working on something having to do with Carl Hannaford and that murder a couple of years ago, in the alley behind the UnaMas Bar..."

"Hold it right there," I interrupted him. "This conversation is over, unless you tell me who you are."

There was silence at the other end.

82

"In that case…" I started.

"Wait! Please wait."

I waited.

After a few seconds, the caller spoke.

"Okay, I'm going to give you my name, but please, if it gets out that I called you, I will be in very deep shit."

"Keep going."

"MY name's Harley Jenkins, and I'm a police officer with the Junction City Police Department."

"And why the deep shit?"

"Because I want to talk to you about…about corruption in Junction City. Stuff that goes right up to, and into the Mayor's office."

"And if it got out that I talked to you about it…well, there'd be serious trouble for me. And…for others."

I still wasn't buying anything, but Jenkins at least got me interested.

"Mr. Jenkins, what's your rank?"

"Patrolman. Been with the Department a bit over two years."

"And how do you know that I'm supposedly doing some investigating of the Carl Hannaford case?"

"Because I'm no dummy. I was in the station when you came to see the Chief. And his secretary told me who you were and what you're doing. It's no secret, right?"

"Okay, I'll admit to that much. But why do you think I'd be interested in any corruption stuff in Junction City?"

I heard a sigh.

"Actually, Mr. Jonas, I don't *know* if you'd be interested. But what I was hoping – what we were hoping – was that we could get you interested. Look, Mr. Jonas, there's a lot of bad shit going on here. And a few of us would like to work to improve things. But we need help. The kind of help we think you can provide."

"And if I'm not interested, then what will you do?"

"Honestly? I don't know. But I suspect it'll be nothing. It's just plain too risky for us."

"Give me a minute to think," I said to Jenkins.

I thought to myself, this could be a trap of some sort, set up by Chief Russell, to smear me and thereby screw up our investigation.

On the other hand, if there really was some corruption going on, I could use that as a wedge with the District Attorney's office. Get them to pay serious attention to the Hannaford case – when I first bring them the results of my investigation – in exchange for me handing them a juicy city hall corruption scandal, and all of the built-in press that comes with it.

Jenkins impatiently interrupted my thinking.

"I've got an idea, Mr. Jonas. Let's meet. You pick the place. Make it up in your area. Let me give you some more details. Then, I hope you'll want to help us. And that would be great. But if you decide not to, then that's the last you will ever hear from me. Fair enough?"

"Fair enough. What's your duty schedule? When do you want to meet?"

"How about Thursday?" I start on duty at 4 PM. So the morning would be best."

"Let's keep it simple," I told him. "There's an IHOP coffee shop in Sherman Oaks, on Ventura Boulevard, a couple of blocks west of Sepulveda Boulevard. Let's meet there. At 10 o'clock. That'll leave you plenty of time to get back down to Junction City for your 4 o'clock shift."

"That's fine," Jenkins agreed. "And don't worry. I'll spot you. Got your picture off of Google."

CHAPTER 21

ONE YEAR EARLIER

LATER ON SATURDAY NIGHT…JUNE 21ST…YEAR 2003…10:00 PM

"Okay," Chief Russell said, as he put down the phone and spoke to Gus Zeterenk and Mayor Crane, "I had the officer on duty delete the UnaMas bartender's 9 PM call-in. That's off the books."

"Now comes the key part of this," Crane said. "To get someone to blame for the homicide. To get your son Donald out of it. Like he was never there."

"Can you do that?" Gus asked, the anxiety clear in his voice.

"We think so," the Chief answered. "Anthony and I have been discussing some angles, while you've been on the phone with Donald, at home."

Crane said, "And based on what we know about Junction City, and some of the people here, we think we've got something that will work."

"To start with," Eli said, "we think we've caught a big break here, Gus. You told us, your son said that the Mexican witnesses cleared out, once the victim went down. But that one white guy stayed, right?"

"Right."

"And say again, what Donald said to you, about that guy?"

"He said it was some tall, stupid looking guy. He looked really dumb, like he wasn't all there. He was drunk. Very drunk. And he was leaning over the guy on the ground."

"Luckily, Gus," Eli said, "both Anthony and I know who that guy is. His name is Carl Hannaford, and he really is close to simple-minded. He drinks too much. Usually at UnaMas. And I know from personal experience in dealing with him, that when he drinks, he gets very, very confused."

"His father, Gordy, is no genius," the Mayor said. "Not quite as dumb as Carl, but not at all bright. Gordy's got a heavy drinking problem. He can't hold down a regular job, and he's always broke."

"And the best part is," Eli said, "whenever I lock him up overnight, for drunk and disorderly, he's always bitching about his family. And especially about Carl, and how Carl's stupidity keeps screwing things up for him. How we wished Carl had never been born. Stuff like that."

"What we're thinking, Gus," said the Mayor, "is that we get Gordy to convince Carl that he – Carl – did the killing. In return,

Gordy gets a steady job in one of your warehouses, plus some extra ongoing money. He gets all that – if he can convince Carl to confess."

"And then he has to bring Carl back to UnaMas, where Carl confesses – on the record – to me," Eli said.

"And then," Eli continued, "here is a very important point. Since we have a confession right from the start, I can then push for all of the other processing to be done – fast. Real fast. So no one has a chance to look too closely at the initial investigation, which I'll handle and write up myself."

"Then, the public defender isn't going to waste any time on a confessed murderer case. And the district DA office also will just paper it through, since there's already a confession. And the same for the Probation Department. And the judge, for sentencing."

"And then what we have," the Mayor says. "Is Carl in prison. And Donald free."

Gus sat still for a moment. Then he said, "Jesus. If you can pull this off..."

Eli interrupted Gus.

"I'll put it to you this way, Gus. Carl stating his confession to me, is the key. Once I have that, everything should go like I've described it. No one is going to give any serious review attention to an already-solved murder of some Mexican illegal in a barroom brawl."

Crane said. "This is the best we can figure out, given the fact that we only have a few hours to set it up. Time is tight. Very tight."

"And that's why," Crane continued, "We've got Gordy Hannaford sitting right outside, in my reception area. Eli had one of his officers bring him in."

Chief Russell looked at his watch.

"We have to get started on him. Now. Get him to agree to do this. We don't have much time, if I'm going to discover that body by 3:08 AM, Sunday morning."

CHAPTER 22

BACK TO THE PRESENT

It was time for Louis The Fisherman to give me his report on Junction City. So he said, when he called and gave me our meeting instructions.

"You know the Encino/Balboa golf courses at the corner of Burbank and Balboa in Encino? I'll meet you at the far end of the Eastern parking lot. Be there at 2:00 PM. Today."

And then he hung up.

No question if I could be there at the designated time. Or if I knew the meeting place.

These were not problems for Louis to worry about. He had information. You want the information? You meet him when and where he designates.

So, here I am, in the parking lot, at 1:55 PM. And sure enough, five minutes later, another car arrives. It parks a few slots away. Out comes Louis, from the passenger side. He walks to my car and gets into the passenger seat.

He hands me a large manila envelope.

"Like they say, Will…everything you ever wanted to know about beautiful downtown Junction City."

"Care to give me a few highlights?"

"Well, for one thing, Junction City is one of those 'charter cities'. At last count, there were 108 such cities in California. Their main attraction is that they have what is called "supreme authority" over their municipal affairs. That means those in charge can pretty much operate without any state control of their affairs. Junction City got its charter status in a special municipal election, back in 2000. Some say the election was rigged. Or at least, it was held in something close to secrecy – only a few hundred people voted – out of a population of 22,584."

"So what's all that mean, Louis?"

"Well, I don't know what business you got going in Junction City, but you need to be aware that the charter status gives the key top officials the authority to do pretty much whatever they want. Big time salaries, overseeing building inspections and cutting corners, issuing bonds for construction to be carried out by favored companies. I'm not saying there's necessarily anything wrong going on there. But there are lots of corruption possibilities, Will."

"Regarding key people in the city, there's Mayor Anthony Crane. Been in office for 12 years now, and still going strong."

"Almost as high up on the power scale as the Chief of Police, Eli Russell. He and the Mayor work together a lot."

"And there seems to be a favorite businessman of theirs – someone who started showing up some time before they became a charter city. Name is Gus Zeterenk. His construction company is Star Development, and it's in Century City. Star owns several warehouses in Junction City, and is now building a couple of mega-warehouses there."

"You'll find biographies on these folks, plus a few more players."

I asked, "Did you find anything about a homicide that took place in an alley next to the UnaMas Bar, back in 2003?"

"Saw one story in the local edition of the Los Angeles Times. Some guy confessed at the scene, the story said. That's the only mention I remember. I guess, since they got the killer right away, there wasn't much else to write up."

Louis looked at his watch.

This was his usual sign that the meeting was about to end. A decision not to be debated, I knew from past experience.

Louis nodded at the envelope.

"It's all in there, Will. More than you'll ever want to know about a crummy little two-by-four city. Or to be more precise, the place occupies 1.8 square miles."

Louis gave me a quick smile, as he looked out of the car window, toward the golf courses.

"This Encino/Balboa golf set-up…I hear they got a couple of nice courses here. In case you play, Will."

So, when did you ever meet a snitch, who could tell you about golf courses? Like I've always said, Louis The Fisherman is truly a unique kind of human being.

CHAPTER 23

Next on my list of interviews were three people.

Doctor Gary Webstein, the general practitioner in Junction City who also served as the part time coroner to the police department. Webstein had said the time of death had been between 11 PM on Saturday night, June 21st and 2 AM Sunday, June 22nd. I wanted to ask Webstein about the lack of an autopsy. I had Chief Russell's explanation…I wanted to hear Webstein's.

Jeb Fisher, a lawyer in the Public Defender's office, who handled Carl Hannaford's initial plea. Just about no activity by Fisher on behalf of Carl Hannaford. I suspected it was because of the guilty confession, but I wanted more details, if possible.

Jesus Morales, an assistant district attorney in the local district office that covered that part of the County of Los Angeles. Morales really didn't have anything to do on the case, what with Carl having pled guilty from the get/go…but I wanted Morales's take on the case itself – if he even remembered it. Probably not, since all he had to do was rubberstamp the file and pass it along.

But I might learn something, so I had Morales on my list.

I caught up with Dr. Webstein in his office in Junction City. Told his receptionist who I was and what I wanted. And a few moments later, I was sent in to see the doctor, but not until I'd run the gamut of dirty looks from patients who'd obviously been waiting before I even arrived.

"Mr. Jonas," Dr. Webstein greeted me. "As you can see, my waiting room is jammed. So, can we please get right to the point. What questions do you have about the victim? I seem to recall his name was Estevez?"

"Good memory."

"Well, that's been the only homicide I've ever been the coroner on. So it kind of sticks in my memory."

"Here's my question. How come you didn't do an autopsy?"

"Chief Russell's call. You should check this out with him, but I believe he felt that, since he already had a confession, and since I'd officially declared Estevez to be dead from that knife wound that cut the carotid, there really was no reason to do an autopsy. Can't say I disagreed with him. It was all pretty clean and clear."

Webstein paused and seemed to be searching his brain for some information.

"There was one point, on which the Chief and I did not initially agree, though."

"What was that?"

"On the estimated time of death."

"How'd you disagree?"

"Well, when Eli first asked me to estimate the time of death, I said it was between about 8 PM and 11 PM, Saturday night. But Eli said he'd reviewed everything carefully, and he felt the TOD was more like between 11 PM Saturday night and 2 AM Sunday morning. And he asked if, based on his knowledge, I wouldn't mind agreeing to that, as the time of death."

"I told him that was fine. Couldn't see any reason not to. Especially since the Chief already had a confession."

Another one of those loose ends, I thought to myself. Two different times of death had been considered. Something I'd have to look into more closely.

To talk with the public defender – Jeb Fisher – I had to go to the Lancaster Court House. That's where Fisher spent most of his time. Like most pd's, the receptionist told me, Fisher was overloaded with too many cases. So I could try and talk to him there, but I shouldn't get my hopes up too high.

I found Fisher, just outside one of the court rooms, and introduced myself.

"Mr. Fisher, I'm a private investigator, and I'd like to ask you about a case you handled. About a year ago. A murder in Junction City, with the offender, Carl Hannaford, pleading guilty. Do you recall the case?"

Fisher looked at me, and I suspect he was thinking I was crazy.

He waved his armful of files at me.

"This is my case load to defend – just this morning. And you expect me to remember a case I probably spent five minutes on...about a year ago? You must be kidding."

"I'm not. And the only reason I'm not...is because I think the guy was railroaded into believing he did the killing – when he did not. And I'm just trying to see if there's a way to get some justice done."

Fisher's attitude softened a bit and he shook his head.

"To get some justice done," he repeated what I had said. "Good phrase." He patted his file of cases. "That's all I'm trying to do here, Mr. Jonas."

Fisher went silent for a moment, and I was hoping he was trying to recall Carl's case.

"Yeah," he finally said. "I do remember that case."

He shook his head.

"But I'm afraid there is nothing I recall, that can be of any help to you. As soon as I saw that the guy had confessed, well, I had no more interest in the case – except to send it on. And that's what I did."

My final visit was to the area office in Inglewood of the Los Angeles District Attorney, this was the office that covered Junction City.

The Assistant DA I wanted to see was Jesus Morales. His name had been on Carl's file as it processed through the district attorney office on its way through the justice system.

It was my lucky day. Morales was in, and after a few minutes of waiting, I was led into his office by an assistant.

Morales gave me a big smile, and I found out why, when he spoke.

"Mr. Jonas. Will Jonas. I'm getting to meet a legend!"

"Excuse me?"

Morales reached out and pumped my hand.

"In law school, periodically, we'd study some actual cases, to see how they were investigated and then prosecuted. And it turned out, that most of these were cases that you had investigated. They were perfect for our use in the classroom. Your stuff was so good. So thorough, that we used to call you and your partner – what was his name – yes, Charlie Black –we used to call you guys…"

"Sherlock Holmes and Dr. Watson."

I grinned.

"Never heard that one before, although I did know that some of our cases were used."

Morales indicated I should sit down on the guest side of his desk and he went behind it and sat.

"So, Mr. Jonas…"

"Please call me Will."

"Thank you. Okay, Will, what can I do for you?"

"I'm doing some investigating on behalf of someone who is serving a manslaughter sentence. And his lawyer and I are convinced he was somehow talked into confessing – when he didn't actually commit the crime. Your name is on the case, so thought I'd see if you can tell me anything that will be useful to us."

I gave Morales the file information, and he pulled it up on his computer.

"Yes, here it is. And yes, I see that Mr. Hannaford did confess. In fact, he confessed to the Chief of Police directly."

"Agreed," I said. "But here's my question. Please take a look at the file itself. Doesn't it strike you as being...thin? Very minimal on detail. Not even an autopsy. And a defendant who doesn't seem to understand much."

Morales clicked through the file.

"Yeah, it is kind of a thin file. But I've seen others like it. Especially when the perp confesses right up front. As you know, that does away with a lot of paperwork involved in mounting a prosecution, dealing with the defense and its motions...you know the drill."

Morales turned his attention back to me.

"Will, is there anything in particular that you're looking for?"

"No. Not really. The thin file is what caught my attention."

"Well, if you do turn up something that can have an effect on how this case was done, please do get back to me. I promise I'll take seriously anything you come up with."

When Morales invited me to contact him with anything I learned about the Hannaford case, I was tempted to switch subjects and mention my phone discussion and upcoming meeting with Harley Jenkins. But I decided not to, for two reasons.

First, my priority is Carl Hannaford.

And second, I didn't yet know enough about Jenkins, to

decide if there was anything to what he was claiming.

Better to wait until I dug more into that one.

CHAPTER 24

Okay, so it wasn't one of the gourmet restaurants in Los Angeles, but the Sherman Oaks branch of the IHOP chain served up a bunch of great breakfast specials – eggs, pancakes, waffles, French toast, potatoes and fruit in different combinations.

I stayed with coffee and a donut. Yeah, I know – very cop-like. But I was one for 30 years, so the habit is still there.

I'd taken a booth facing the front entrance and was playing the usual "maybe that's him" game with each man who entered, when the right candidate did come in.

Tall. In good shape. Mid to late 20's. Crew cut. Too many donuts and sitting in a patrol car hadn't yet affected his physique.

Jenkins spotted me at the same time that I made him, and he came right over to the booth.

I stood up and held out my hand.

"You have to be Jenkins," I said. "I'm Will Jonas."

We shook hands as Jenkins grinned.

"Takes a cop to spot one."

"Something like that," I agreed. "Why don't you sit down?

Order some breakfast."

"Just coffee. Ate before I left home."

"And where's that?"

"Right in Junction City."

I guess I looked a little surprised. All I'd seen of the City was a small business district, a few beat up houses, like where Gordy Hannaford lived, and warehouses.

Jenkins saw my reaction.

"There's a new section of town, out past those beat up homes. Development went up about five years ago. We live there."

"'We' meaning...?"

"My wife and I. And our baby daughter." Jenkins shook his head. "Well, not a baby anymore, I guess. We just celebrated her first birthday."

"Nice."

"Yeah, nice."

Jenkins turned serious.

"And the living is nice, too, Will. And I'm hoping it'll stay that way. But not with how things are developing, with the bunch who're running the City."

"And that's why you want to talk to me? Because of what you think they are doing?"

Jenkins shook his head.

"I don't *think* it. I *know* it," he said strongly.

I nodded.

"Okay, why don't you tell me more. Starting with some

background on you."

"About me? I'm 28. Been on the Job for a little over two years. Spent the previous eight years in the Army. Most of it in the Middle East. Was an MP for the final 5 years of my service. Came back from Afghanistan and decided I liked being a cop. Junction City had an opening for a new patrolman. My MP experience helped. And I landed the job."

Jenkins shook his head again.

"And it was great – in the beginning. Liked the work. Right from the start. Still do."

"But for a year, now, I've been aware that the folks up at the top are taking way too much advantage of the fact that Junction City is a charter city, and has been one for the last five years. You know what a charter city is, Will?"

Thanks to Louis The Fisherman, I did know what a charter city was.

"Yes, I do," I said.

I asked, "So, what are those folks doing? Who are they? And how do you know about it?"

"First thing I heard were some rumors around the Job. How Chief Russell was making a salary way above the usual. Not a crime, of course. It's legal. But not right."

"But when I really got into it, was when one of the city hall staffers started confiding in me. And she knew…and knows…a lot. She's been telling me about way-inflated salaries for the chief, for the mayor, and for some others. And also, about kickbacks in the building inspections department. And contracts being awarded on a non-competitive basis. And about big time cash withdrawals from the general fund going into overseas accounts for the mayor and others."

"That's pretty heavy stuff. Do you believe her?"

"Yes."

"Why?"

"Because she's shown me some of the paperwork, to back up what she's telling me."

'But why has she come to you? Why hasn't she gone straight to the authorities?"

"What authorities would that be, Will? Someone in the city administration? Right where this stuff is going on?"

Jenkins sighed.

"Besides, there's another problem. And this one's got her scared. Really scared."

"Tell me about it."

"My friend has been working for the City for almost 28 years. Just two years to go now, and she retires. Full pension. Full healthcare benefits. A nice package. And she's afraid she could lose it all. Which would be a bitch. She's got two teenage kids. No husband. He cut out years ago, and doesn't help out in any way at all."

"Well," I pointed out, "Under the right conditions, all that can be cleanly handled and protected, if she comes through, like a whistleblower."

Jenkins looked at me, as if I was born yesterday.

"You read up lately, about whistleblowers, Will? Most times – *if* – they get rewarded, it can take months...years...before the rewards come through. And she's got nothing to fall back on, in the meantime."

Again, Jenkins shook his head.

"But that's not even the worst of it. Listen to this, please."

Jenkins paused, organized his thoughts and then continued.

"This all started about three years ago, when the mayor called my friend in for a private meeting. Not unusual, she thought. By that time, she'd been on staff at city hall for 25 years and had worked her way up to one of the senior city clerk posts."

"The mayor explained to my friend that she was going to be put in charge of certain bookkeeping matters. And because of their importance and their sensitivity, she was going to be getting special cash bonuses for herself, in order to assure the confidentiality of these matters. Of course, the mayor pointed out to her, he hoped she welcomed this promotion and felt she could handle it. Otherwise, they would have to consider – as he put it to her – the status of her employment."

"Yeah, they had her by the balls, even if she didn't have a pair," Jenkins said. "The way my friend saw it – and the way it was – she had two choices. Go along with what they wanted. Or refuse, and end up getting terminated. And how does she then support her family? And what about her pension? What would happen to that? How long could they tie that up, while her debts kept growing?"

"My friend accepted. She took care of the books, real and otherwise. And for that, she received an envelope, every two weeks, right from the mayor, with $2,500 in cash. In other words, $5,000 per month. Sixty thousand a year. That's continuing, right now."

"Look," I interrupted, "I realize your friend was between a rock and a hard place. But she *did* accept the deal. And the money. That doesn't look good for her."

"Except for one thing," Jenkins came right back at me. "She's never spent a cent of that money. When she started getting the payments, she opened up a savings account. In a bank in Long Beach. Every payment has gone into that account. And – there – has – never – been – a – withdrawal."

"What's her reasoning?"

"Right from the start, my friend felt that what was most important, was for her to complete her 30 years – that'll be in 2 ½ years now, retire – and then give the money back to the mayor."

I laughed.

"Your friend is a real optimist, if she thinks that's going to work."

"Why? What do you think will happen if she does that?"

"I figure…the mayor will take the money back, then tell your friend that she better shut up, or they'll go after her pension, and tie it up in litigation. Which will result in legal fees that she can't afford."

"And he'll also warn her that – if she gets the least little bit out of line, they'll come after her."

"And then, there's your friend, looking over her shoulder, for the next – who knows how many years – worrying."

"Or, try this on for size. Suppose the administration's dirty deeds start getting investigated by the L.A. County DA's office? And they find out about the bonuses she's accepted. They're not going to care that she never spent a cent of it. Only that she did receive the money. And she did keep quiet."

"In fact, they'll probably decide that the only reason she hadn't spent any of the money was because she was waiting for her retirement. To use the money on vacation cruises and trips."

Jenkins leaned forward to emphasize his next comment.

"Will, all of what you just said? That's what I told my friend. And that's why I now have her convinced...or almost convinced...that she has to blow the whistle. Now. When her story about never spending the money and being frightened for her pension...when those reasons do make some sense."

"So?"

Jenkins shook his head.

"I've told her. But she's afraid to do it on her own. And that's when I thought about you. Someone who can help my friend approach the DA, to work things out."

I stayed quiet for a while, as I thought things through. At least to the point of deciding that I'd like to meet Jenkins' friend, and gauge for myself, her degree of innocence...or guilt.

"How about you set up a meeting for me, with your friend?" I suggested. "Again, up here in the Valley. Away from your home grounds."

CHAPTER 25

"This investigator – Jonas – he's going around, asking some solid questions that could make our whole plan start to have problems," Eli said to Mayor Crane and Gus Zeterenk. They were meeting in the Mayor's office.

"How so?" Zeterenk asked.

"Well, I've followed up with the people he's been interviewing. And he's questioning several things in our file. When did we first get notified about the body? What was the time of death? Why wasn't an autopsy done? Stuff like that."

"Hey, Eli, our scenario holds up against those kinds of questions," the Mayor said. "I mean, this Jonas can ask all he wants, but we've got the official record, and that's what we go by."

"And I'm no lawyer," Zeterenk added, "But even if someone started – officially – to review everything…there's nothing there to warrant any sort of a re-trial or whatever. At least, that's the way I see it."

"Yeah," Eli said, "Everything you're saying is so –but only so long as Carl remains convinced that he killed that Mexican. There's our weak spot."

"But we've got that covered, right?" Gus asked. "You're staying on top of Gordy, and making sure he's out there, at the prison, talking regularly with Carl?"

"Yes I am."

Gus reached out and touched Eli on the arm.

"Eli...we all worry. And I thank god that we've got you to do all of the planning on this. We could not have done this, otherwise."

Gus spread his hands.

"But let's look at the good side. Ever since I came here, and suggested to you two that you hold a municipal election and make Junction City into a charter city...well, it's been good, hasn't it? Your salaries have gone from damn near nothing to where they are today. Over a hundred thousand. Plus, the kickbacks."

"Gus, we'll always be grateful for what you've done," the Mayor said. "And our working together has been good for you, too. The lower appraisals on new construction, so lower taxes on what you own here. The easier building inspections, so that you can cut building costs. The no-bid construction jobs."

Gus nodded in agreement.

"What we're doing is good for all of us," he said. "And how we've handled the killing has worked out very well – despite Jonas. So...Anthony...Eli...we all set now? In this together?"

He leaned toward the two of them, to give emphasis to what

he was about to say.

"All we have to do, is keep strong. Because this'll pass. You'll see."

Zeterenk looked at his watch.

"Whoa! I've got a meeting back in Century City. Got to go."

Gus shook hands with the Mayor and the Chief, and then left.

The Mayor spoke first.

"It's getting kind of hairy, isn't it, Eli?"

"It sure is," the Chief agreed.

"True," Anthony said, "Gus has brought us a lot of good stuff here. With his ideas on how to run things. I'll give him credit for that,"

"But," Eli answered, "Covering up a murder is a whole different deal. And it does not make me happy."

Anthony sighed. "I guess I'm sorry we got into this in the first place."

"Well," Eli said, "It looked okay. And simple. Gus's kid called him with the problem. We were all together. We came up with the solution. Seemed to make sense. And if it weren't for this Jonas, everything would be just fine."

The Mayor said, "Eli, we've got to stick together on this. Wherever this is headed, we need to stick together. You agree?"

"I agree."

CHAPTER 26

As his driver neared Century City and his office at Star Development, Gus Zeterenk was reviewing his meeting with Anthony Crane and Eli Russell. There were pros and cons, Gus decided.

The pros? Together, he and they had worked out a really good solution to the problem. His son, Donald, was not in any way connected to the killing of that Mexican. Indeed, with the short amount of time they'd had to put it together, the solution was solid. It cost him a lot of money – with that Carl Hannaford – but it certainly was well worth it.

The big con – though – was this private investigator. This Will Jonas. Gus was more worried about him than he'd been willing to admit to Anthony and Eli.

Yeah, Jonas had been retired for nine years now. Maybe getting a little old? Didn't look like it, though. Judging by how he'd proceeded thus far, Jonas seemed to still have all his *cajones*.

Gus sighed. It was at times like this that he most missed his wife, Gloria. When things got tense, she could always calm him down. When he needed, somehow, to relax.

Gus shook his head and rubbed his temples.

And of course, as he knew it would, whenever he thought about Gloria, his thoughts drove him back to the day of the airplane crash, two years ago.

And his guilt.

He remembered every word of their discussion about that flight, and Gloria's reluctance to take it.

As a special surprise for their 30th wedding anniversary, Gus had chartered a private plane to fly them down to Acapulco. The whole family. Gloria, their two young daughters, Dorita and Dalina, their son, Donald, and himself.

But at the last minute, there was a problem at the office. And Gus had to delay his departure. Donald's, too. His son was in the office, working as an apprentice, in anticipation of joining the company, once he graduated from college the next year.

"Listen, Gloria," Gus said to his wife when he called her, "The plane's ready. I want you and the girls to take it. Then, by the time the plane returns to Santa Monica Airport, Donald and I will be at the airport, and we'll fly down and join you."

"Gus," Gloria had said, "You know me and flying. How nervous I get. And how much better I feel, when you're with me. So, why can't the girls and I just wait here for you? At the airport. Then, when you and Donald get here, we'll all fly down together."

But, Gus recalled – whipped by the force of the guilt that never left him, he had insisted that Gloria go ahead with that earlier flight.

Not that he was one of those husbands who required that his wife do whatever he told her.

No, it wasn't that.

Rather, it was because he suspected that the office problem that was delaying his departure for the airport, was going to take quite a bit longer than he had indicated to Gloria. The wait at the airport would have been considerably longer than anticipated. And so, he had insisted Gloria and his daughters take the more immediate charter flight.

He had insisted.

And it had cost them their lives!

Shortly after takeoff, both engines shut down, and the plane had plunged into the Pacific. No survivors.

Just like that! His wife. And his two daughters were gone.

If only he hadn't insisted that they go ahead!

The guilt always hit him.

If only he hadn't pushed them into taking that earlier flight.

The impact never lessened. The loss of most of his family. A loss that left him now with only Donald.

Donald and he. The only family that was left to him.

And once again, Gus thought about the mantra by which he now lived, when it came to Donald and himself.

This remnant of family was all that he had.

Nothing more. Nothing more can happen to this family.

CHAPTER 27

"You're getting into some interesting territory there, my friend," Marty Gershon said later that day, when I told him about my meeting with Harley Jenkins.

"This is the kind of stuff that district attorneys have orgasms over," he added. "Corruption involving our civic leaders? Good for all sorts of headlines."

"And," I pointed out, "If this one turns out to be real, then it's good for our side, too."

"How so?"

"Well, I figure we can push the DA pretty hard on the Hannaford case, once we get our investigation squared away, and give them our report. Normally, they'd probably drag their feet a bit. Not want to admit that the case passed through their office with no real review."

"But if we do also have some solid corruption stuff for them, I'm sure we can get them to push on Hannaford."

"So, what's next on this one?" Marty asked.

"I'm meeting with the potential whistle blower, as soon as

Jenkins can arrange it."

....

And that turned out to be on Saturday morning, because Jenkins' friend could not get away from the office for a meaningful stretch of time during any weekday. So, Saturday, she and Jenkins took the 405 up to Sherman Oaks to meet me at the same IHOP where Jenkins and I had met before.

When they came in, I saw a nice looking, middle aged woman, very much on edge. Jenkins took her by the elbow and guided her toward the booth where I was sitting.

The woman – whose name I didn't know – Jenkins had been careful to keep that information from me – was casually, yet neatly dressed, in a pair of denim slacks and a blouse, looking every bit like a senior level civil servant. Someone whom I suspected operated with a good deal of self-confidence in her job.

But the strain of her present circumstances showed. Her smile was tentative. Her shoulders were sloping, and she kept looking at Jenkins for reassurance.

I got up to greet her. And I smiled, in a conscious effort to put her at ease, and to set a friendly tone for our meeting.

I held out my hand to shake hers.

"Hello. Thank you for coming here this morning. My name's Will Jonas. Please call me, Will."

The woman took my hand, but she looked at Jenkins, and I guessed at what was bothering her.

"It's okay," I assured her. "You don't have to give me your

name. Let's see how our meeting goes. And then, hopefully, you'll feel more comfortable about doing so."

She smiled, and I could see just a bit of relaxation working its way in to her shoulders.

"Thank you," she said.

We sat down and placed our orders with the waitress. Varied egg dishes all around. The waitress completed writing our orders, took our menus and walked away.

I gave what I hoped was another reassuring smile.

"Now, why don't you tell me what you want to tell me, about this situation you're in? Let's see if I can help you. Okay?"

She nodded, and seemed to relax a bit more.

"Thank you," she said. Then she took a deep breath and continued.

"I have this terrible problem. And it's not my fault! But I am very much afraid that it could blow up and ruin everything I've worked for, for the last, almost 28 years!"

She took a sip of her coffee.

"For almost three years now, I've been forced to take cash bribes from the mayor. Of course, he doesn't call them that. He calls them 'special payments' because of special work that I'm doing with certain accounts. But they're bribes. That's what they are."

"And what are these special accounts?" I asked.

"Large payments into overseas banks," she answered. "Accounts controlled by the mayor and by the chief of police.

"I also am making payments from the Junction City general fund to outside vendors, for some contract work that I don't think is being done. But the invoices are being produced. For new construction. For road repair. Things like that."

I asked, "To the best of your knowledge, is anyone else doing the kind of work you're doing? Do you think the mayor or the chief of police might have other people like you, working in a similar way?"

She shook her head.

"I don't think so. Mayor Crane doesn't trust many people. I know he trusts me. Oh god, I wish he didn't! But he does."

"Can you produce proof of what you're claiming? Paperwork on the overseas accounts? And on the phony work orders? Other examples?"

The woman looked at Jenkins. He nodded. Then she looked back at me.

"Yes. I can put a package together."

"Give it to Harley," I said.

Then I spoke to Jenkins.

"Harley, can you get that package to me, without any problems? I can meet you somewhere between here and Junction City."

"Can do," Jenkins said.

"Now," I continued, "assuming the paperwork is what I hope it will be, then you and I need to make sure we trust each other."

"From my end, I already feel certain. Harley's told me what you've done – or more correctly – not done, with that bribe money. Your concerns are real. And I want very much to help you. But before we can go any further, you've got to decide if you can trust me."

I stopped talking and looked at the woman.

"Do you trust me?"

She pushed her fork around her plate, looking downward, as she nudged at some of her uneaten breakfast. Then she looked up, and directly at me.

"I…I'm sure I can trust you. I do trust you. Can you help me?"

"Yes. But with a few conditions that I need to discuss with you."

"And what are those?" Jenkins asked.

"Pretty basic, but important," I answered, and then went on to explain, still concentrating my attention on the woman.

"As Harley knows. I'm now investigating the conviction of a man whom we believe was framed for a murder he didn't commit. He's now in prison. And my priority is to get him out of there."

"I'm right in the middle of that investigation. And I need to finish my work on it. Then, I'll be ready to report my findings to the regional district attorney's office in Inglewood."

"At that time, I'll also present your findings to the DA. Sorry, but I can't jump your stuff ahead. It wouldn't be fair to the man in prison. Yes, I know how difficult your situation is for you – right now – but you've got some time, until things come to a head. So I need to go – first – with the other investigation."

I paused and looked at the woman.

"So…what do you think? This okay with you?"

The woman looked at Harley. They exchanged nods.

"Yes," she said to me. "It's okay with me."

She smiled at me.

"And my name is Tia Ruiz."

CHAPTER 28

As usual, Louis The Fisherman's report was about as complete a document as possible, regarding what I liked to call the "underbelly" of whatever subject matter I had asked him to look into.

In this case, I wanted to know about two subjects – Junction City, and four people:

Mayor Anthony Crane

Chief of Police Eli Russell

Gordy Hannaford

Gus Zeterenk

Nothing much exciting about Mayor Crane. A life-long, small-time politician, he'd been mayor of Junction City for 11 years. The usual municipal routines – until four years ago, when Junction City held an election and became a charter city. There were rumors that the election was rigged. It wasn't publicized in advance. Only a few hundred voters turned out, and even some of those were suspect. But the charter city status was achieved. And from that point on, things got interesting. One example: there were rumors that some salaries had increased many times over their original figures.

Chief Russell, according to Louis, was pretty much what you might expect of a cop who headed a department, even a small one like Junction City's. Russell was a guy who worried the details. The Chief was close to Mayor Crane, Louis reported, and so it was believed that he benefited from whatever deals the city might set up, for the benefit of the key players.

Regarding Gus Zeterenk – Louis reported that he was a key figure in whatever went on, in Junction City. It was believed that it was Zeterenk who gave Crane and his associates the idea to become a charter city. And a number of the pocket-lining schemes that were rumored, seemed to be under Zeterenk's guidance. His Star Development, was the most active construction company in Junction City. Louis also reported that Zeterenk had suffered a personal tragedy two years ago, when his wife and two young daughters were killed in the crash of their chartered plane. Zeterenk and his son, Donald, a recent college graduate who now worked at Star Development, were not on the flight, and are the surviving members of the immediate family.

As for Gordy Hannaford, Louis reported he was no player in the city. Just an alcoholic who had never seemed able to hold on to a job – except in the last couple of years, when he had been hired as a maintenance man for one of the Zeterenk warehouses in Junction City. The only other thing to be noted about Hannaford, was that he was the father of Carl Hannaford who, about two years ago, had been convicted of killing someone in a bar room brawl. Carl was currently serving his sentence at the California State Prison in Lancaster.

After my first read-through of Louis's report, I went back and read it again. And this time around, something hit me right up on center stage.

I mean the information about Gus Zeterenk. That his wife and two daughters had died in a plane crash, leaving Zeterenk with one surviving child, his son, Donald.

And based on how Louis had described Donald, the man seemed to be just about the same age as…Carl Hannaford!

So! Think about this! Right from the start, Marty Gershon and I had wondered why Carl Hannaford was being set up, to take the place of the real killer.

Why such an effort?

The obvious answer? Because the real killer was someone with enough clout to possibly squirm away from responsibility, if a substitute fall guy could be found.

"Someone with enough clout," I said aloud, to myself.

And who fit those key words?

Certainly, Donald Zeterenk – through the clout of his father, Gus.

I recalled what Fred the bartender had told me about the fight at the UnaMas Bar. It was, he said, "between a Mexican guy and a white guy."

The white guy was in his early twenties. And Fred said the

white guy definitely was not Carl Hannaford, although Carl had gone outside with the other onlookers.

Damn! Could this Donald Zeterenk be the white guy in that argument that the bartender described?

Was he the real killer of Manny Estevez? With his father, probably helped by the mayor, and the chief, coming up with Carl Hannaford as a replacement candidate?

Was this more of the loose ends stuff that I kept running into as I did my interviews?

First, there was Fred, telling me that he had identified himself and had called the killing in to the Junction City Police Department at about 9:00 PM Saturday. But Russell's report stated that the call in came from an anonymous source at 2:35 AM Sunday.

Second, there was the difference between Russell and the coroner, Dr. Webstein, about the time of death. Webstein originally said TOD was between 8 PM and 11 PM, but Russell wanted it to be between 11 PM and 2 AM.

Third, there was the fact that no autopsy was done. They usually are, in a criminal death case. But Chief Russell had ruled against doing one. For budget reasons. Hard to accept that. Looked more like Russell just wanted to get rid of as much hard evidence as he could. And that not only meant no autopsy – it also meant shipping the body back to Mexico.

Fourth, of course, and as had been true right from the start, there was the question of whether or not Carl Hannaford really did do the killing. He didn't remember any details. And he kept referring to the fact that he was guilty because his father told him so.

Trying to take the long view on all of this, I asked myself the question: why had Chief Russell pushed so hard and so fast, on the original conviction? Even got a full confession from Carl at the scene of the crime?

"The whole deal was a set-up from the start," I said aloud. "Put together to save Gus Zeterenk's kid, from being arrested for the Estevez murder!"

I mulled and re-mulled these thoughts.

And the more I did so, the more it made sense to me.

"Rose!" I shouted. "I need you."

Rose came into my office.

"Listen, Will," she said. "We paid good money for the intercom. Why don't you use it – at least once in a while?"

"I promise. I really promise. But right now, I've got something important that I need you to do."

"And what is that?"

"Get on your computer and see if you can come up with a picture of a Donald Zeterenk. A guy in his early 20's. He's with a company called Star Development, in Century City."

"And you need this…yesterday?"

"Maybe even the day before that."

CHAPTER 29

"It makes sense," Marty Gershon said to me, a few hours later. "This is a hell of a deduction, Will. I'm impressed."

"Well, Marty, get unimpressed. Because it's all just smoke."

"You mean, it's circumstantial. And we need some hard facts to back everything up?"

"Exactly."

Marty shook his head.

"Will, I don't see where we're going to get that from. I don't know them, but I suspect that Crane, Russell and Zeterenk aren't going to cave that easily."

"No, they won't," I agreed. "But there is one person I think will be ripe for cracking, at the right time."

"You mean...Gordy Hannaford."

"The one and only. He's an alcoholic. And since I'm one, too, I know how hard it is to handle outside pressure. So, what we need to do, is to put enough pressure on him, at the same time that we show him how he can get out from under –if not all the shit that is about to come down –at least a good part of it."

"And how do we do that?"

"Damned if I know, Marty. You're the lawyer. You're supposed to figure out the summations. The stirring words that bend the jury to your will."

I was interrupted by Marty's secretary knocking on the door and then coming in, carrying a piece of paper.

"Your secretary just faxed this over," she said, handing me the paper.

It was a picture. A headshot of Donald Zeterenk, newest addition to the staff of Star Development. The original photo was in Star's company newsletter; Rose wrote on the bottom margin. Good going, Rose!

I showed Marty the shot.

"Meet who I think is our *real* murderer," I told him. "Donald Zeterenk."

I handed the sheet back to Marty's secretary.

"Please trim the picture, so the name doesn't show," I said. "Then make a few copies. Keep one for Marty and one for your files. And let me have a half dozen. But please, don't leave yet, okay?"

I turned back to Marty.

"Have you got a firm brochure with pictures of at least five of your young male lawyers, in their early to mid-twenties?"

Marty knew what I was thinking.

"You want to make up a six-pak of pictures to see if the bartender can pick out Zeterenk?"

"Right. Much stronger ID if he picks Donald from among a group of six. Better than my just handing him one picture of Donald, and asking him if he recognizes the guy."

"Barbara," Marty spoke to his secretary, "We've got that brochure with biographies and head shots of the new associates joining the firm."

Marty said to me, "Those should be fine. They're all in their mid-twenties."

To Barbara, he said, "Please bring one of those brochures back to us. And ask Gerry to come with you."

Marty explained to me, "Gerry is our graphics guy. Once we pick out the pictures, he can set them up in a six-pak, in whatever way you want."

"Great."

Barbara left and Marty looked at me and grinned.

"I like this better than working on those damned leases and agreements," he said. "Maybe I'll quit and we can go into business together."

"Definitely not." I countered. "Dealing with a lawyer once in a while is okay. But all the time? No."

CHAPTER 30

It took the good part of an hour to pick out the faces, and then for Gerry to put the six-pak together. But it was worth the effort. If Fred made a positive ID of Donald Zeterenk, there would be less of an argument about the validity of the identification process, because of the use of the six-pak tool.

Since it was rush hour, plus the fact that Junction City was in that part of Los Angeles County where "too many cars" was an understatement, it took me an hour and a half to reach UnaMas.

It was still early enough in the evening, so that only a few dedicated drinkers were in place, along with Fred, behind the bar, doing the usual – that is, cleaning glasses.

"Look whose back," he said, smiling. "Welcome. The usual?"

"Thanks," I said, sitting down at the bar and taking a drink of the club soda that he poured for me.

"What brings you down here, again? Still working on that Hannaford case?"

"Yes. And the reason I'm here, is that I'd like to get some

more information from you. About the guy – you called him 'the white guy' – who was in that fight with the victim, Estevez."

Fred shrugged.

"Not sure what more I can give you. I never saw the guy before. Or not ever again."

"Well, I'd still like to give it a try. Okay?"

"Sure."

"Thanks. So, here's what I want to do. I want to show you some pictures. And let's see, if among them, you can pick that guy out."

"Man, that was two years ago," Fred protested.

"That's okay," I said. "Now, let me explain the process. What I've done is take the pictures of six people and put them together in what we call a 'six-pak.'"

"And I'm supposed to pick out they guy, from among those six?"

"Only if you recognize him. Fred, let me be absolutely clear about one thing. You should only pick out someone, if you truly do remember him as the person who was in that fight. If you don't see anyone who you think is the right guy, then that's okay. Under those circumstances, just don't pick anyone. Understand?"

"I understand."

"Okay, then here are the pictures."

I took the six-pak from the envelope in which I'd carried it, and laid it on the bar, right side facing Fred. Then, I sat back, out of his direct line of sight. I didn't want any of my body language to interfere with, or influence, Fred's ID processing.

Fred took his time looking at the six-pak. At first, he didn't seem to recognize anyone. Then, he started coming back to the picture of Donald Zeterenk. Left it. Came back. Left it. Came back again.

He tapped the picture.

"This guy," Fred said, "I'm not that sure. But he looks...familiar."

I didn't say anything. Didn't want break his concentration.

Fred stared at Zeterenk's photo, then at me.

"Look, here is where I'm coming out."

He tapped Zeternek's photo, again.

"Like I said, this guy looks familiar. But can I swear he's the guy – the white guy in the fight? No."

Fred did some more thinking.

"I'd say this. I'm about 75 per cent sure he's the guy from two years ago. But that's as far as I can go."

"Of course, I'd have been happier if Fred had absolutely recognized Daniel Zeterenk. But I could live with 75 per cent. It would serve my purposes, at this point in the investigation."

"Don't worry it, Fred," I assured him. "Your 75 per cent is good enough."

"Do you know him? Do you know who the guy is?" Fred asked. "Is he under arrest?"

I didn't want to lie to Fred, but I didn't want to answer his questions, at this point. So, I gave him a partially truthful answer.

"I have a pretty good idea who he is. But I've got to verify some things before I go any further."

Truthful enough, right? Like the kind of "lawyer talk" Marty Gershon might have used.

CHAPTER 31

Sometimes, some things are right with the world.

And I walked into one of those "right times" when, later that night, I opened the door of our condo in Tarzana, to be greeted by my beautiful wife, Lu, with an on-the-lips-no-kidding-around kiss, and a fresh glass of club soda.

I returned the kiss with equal enthusiasm, even as my sense of smell was being activated by a wonderful aroma floating out from the kitchen.

"One of your favorites...Beef Bourguignonne," Lu said.

"What's the occasion?"

"I'm still in charge," Lu said with a smile. "At the office."

"Things are okay?"

"Better than okay."

"Explain, please."

"The deal is going through. We are being acquired by General National Bank. But the way they're setting things up, I'll be in charge of all Information Technology work, for the western half of the country. Not just California, but everything west of – as they say – the Mississippi."

"That *is* good news."

Lu hooked her arm into mine and guided us toward the dining room.

"Come on. Let's eat. And then we can talk," she suggested.

So, we did. And now we were sitting in the den, with our coffee.

"No more worrying about getting old?" I asked Lu. "You were definitely thinking along those lines, last week."

"Oh, it's still something that concerns me. And I'm sure I'll be thinking about aging, more and more, in the future. Got to be inevitable."

Lu looked closely at me.

"What about you, Will? Any more of that old age feeling creeping up on you? Like it did last week?"

"At the moment? Absolutely not. Of course, my feelings are influenced by the fact that things are going great right now."

"How so?"

"The Carl Hannaford investigation. Everything is starting to fall into place."

"You getting closer to figuring out who influenced Hannaford to confess? If indeed, he actually was influenced."

"Oh, he was influenced, alright. And I'm pretty sure I know where it came from. The key, now, is how to proceed, how to get Carl cleared, and out of prison."

CHAPTER 32

A couple of days after Tia, Harley and I met, Harley delivered the package of documents that Tia had promised. And as I reviewed the documents, it was clear that the officials in Junction City should be in prison.

I asked Marty Gershon to meet with me, and to review the package. I felt it was important to have Marty, a lawyer, assess the documents as to validity and culpability for wrongdoing.

Tia had included samples of the following:

...A contract between the City and Star Development for building some new streets, for paving other streets, and for general street repair and maintenance. Cost: $1,250,000. Tia attached a note: "None of the work was ever done. And there is nothing in our records to back up the charges."

...Paperwork indicating that Mayor Crane's salary for the previous year was seven hundred and twenty-five thousand dollars. And that Chief Russell's pay had been five hundred and twenty-five thousand dollars.

...Copies of deposit slips for Crane and Russell bank accounts in the Cayman Islands.

The Crane paperwork showed a balance of eight hundred and forty-seven thousand dollars. The Russell account had a balance of five hundred and thirty-seven thousand dollars.

...A copy of an assessor's report on a newly constructed warehouse, with a handwritten note on it, which said – "Anthony...can you get this appraisal lowered? Need the lesser amount in order to be able to return anything worthwhile to you. Thanks." And it was signed: Gus.

After he finished going through the documents, Marty said, "If this stuff is valid, then it's like gold for the prosecution."

"Yeah, I figured the same," I said.

We were interrupted by the intercom on Marty's desk. It was his secretary, Barbara.

"Marty, I've got a collect call for you, from Jack Lewis in Lancaster. He's on line two."

Marty picked up the phone.

"Jack...?"

"Hello, Marty. Listen. I've got some good news. It looks like Carl Hannaford is starting to remember the real...the true circumstances...surrounding the killing that night. To be specific, here is what he's saying, word for word. 'I don't think I killed that man. My Dad told me I did, but I think my father made a mistake. The other man did it.'"

"That *is* good news, Jack."

"Yeah. And he didn't just say it once. When we met in the

Yard a little while ago, he kept repeating it to me. That is, until one of the guards separated us."

"They're still not letting you be together?" Marty asked.

"Right," Jack confirmed. Then he asked, "Marty, does this information help?"

"Jack," I broke into the conversation, "This definitely helps."

"Hi, Will," Jack replied. "How are you feeling about the investigation?"

"Good, Jack," I answered. "Good. Hopefully, we can wrap it up, soon, and present our findings to the district attorney."

The call with Jack ended, and Marty said to me, "I'm going up to Lancaster tomorrow. I want to tape record Carl. Hopefully, he'll still be saying the same things when I do the tape."

"Good idea," I agreed. "At some point, we'll need that recording."

I shook my head.

"Listen, Marty, the fact that Carl is seeming to remember things – well – that is good. But there is a problem with it. And you know what it is, just like I do."

Marty sighed.

"Yeah, I know. Most third parties, especially judges, would conclude that Carl was just changing his words in a typical jailhouse maneuver. Change the testimony. Try for a new trial."

I said, "I think it's great if Carl is starting to remember what really happened that night. And at some point, this new testimony of his will be important."

"But Marty, what really concerns me right now, is the same problem we've been facing all along. No hard evidence. What we've got is mainly circumstantial. I think it's good. Strong. But not hard facts."

"So, what do we do, Will?"

"We start getting more confrontational. That's what we do."

"First, as soon as we finish this meeting, I'm going over to Star Construction. And I'm going to ask to see Daniel or Gus Zeterenk. They probably won't see me. But my visit will put them on the defensive. Maybe goad them into doing something that we can latch on to."

"Next, I'm going to see Gordy Hannaford. I figure he'll know about Carl's revived memory. Chief Russell has to bring Gordy up to date, so Gordy can get back up to Lancaster, and try to convince Carl that these new thoughts of his are wrong."

"And after that, I'm going to go after Chief Russell and Mayor Crane. Get them worried. That's what I aim to do."

"You think it'll work?"

"Maybe not one hundred per cent. But I bet I open up some more things for them to worry about. And the more they worry, the better our chances."

CHAPTER 33

It took me about 40 minutes to get from Marty's Encino office to the Star Development office in Century City. On the drive in, I thought about how I wanted to handle the confrontation. And that's what it was going to be...a confrontation.

One way to do it would be to go to Star and ask to see Donald Zeterenk. See if that got me anywhere.

An alternative plan would be to ask to see Gus Zeterenk.

I decided confronting Donald would be potentially more productive. I had the feeling that he would wilt faster than his father.

Most folks living in Los Angeles and the surrounding area do know where Century City is, and what it is. But for those uninitiated, Century City is a 176-acre neighborhood and business district in Los Angeles' Westside, just outside of Downtown Los Angeles, and adjacent to Beverly Hills. It's a metropolitan area of skyscrapers, giving it its own distinctive skyline. Large numbers of prominent and successful companies are headquartered in the area.

Star Development was one of these. Its HQ was in a high-rise on Avenue of the Stars, between Santa Monica Boulevard and West Olympic Boulevard. Turning right, off of Santa Monica Boulevard, I drove a short way on Avenue of the Stars and then turned right, into the underground parking for number 12715, took the ticket that popped out of the entry box and eventually found a parking space on the second floor of the garage.

According to the lobby directory, Star Development was on the 9th floor, so that's the button I pushed in the elevator. When I arrived on the 9th floor, I followed the hall signs to Star Development, suite 908, and went in.

The reception area was standard leather, iron and glass, along with a reception desk and a young and attractive woman who gave me her professional smile.

"Greetings to Star Development, Sir. May I help you?"

"Thank you. I'd like to see Donald Zeterenk, please."

"May I ask your name? And do you have an appointment?"

"No appointment. And my name's Will Jonas."

I figured I might as well heat things up a bit, so I added, "And please tell Donald that I'd like to talk to him about…UnaMas. That's spelled…u…n…a…m…a…s."

The receptionist dialed a number, and then I listened to her side of the conversation.

"Donald? Hello. There is a gentleman here to see you. No appointment, he tells me. But he said he'd like to talk to you about" …and here, the receptionist checked her notes… "UnaMas. He spelled it out to me as…u…n…a…m…a…s."

Evidently, Donald was answering the receptionist, and the answer wasn't one she expected. Although it was the answer I expected. That Donald did not want to see me.

No surprise. The surprise would have been if he *had* agreed to see me. That would have been an interesting confrontation – Donald and the six-pak ID.

But this was okay. My main purpose in coming to Star had been, as that old saying goes, "To shake some apples from the tree."

And I was sure I was doing just that.

Now, both Zeterenk's would know that I was closing in on them. That I wanted to talk to them about UnaMas.

Damage done.

I thanked the receptionist and left Star, on my way to my next tree shaking.

CHAPTER 34

While I was shaking Donald Zeterenk's tree at Star Development, Gus Zeterenk was meeting in Junction City with Mayor Anthony Crane and Chief of Police Eli Russell.

Chief Russell had called for the meeting, and now, he explained why, to Crane and Zeterenk.

"I went up to Lancaster yesterday, to see Carl Hannaford," Russell said, "Because one of my prison contacts said that Carl is beginning to remember the details of what happened at the UnaMas Bar. Most important, he's beginning to question his involvement in the killing."

Eli read from his notes.

"Here is what he's saying."

"'I don't think I killed that man. My Dad told me I did it, but I think my father made a mistake. That other man did it.'"

"That other man did it?" Gus Zeterenk questioned.

"That's what he said," Ira answered.

"Did Carl say anything else?" Mayor Crane asked.

"No," Eli answered, "What I read you is what Carl was saying yesterday. Don't know about today. But if there is any more, then my contact will call me."

"Shit," Gus said.

"Yeah, shit," Crane agreed.

"Has Gordy been going up there? Like he was supposed to?" Gus asked.

"Yes," Eli answered. "I've made sure of that. Gordy has been going. And he has been pushing. Carl. But it isn't working, anymore."

No one said anything for several seconds, and then Gus spoke.

"If Carl is starting to remember, then he very well may remember that…that Donald…was the guy who was arguing with that Mexican. And I can't have that happen!"

Again, there was silence. And again, it was Gus who broke it.

"Carl has to be killed."

"Kill Carl?" Mayor Crane's voice was almost shrill. "Are you listening to what you're saying? You want to commit murder?"

"I don't know what else we can do," Gus said. "If Carl starts denying he did it, then that will open up one hell of a mess for us. What else can we do?"

"I don't know the answer to that, Gus," the Mayor objected, "But I do know, that I don't want to commit a murder!"

"We're talking about my son," Gus said strongly. "I will not let anything happen to him! No way!"

The three of them were silent, until Gus spoke again.

"Here is how I want to handle this."

He challenged Eli and Anthony, but neither said anything.

He asked Eli, "With your contacts at the prison in Lancaster, can you arrange for someone to kill Carl? Make it look like an accident? Or suicide? But done, so that it doesn't point back toward us? Is this something you can do?"

Eli nodded.

"Yes. It can be arranged. But it's going to cost you."

"How much?"

"Maybe five, ten thousand."

"I want you to tell them the payment will be $15,000. But only if it is absolutely not traceable back to us. Can you do that?"

Eli nodded.

"For that kind of a payoff, it can be done."

"How fast?"

Eli thought.

"Within a week."

Gus stared at the Mayor and then the Chief.

"Look, Guys, I really wish there was another way to handle this mess. But there isn't. And I've got to protect the only family that I have left—my son, Donald."

"We have our families, too," Anthony said. "We have to think about all of this in relation to our families, Gus."

"Up to now," Gus snapped, "Your families have done pretty damn well, with all of the ideas I've been bringing to you. Thanks to what you've been able to pull off as a charter city—and remember, that was my idea – you both have more money than you ever dreamed of having!"

"Gus," Anthony said, "We know all that. And we acknowledge our debt to you. But…ordering a murder? No! That's not something I thought we'd ever be doing."

"Anthony," Gus replied to the mayor, "We put Carl Hannaford into prison for something he didn't do. And we made it possible for my son to get away with murder. We've already played with people's lives. So, how much more of a deal is it, to arrange for Carl Hannaford to die?"

Eli gave a deep sigh.

"Gus, you make it sound so…kind of like a textbook. A lecture. Clean murder. No bodies."

He sighed again.

"Okay, Gus. When you lay it all out – I can see your logic."

Eli turned to Crane.

"It does make sense, Anthony. And it does look like it's the smartest thing we can do. We have to do it."

The Mayor did not reply at once. Instead, he kept his head bowed, almost in a praying position. When he finally did speak, his voice was soft, almost a whisper.

"God help us…"

CHAPTER 35

On my way to see Gordy Hannaford, I figured that, by now, he would have been told – probably by Chief Russell – that Carl was beginning to remember things differently.

And I suspected that Gordy would not be handling that information well. Probably drinking heavily.

Hell! I was *hoping* he'd be drinking.

Yes, I know. It was terrible for me, an alcoholic, to hope another alcoholic was drinking. But I had some special circumstances going here, so I figured no attendees at an AA meeting would object. And even if they did, I wasn't going to listen. I had a chance here, to help Carl Hannaford beat a wrong conviction. So I had to go at it, with everything that I had.

I reached Gordy's beat-up house shortly before noon. And although it was a work day, I figured he was home. Not at work. Not in view of today's developments.

I went up to the front door and pounded on it.

"Gordy! Gordy Hannaford! I need to talk to you!"

I went at it loudly and harshly, hoping that to be the best way to frighten him. To break him down, which is what I wanted to do.

No answer.

I banged on the door again.

"I know you're in there, Gordy. Open up."

I heard someone moving around inside, coming to the door.

It opened. But it wasn't Gordy. It was Melanie, his daughter.

I had only seen Melanie for a moment, during my earlier visit to Gordy. She'd been in the hallway, leading out of the living room and to the rest of the house.

I knew that she was twelve years old, and looking at her now, I saw the first traces of someone who would grow into an attractive woman. And I could see, too, that unlike the confused Carl, or the beaten down wife, Hazel, or the alcohol-driven Gordy – Melanie was different. She seemed bright. Alert. And despite her circumstances – or maybe because of them -- she seemed ready to face the world.

"He's in the kitchen," Melanie said.

She stepped aside, to let me in.

For a moment, I delayed going to the kitchen. This young lady, obviously so different from the other members of her family, deserved some attention.

"Melanie," I asked her, "Are you okay? There's a lot happening here right now. Are you okay? Where's your mother?"

"She's in bed. One of her headaches."

She nodded toward the kitchen.

"He's in the kitchen," she repeated.

Then she turned and disappeared into the hall leading to the rest of the house.

I went into the kitchen, and there was Gordy, sitting at the kitchen table, a bottle of cheap whiskey next to him, and next to that, a half empty glass.

"Hello, Gordy," I said, sitting down opposite him. I nodded to the glass and bottle.

"Been drinking, some?"

"Why the hell not?" He said, with just a slight slur in his voice.

I guessed he hadn't been drinking that much – yet.

"Because I need to talk to you about Carl, and what he's now beginning to remember about that killing at the UnaMas Bar. I'm sure Chief Russell has told you the latest? What Carl's now saying?"

Gordy nodded. "Yeah, he told me. Doesn't change a thing. Carl's so brain dead that he never remembers anything. Right or wrong."

"You mean, that what he's remembering now…that he didn't kill the guy? That's not the truth?"

"The truth is…like I told it originally to Chief Russell."

Gordy took a good swallow from his glass, then continued.

"What Carl is saying now, doesn't mean a thing. What counts is what Carl said before. When he confessed to the Chief."

Gordy looked at me and smiled.

"The Chief says nothing's changed. Not really. And that's the way it's gonna be."

CHAPTER 36

I got back to my office in Woodland Hills about an hour later. Rose greeted me as soon as I came in.

"You have your pager with you, right?"

"Right."

"So, why wasn't it turned on? I've been calling you, every few minutes for the last hour. There is someone who says he needs to talk to you. About Carl Hannaford. But he won't tell me his name. And he won't tell me his number. In other words, he is giving me nothing. Except...except he says he must talk to you. And he said he would call back at 2 PM."

We both looked at our watches. Two PM would be a couple of minutes from now.

Rose directed me, "Go sit at your desk...and stay there."

Dare I do otherwise? I dare not.

I went and sat at my desk, and wondered who was trying to reach me. Couldn't come up with any name, but it was now just about 2 PM, and my phone started ringing.

I picked it up.

"Will Jonas…"

"Will?" The man was speaking softly. "This is Ed Chomsky. Remember me?"

"Of course, Ed," I answered. "Saw you up in Lancaster."

Chomsky was the prison guard who'd met Marty and me and escorted us to the interview room for our first meeting with Carl Hannaford.

"What can I do for you, Ed?" I asked.

There was a short pause at the other end before Chomsky replied.

"Will, this is a dangerous call for me to make. Before we go any further, you have to promise that you won't identify me to anyone. And I mean…anyone. Can you make me that promise, Will?"

"It would help if I knew what this was about, Ed."

"No! Either you promise, or I hang up! Right now!"

I decided to meet Ed's condition.

"Okay, Ed. I'll never reveal you as the source for whatever it is, you tell me. I promise."

"Alright. Here's what you need to know. A contract has been put out…on Carl Hannaford. A contract to kill him. Make it look like suicide. Or an accident."

"Shit! How reliable is this information?"

"Very reliable. I was in the wrong place at the right time. So, I overheard the discussion. Just a few hours ago. The price tag is $15,000."

"Yeah, and one more thing. It's supposed to be done within one week. I also heard that."

"Ed, I appreciate this information. Is there anything I can do for you?"

"If you mean, a payoff? Absolutely not. Look, Will, like you, I take pride in my work. True, the last several years, it's been harder to do that. Too much corruption in too strong a union. But I'll be done in a year and a half. And I'm all set and ready for that."

"So, I just hope that this information is of help to you, Will. I've gotten to know Carl Hannaford a bit. True, he's not very bright. But he's a sweet, simple person. And if he's been railroaded … well, if what I've told you, helps to straighten things out for him…that'll be payment enough."

"Goodbye, Will."

The line went dead. I put down my phone and thought about what I'd just heard. And what to do about it. And indeed, what to do about our entire investigation.

I picked up my phone and dialed Marty Gershon's private number. He answered, and I said, "Marty, can you get out to my office as soon as possible? We need to talk. And we need to make some decisions."

CHAPTER 37

Marty was in my office an hour later…about 3:30 PM…and I brought him up to date.

I told him about my visit to Star Construction and not being able to see Daniel Zeterenk.

I told him about my meeting with Gordy Hannaford, and how Hannaford was sticking with the official view of the facts, despite what Carl was now starting to remember.

And about the telephone call I got, telling me about the contract on Carl. True to my promise, I did not mention Ed Chomsky's name or the fact that he was a guard up at the prison.

"Marty," I then said, "Here's what I'm thinking."

"On Hannaford, we're not going to find out anything more. Because we don't have the official standing, to confront any of the key players. To bring them in for questioning. To start an official investigation. Instead – we've got to go with what we have. What do you think?"

"Yeah, I've got to agree. What we have is solid. But it is circumstantial – and not likely to get any better."

I continued.

"And now, I'm worried about this contract on Carl. We've got to get him into some sort of protective custody."

"Agreed." Marty said. "Then he switched subjects."

"What about the other investigation?" he asked. "About the corruption? That one looks even stronger to me. And it involves many of the same players."

"Yup. And that's going to be our leverage," I told him.

"Our leverage?"

"With the L.A. District Attorney. And more specifically, with the branch office in Inglewood."

"That's where you met that assistant DA, right?"

"Yes. Jesus Morales. And when we met, he said to me... 'I promise I'll take seriously anything that you come up with.' Well, I figure it's time to take Jose up on that offer. And I'm hoping, too, that when we give him the very solid corruption stuff, then he'll seriously follow through on the Hannaford case, despite it being so heavily circumstantial."

CHAPTER 38

Before calling Morales, I wanted to alert Tia Ruiz that we were going to bring her information to the attention of the district attorney. I wanted to make sure that she still was comfortable with our doing so.

It being mid-afternoon, I knew Tia would still be at work, and I didn't want to call her there. So, I called Harley Jenkins at home, hoping that he might be working the night shift. Turned out he was.

"Harley," I told him, "I want to let Tia and you know that we're ready to discuss her information with the DA's office. Trying to set up a meeting as soon as possible."

"Wow! We're down to the short hairs, huh?"

"Yes, we are. But we don't want to move ahead, unless she gives us a final okay to do so. Here's how we plan to proceed, provided Tia agrees."

"We will present the documents Tia gave us, and describe what Tia told us – but we are not going to reveal who she is, until we get assurances that she won't be in any trouble for having taken the bribe payoffs. The DA has to agree with Tia and her claim that she only took the payoffs because she was frightened, and concerned about her pension and her benefits."

"That sounds good to me," Harley said. "But it's really Tia who has to agree with what you're proposing."

"Right. But I don't want to call her at work. Or even at home, to discuss this with her. I have no proof or anything, but it could be that her phone line is bugged."

"I'll call her at her office," Harley said. "Ask her to take a break and go to the cafeteria. I'll meet her there. Not unusual. Plenty of cops go to eat there. Good food."

"When can you do this?"

"I'll call her now. See when she can meet. I'll call you back."

And he did. About ten minutes later.

"I'm going to meet her now. In the cafeteria. Call you back within a half hour."

In just under that time, Harley called back.

"Tina says go ahead. She's ready. Nervous as hell. But ready."

CHAPTER 39

By now, it was later in the afternoon, but Assistant DA Jesus Morales was still in his office.

"Will. Nice to hear from you."

"Hello, Jesus. Do you remember what you said when we met?"

After a short pause, Morales answered. "Sure do. I told you to get back to me, if you discovered anything of interest. So, have you got something for me?"

"Jesus, I've got *two* 'somethings' for you. Two solid investigations. Ready for you to take over."

"Two? I only remember one. About that Hannaford person convicted of killing someone at the UnaMas Bar in Junction City."

"And I've got enough on that one, I believe, to get Carl Hannaford out of Lancaster – and – the real murderer arrested and convicted."

"But Jesus, the other investigation report I have for you, has the potential for turning into a very high visibility case. Lots of major media."

Morales laughed.

"Okay! Enough with the buildup, Will. What's the deal?"

"The deal is...major corruption in Junction City. Involving the mayor, chief of police, a prominent Los Angeles businessman, secret overseas bank accounts, payoffs for phantom works projects. Got the picture?"

Morales did not respond right away. And when he did talk, he was all-business.

"Will, this is very heavy stuff. Can you back it up?"

"With a solid paper file, Jesus. And...that file comes with a live, whistleblower."

"Who is...?"

"The identity of the whistleblower is a point we have to discuss, before I can tell you. Here's what I mean."

Without revealing her name, gender or position, I told Jesus about Tia Ruiz and how she had banked all of her payoff payments. Never withdrew or spent a cent of it. And why she did what she did.

"Jesus, I'm convinced the whistleblower is innocent. Caught in a tough situation, and handled honorably. If you can assure as to innocence, the blower is ready to give you everything you need to break this one wide open."

There was a pause of several seconds. I let it go. Time for Jose to think.

He finally said, "On this corruption stuff, with what you've given me, I'm going to have to go higher up. I'd like to get a meeting – with the right people – set up by tomorrow afternoon."

"That's fine, Jesus. But listen…let's not forget about Hannaford. Yes, I know the corruption case can be the hot one. But Hannaford's important. And if what we give you, proves our claim of his innocence, then I'll need your word that you'll move ahead on that one, too. Hopefully, to ask for a favorable ruling by a judge that gets Carl out of that cell in Lancaster."

"Of course you're right, Will. Corruption is sexy. But I promise you, that if you have a strong case for Hannaford, I will move on it. I feel personally responsible for that one, since I reviewed the original case, and just plain rubber-stamped it."

"Good. Now, on Hannaford, we have an immediate problem."

"What's that?"

"I can't reveal my source, but I've learned that a contract has been put out on Carl Hannaford. I believe my source. And I am convinced that Carl's life is in danger. So, can you get him into protective isolation…right away?"

"That's a tough one, Will."

"The man is innocent, Jesus. The system fucked him once, already, by imprisoning him. It would be terrible if he got shafted a second time—by someone killing him."

"Okay, your point is well taken. I'll see what I can do. I will push to have it happen just as soon as possible."

Morales shifted subjects.

"Will, I'll get back to you soon. Hopefully to confirm a meeting for tomorrow afternoon. Here in our office. I want one of our key guys from the L.A. office to be in the meeting. He specializes in corruption investigations, and he'd be the one handling this. And I want the head of our branch office here, also at the meeting, because we'll handle Hannaford out of here."

"Good. There will be two of us. I've been working the Hannaford investigation with Carl's lawyer, Martin Gershon. Marty brought me in on Hannaford, originally."

Jesus asked, "What about the corruption source? The whistleblower? How'd you get on that one?"

"A source in Junction City knew about me and my working the Hannaford investigation. That source's friend is the whistleblower. They were stuck and didn't know what to do. Who to talk to. So the source contacted me."

"Do we get to meet these people tomorrow?"

"No. We'll have a solid package of documents from the whistleblower, to show you. But I can't reveal who the blower is, until the district attorney's office agrees – in writing – that there will be no prosecution of that person."

"Will…" Jesus interrupted me.

I interrupted him.

"Yeah, Jesus…I know you can't give any such assurance, just on what I've told you now. Based on the documentation I've seen –though – I'm pretty sure the DA's office will feel comfortable with no prosecution of the whistleblower. Please just hold up on any judgement here, until you get the full picture."

"Fair enough," Jesus agreed. "Let me get to my people now,

and see if I can get this meeting set up for tomorrow afternoon. Let's say, at 2:30."

Jesus hung up, and I asked Marty, "Ever pull an all-nighter?"

"Yeah, when I was a lot younger."

"Well, it may not be a full all-nighter, but here is what I suggest for our meeting tomorrow. Let's do things in three parts."

"Part One should be a document that you write, reporting on what we've found out, about the Hannaford conviction. Done as much like a legal brief as is possible. I figure these folks are going to need something like that. It just goes with their DNA."

"And Part Two," Marty said, "is you giving them, verbally, the key points from the brief."

"Make sense?" I asked

"Makes sense," Marty said. "And then I assume you're going to hit them with the corruption file? That's the one they're really going to be looking for."

"That's the one," I agreed. "But not until we're comfortable that they *will* work strong and hard on Hannaford."

Marty looked at his watch. "Got to get back to my office. To work on the brief."

"And I'll be here with Rose, working on my end of the report."

CHAPTER 40

By 9:30 that night, Rose and I had pretty well wrapped up my report. I'd made a few final changes to the text, and Rose was inserting them. When that was finished, we'd be done. Time to go home.

Rose shouted into me, from her desk outside.

"Will, the night line is blinking. Someone is trying to call us."

I usually don't pick up the night line. It most often is a wrong number, anyway. Or if it isn't, then it's a client, with a question, that could wait until the next morning.

But I thought it might be Marty, for some last minute discussion, so I picked up the line.

"Hello, this is Will Jonas."

There was a pause.

"Mr. Jonas? Mr. Jonas? Can you help me, please?"

I recognized the voice. It was Melanie Hannaford, and she sounded frightened.

"Melanie? What's the matter? How can I help you?"

"You left your card on the table. I need you, please. I need you."

"Of course, Melanie. Whatever you need, I'll help you. Just tell me what you need."

"Can you please come and get me? I need to get away from here. Away from him. I need to get away!"

"Melanie, is someone chasing you? Where are you?"

"I'm at home. But I have to get away from my father. He…he tried to come into my room before. I locked the door. But he banged on it so hard, that, it's almost broken."

Oh shit! I was afraid of what I was hearing! Of what it sounded like. Got to help her!

"Melanie, I *will* help you. I will. Where is your father now?"

"He's in the kitchen. Passed out."

"What about your mother?"

"In bed! Where she always goes at times like this! Please help me!"

"Okay. I'm going to come and get you. Can you get out of the house? Can you do that? And is there some place nearby, where I can meet you?"

"Yes, I can get out. He'll be passed out for a while, now."

There was a pause, and then she continued. "Two blocks away from here, there's a gas station. A Union 76 station. With a little market. Can you pick me up there?"

"Absolutely!" I assured her.

"Listen, Melanie…it is going to take me about an hour to get there. But I'm coming."

"Melanie, I promise. I am coming to get you. Everything is going to be alright. Just get out, and then wait for me. Can you do that?"

"Yes..."

And then she hung up.

By this time, having listened in on the conversation, Rose was in my office.

"Is it what it sounds like? Her father is abusing her?"

"It sure sounds that way."

"What are you going to do?"

"What I promised her I'd do."

"I'm coming with you," Rose said.

CHAPTER 41

On the way to Junction City, Rose and I discussed what to do.

"One thing I know," I said, "I don't want Melanie to end up with the County Department of Children and Family Services. I've heard too many horror stories about what happens to kids in that set up. I hope she has some relatives that we can contact, who will look after her, until this all gets resolved."

"So fast it's not going to get resolved, if her father has been abusing her," Rose said. "But I agree with you. No Family Services."

Rose was silent for a moment, but I could almost hear the gears meshing in her brain. It's not that she specifically, like the saying goes, "thinks out loud." But she was going through something kind of like that. Then she spoke to me.

"The girl, she stays with me. I have the extra bedroom. We get her a few new things to wear. She stays with me."

Rose looked over at me and smiled.

"Of course, this does mean I may not be in the office very much, for the next few days. Do you think you can get along

165

without me?"

"If I have to, yeah. But you know, you might want to bring her in to the office. To sort of...help you out. Make some work for her. Try to keep her mind occupied."

"Good," Rose agreed. "Sometime at home. And sometime in the office."

By now, we were in Junction City and I saw the Union 76 station a few blocks ahead. When I got there, I pulled into one of the parking spaces serving the small market attached to the station.

"I think I should go in alone," I said to Rose. "She knows me. She doesn't know you. And I don't want her to panic."

"No," Rose said. "She needs to see that a woman is going to help her. I should come with you."

We got out of the car and went into the market. There were just two, short aisles of shelves, so it was easy to spot Melanie down at the end of one of them. When she saw me, she sort of half-waived and drew herself up, from the slumped over stance she had, when I first spotted her.

I smiled and walked toward her, followed by Rose.

"Melanie," I said softly, "As I promised, here we are. We're here to help you."

I held out my hand in her direction.

She hesitated.

Rose stepped around me and walked up to Melanie. She smiled at her, and then she put her arms around the girl.

"Melanie, I'm Rose. Nu? You come home with me now. We

will tell each other good things. Nice stories. About nice things. Come."

The girl looked at Rose and made her decision. She folded herself into Rose. Rose then led her out of the store, me following. It was clear that I had been demoted to being the driver. And that was fine with me.

CHAPTER 42

In my office the next morning, I called Marty and told him about Melanie and what had happened.

"Will, you need to be careful on this one," Marty said. "I mean, the girl is a minor. Both her father and her mother could claim that she was abducted. This, despite anything Melanie would say in your defense."

"And even if the parents didn't come after you, the L.A. County Department of Children and Family Services will. And in particular, the Abused Child Section. That Department has gotten a lot of bad press lately. And they would love to look like knights in shining armor, going after you. A private eye, along with his secretary, grabbing this young girl in the middle of the night."

"But it wasn't anything like that," I protested.

"Will, come on. We're not talking reality here. We're talking perceptions."

"No! What we are talking about is a young girl's entire future life. And if I have to take some chances to make sure she *has* a good future life...well...so be it."

"Of course," Marty came back at me, thoughtfully, "If Melanie could be cast as someone who can provide important testimony in our investigation, maybe she can be declared a material witness who needs to be kept in protective custody. And if she is spending that custody with a nice Jewish grandmother-type, like Rose – it all might just work out."

"Sounds right," I said. "So we have to get the District Attorney's office to agree to that, when we meet with them later today."

Marty said, "Agree to that. Agree to protect Carl Hannaford. Agree to pick up and run with our investigation. That's a lot for them to agree to, Will."

"Yeah, but we're going to be brilliant, Marty," I joked. "Can't you just feel it?"

"What I feel, is something I need a Tums for. That's what I feel, Will."

"Take two, Marty. And I'll meet you a few minutes before 2:30 in Inglewood, at the ADA field office."

CHAPTER 43

I was alone in the office. Rose was at her apartment, with Melanie. I called, to check in. Rose picked up.

"Hello, Will." Rose had one of those phones that identified the caller.

"Rose. How is it going?"

"Melanie is asleep. We stayed up until 2 AM. Just talking. I learned a lot, Will. And it wasn't good. He's been abusing her for years. But she fought him off, about a year ago. And he hasn't bothered her since then. Except, last night, when he was drunk, he tried to get into her room. That is when she called you."

"How is she holding up?"

"She is one strong young person. She is going to need help. No doubt. But she is going to come through, just fine. I have great hopes for her, for the future."

I decided I had to alert Rose to the legal problem Marty had outlined.

"Rose, I need to warn you, that by keeping Melanie, you probably are breaking the law. And the Department of Children and Family Services will probably come after you, and me, once someone figures out where Melanie is. And someone will figure it out. Maybe her mother. Who knows?"

"So what are we supposed to do, Will? Turn the girl out? Send her back to her wonderful family?"

"No. Just alert Family Services and turn Melanie over to them."

"Will Jonas! Are you really suggesting this craziness? You want to do this…this meshugana thing?"

"No. But I want you to know the consequences of what we are doing."

"The only thing we are doing, is saving the world."

"Huh?"

Over our years together, Rose occasionally came up with sayings, sometimes in Yiddish, translated into English. Sayings that she felt fit whatever situation she and I might be discussing.

But – "saving the world?"

That was a new one for me.

"Rose," I told her, "You're going to have to explain that one, please."

"Very simple," Rose said. "It's like my rabbi says… 'if you save one person, you are saving the world.'"

"So, what a deal, Will. We save Melanie -- and we end up saving the world."

She laughed. "Can we get better odds than that? How can we resist? Make sense to you, Will?"

I couldn't fight that bit of logic, now could I?

"Makes sense to me, Rose."

CHAPTER 44

At 2:30 the next day, Jesus Morales led Marty and me into a conference room at the L.A. County District Attorney regional office in Inglewood. Two people were already in the room.

A man in his mid-fifties, medium height, well dressed, and reserved in his manner, was seated at the head of the table. To his right, equally as well groomed, was an African American woman, perhaps in her late thirties.

Jesus did the introductions.

"Will Jonas and Martin Gershon, I'd like you to meet Geraldo Baez, from our home office in Los Angeles. Geraldo is in charge of our corrupt cases investigations. And this is Clarissa Johnson, ADA in charge of this office."

Jesus indicated that we should sit in the seats to the left of Baez, and we did.

Once we were seated, Baez took charge. No preliminaries.

"Jesus tells us you have a file purporting to show several areas of government corruption at City Hall in Junction City. And that you have a whistleblower who has put this file together."

"Yes, to both points," I answered. "But first, we need an update on Carl Hannaford and his well-being."

Clarissa Johnson spoke.

"As of 10:30 this morning, Carl Hannaford was moved into an isolated protective location. And he will remain there, until such time as the evidence shows that he has been wrongfully incarcerated and should be released. Or, it is determined that his conviction will stand, and he is returned to the general prison population."

Johnson leaned across the table, toward Will and Marty, and continued.

"Jesus has made clear to us your concerns about how strongly we will follow up on your Hannaford file. Let me emphasize to you that we will thoroughly review what your investigation shows, as regards Carl Hannaford and his status. And before this meeting ends today, we will want to hear the results of your investigation."

Geraldo Baez then spoke.

"But we would be less than honest if we didn't admit – as an entirely separate issue – that the hints you have dropped about municipal corruption in Junction City have gotten our attention. So, can we please start with what you have on this subject?"

I looked at Marty for confirmation. Carl Hannaford was his client, and it was Hannaford's interests that Marty had to look out for. I felt the same way, too.

Marty nodded his agreement.

"Okay," I answered Baez. "We can go along with that."

I opened up my Ruiz file – no name attached, of course – and passed out copies to Baez, Johnson and Morales.

"What you are looking at are copies of the following items:"

"…Statements from two separate bank accounts in the Cayman Islands. These are the accounts of Junction City Mayor Anthony Crane and Chief of Police Eli Russell. As you will see, Crane's balance is over eight hundred thousand dollars, and Russell's is over five hundred thousand. These agree with several withdrawals from the Junction City General Ledger, as authorized by Crane, that total the amounts of the two bank accounts."

"…Next, salary stubs from both Crane and Russell, showing Crane's annual salary to be seven hundred and twenty thousand dollars, and Russell's to be five hundred and thirty-seven thousand dollars. Prior to when Junction City became a charter city, some five years ago, Crane's annual salary was fifty-five thousand, and Russell's was forty-five thousand."

"…The next item you will see is a contract for street paving, as well as an invoice for the work, and a check made out to Star Development. This deal is stated as three hundred and eighteen thousand dollars, and the work was supposedly done just three months ago. However, our contact has physically checked the streets listed, and none of them has been paved. The whistle blower says phony payments like these are done periodically, and documentation is available."

"…Our source assures us that what we've just given you is only the beginning of the corruption. The source says several paper trails can be provided, tracing transactions that result in cash payoffs to various people."

Baez, Johnson and Morales spent the next few moments reviewing the paperwork I'd given them. Baez was the first one to speak.

"If…and I emphasize, if…these are real, then there definitely is a case pending here. And a big one."

Baez looked at me.

"So? Who is your whistleblower? Who gave you this file?"

"I'll answer that, but only after we agree on some conditions about that person's future," I said.

Baez waived aside my comment.

"Look. As much as I would like to move ahead on this thing – with the help of the whistleblower – I'm not going to give anyone a free pass – if – and I emphasize this – the person is someone who is part of the corruption, and is now hoping to get out, unscathed, by helping us."

Hey, I asked myself, did he really say… "unscathed?" Baez may have been bright. And competent. But it was clear to me that he also was a pompous bureaucrat, who liked words like unscathed.

Okay. I know how to deal with folks like that, I said to myself.

And to Geraldo, I said, "You're absolutely right, Geraldo. No one should get out of it –unscathed, as you so correctly put it. Any last minute change of attitude shouldn't help someone get away clean. You agree?"

"Yes."

"The only way the whistleblower can get away clean is if…and I emphasize, if…that person can show they never did take part in the corruption. Never did 'enjoy the spoils,' so to speak. (Hey, I can use the King's English, when I have to).

Would you agree with me, Geraldo, on this as a reasonable litmus test for the whistle- blower? If the person – by design – has not taken any benefit whatsoever, from any of the corrupt money? Can we agree on this, Geraldo?"

Baez sensed that something was going on here, but he wasn't quite sure what.

I was about to try and nail him in some other way, when Clarissa Johnson came into the conversation.

"Geraldo," she said calmly to Baez, "What you're saying, and what Will is saying, are the same. Will believes the whistleblower has not been involved in the corruption. And if he can show this to be so, then I recommend that we agree. At that point, I'm sure Will would be willing to tell us who the whistleblower is. Right, Will?"

"Right," I answered.

Baez thought for a few seconds. Just to show he was in charge.

"Okay," he said. "I agree. So, who is the whistleblower?"

"Your dream come true, Geraldo," I said.

I picked up another of my files and passed out copies to the

DA people.

"This bank ledger shows three years and three months of bi-weekly payments of $2,500 each, into a savings account at a bank in Long Beach. What you will immediately notice is that – despite the regular deposits – not one cent has ever been withdrawn from this account."

"This, Geraldo, is how our whistleblower –who was compelled by circumstances to take part in the corruption –actually kept herself – and yes, it is a woman – from benefitting from the activities she was forced to carry out."

"Yes, she took the bi-weekly cash bribes of $2,500. Because she had to. The alternative, she was told by the mayor, was that she'd be out of a job. A job that is critical to her very life and well-being. You see, she is a single mother of two, who has her life invested in her pension and health care benefits. And she absolutely cannot stand to lose these benefits. She is now due to retire in two and a half years."

"But, what to do?"

"She saw only one path to take. Yes, accept the bribe money. But deposit it. Never take even a cent of it."

"So, what's changed?" Geraldo asked. "Why – now – does she want to become a whistleblower? Why not just wait another – what'd you say? Two and a half years? Retire. Get her pension. Get her healthcare. Be done with it."

"Ah, but she wouldn't be done with it," I answered. "There's all that bribe money sitting in that savings account. Money she will not touch. But money that could potentially hurt her, if ever there was an investigation of things in Junction City. And she believed there would eventually be one. The corruption is getting worse and worse."

"So, she thought…maybe she'd go to the Mayor…who got her to take the bribe in the first place, and simply give him back the money, at the same time promising never to say anything."

"Well, a friend of her…and the person who first approached me on her behalf…correctly pointed out that this would never work. The Mayor would take the money back. And then he'd threaten to pull her pension, her health care, unless she remained silent. And this sword, if you will, would be hanging over her head all the rest of her life. Making things miserable, of course."

"And that's the point at which her friend – a police officer in the Junction City Police Department – approached me, to see if I could help."

"Why'd he come to you?" Geraldo asked.

CHAPTER 45

"He said he heard around the department that I'd been in to see Chief Russell, because I was investigating the conviction of Carl Hannaford. So, he looked me up on the computer, felt comfortable with what he read about me, and decided to take a chance and call me. We then met. He told me some things about the whistleblower. He arranged for us to meet, and based on meeting her, and documents she showed me, I decided I'd try and help her. In my mind, she definitely needs the help, she deserves it, and she can help you clean up a criminal mess in Junction City."

I paused for a few seconds and then continued.

"Geraldo, this lady is as straight and plain and honest as they come. I'm convinced of that. And I think she handled her situation, with the payoffs, in a kind of imaginative way. And now, she's ready to blow that whistle. Long and hard."

"What's her position in Junction City?"

"She's one of two senior clerks in the overall City Administration. She's been there for almost 28 years, starting at the bottom, and working her way up to near the top. She can deliver, Geraldo. Deliver documentation to the point where your prosecution will be a slam dunk. So – what do you say? Do we have a deal?"

Geraldo sat silently – just to show who was boss, I figure.

So, I waited, too. I just knew he'd have to agree. Couldn't give up such a media-heavy opportunity.

Geraldo nodded.

"Okay. We have a deal."

He turned to Clarissa Johnson.

"Can you have Jose write up such an agreement while I'm still here? So I can okay it and sign it? Then Will can take it to his contact, and we can get things moving."

Clarissa looked at Jesus.

"Jesus, can you do the document now? Reflecting the discussion Geraldo and Will have just had?"

"Sure can," Jesus said, getting up and leaving the room.

CHAPTER 46

Clarissa Johnson now took over the meeting.

"Okay, Will, let's turn to the Hannaford investigation. What do you have for us?"

"What we have is, our belief that Carl Hannaford is wrongly serving a term in Lancaster for voluntary manslaughter. We believe that he has been convinced, coerced or fooled in some way, into believing that he had committed the crime, to which he confessed."

"Our investigation was prompted by another convict in Lancaster, name of Jack Lewis. Jack is a life-long friend of Marty. Jack is about a third of a way through serving a 20-year sentence for murder."

"I need to stress, here, that Lewis has made it clear to us that he does not expect any change – any reduction – in his current sentence – if, as a result of what he uncovered, it eventually leads to the righting of what Jack believes is a wrongful sentence."

"I want to emphasize, too, that – despite what this might look like at the start – we have not found this to be an imaginative variation of a typical jailhouse lawyer caper. Before prison, Jack Lewis was a successful Beverly Hills psychologist. He held multiple degrees, including a doctorate. He'd written several serious papers for the professional journals, and he was an adjunct professor at UCLA. And since he's been in prison, he's had a record of helping prisoners with their mental problems."

"Now, some information about Carl Hannaford, until recently, he was assigned to the unoccupied bunk in Jack's cell. Hannaford, age 22, was convicted about two years ago, for killing someone in a barroom brawl. At the time, Hannaford did confess to the crime."

"Jack tells us that right from the first night Carl was in the cell, he exhibited signs of severe disturbance in his dreams. In his sleep, he kept repeating this phrase: 'He says I killed the man. Don't remember. But he says I killed the man.'"

"And when he is awake, Hannaford wanders around, saying this same thing."

"Jack also tells us that he estimates Carl's IQ to be somewhere around 60 or 65. And he points out that this is an ideal range if you are trying to convince someone that they did something, when in fact, they have not."

"In the brief we've prepared for you, there is more detail about a series of discussions Jack conducted with Hannaford."

"As a result of these discussions, Jack became convinced that Carl was framed. He called Marty, and that's the point at which Marty and I became involved."

"Our job: try to prove that Carl Hannaford was innocent. And find out who had convinced him to confess."

"Now, a few words about the crime itself."

"It started out as a normal bar brawl at a place in Junction City, called UnaMas. According to the bartender, two guys were jawing at each other. He told them to take it outside. They did. Into an alley adjacent to the bar. And one of them ended up dead. His carotid was slashed, and he bled out. And later that night, Carl Hannaford confessed, directly to the Chief of Police, at the scene of the crime."

"Now, please let me tell you, that I spent thirty years with the Los Angeles Police Department, with most of those years as a homicide detective. So I believe I have a good background in how homicide investigations are run."

"And I am here to say, that the homicide investigation on this one, smells bad, from start to finish. Here are some examples of what I mean."

"The first thing that struck me is that the Police Department's file was about as short of details as is possible. I have never seen one, so barren. Nothing about the site, what the argument was about, no scene of crime work done, no details about any witnesses."

"Next, this entire investigation was handled directly by – the Chief of Police. That's very unusual. Even for a small police force like that in Junction City. This is when I began to have my first suspicions that the investigation was being manipulated. Or at the least, being subject to influence, rather than to objectivity. And please note, this is the same Chief Russell whom we discussed in the corruption investigation."

"I didn't know *why* it was being manipulated, but as our investigation proceeded, I grew to believe, that it was in order to railroad Carl Hannaford into confessing, be convicted, and then get sent off to prison…in place of the real murderer."

"Next, the bartender/owner of the UnaMas Bar told us he called the Junction City Police Department at 9:00 PM, Saturday, to report the killing. And he identified himself. But the official Department report, said that an anonymous person had called the event in, at 2:35 AM, Sunday. Why was there this five hour and thirty-five-minute difference? And although we have not been in a position to check it out – we bet that the bartender's 9:00 PM call is no longer on the Department's call-in log."

"Next, the coroner told us that he had figured the time of death at between 8PM and 11PM Saturday. But Chief Russell asked him to change that to between 11PM Saturday and 2AM Sunday. Again, why this three-hour time difference?"

"We have now concluded that these time differentials are because time was needed to figure out how to get Carl Hannaford to confess to the murder."

"Next, in just about 100 per cent of killings, an autopsy is an automatic part of the investigation. But not in this case. No autopsy was done. According to Chief Russell, he decided no autopsy was needed because the cause of death had already been observed – the bleeding out of the carotid artery. And, because skipping an autopsy was better for the Department's budget. Those are unacceptable reasons for not doing an autopsy in a homicide case."

"Next, after the death of the victim, Manny Estevez, his body was shipped off to Mexico, supposedly at the request of his family. Chief Russell said he couldn't see why not. Of course, I would point out that by doing so, the Chief severely limited any future possibility of exhumation, and an autopsy."

"Now, as regards the bar brawl that led to the death of the Mr. Estevez, you should know the following. The bartender told me there were two participants in the brawl, and he identified them as – and I quote – 'A Mexican guy and a white guy.'"

"Because of information we were accumulating in our investigation, I grew to suspect that the white guy was – NOT – Carl Hannaford, but -- WAS -- Donald Zeterenk, son of Gus Zeterenk, the head of Star Development. And yes, the same Star Development that is mentioned in the corruption file."

"Because of my suspicions about Donald Zeterenk, I prepared a six-pak which included his picture. I showed the six-pak to the bartender at UnaMas. He said, and to use his words, he was '75 per cent' sure that Donald Zeterenk was the white guy in the brawl.

"There is another point to note – and I present it – although it is totally circumstantial. You have to know that Gordy Hannaford, Carl's father, is well known around Junction City, as an alcoholic who cannot hold a job. He picks up day work in the lineup outside of Home Depot."

"But – as soon as his son, Carl, was convicted, Gordy was put on the maintenance staff at one of the Junction City warehouses that Gus Zeterenk's company owns. I need to point out to you that Gordy is the person who brought his son to the scene of the crime, and as soon as they got there, Carl – at Gordy's urging -- confessed to Chief Russell."

"To put this in its plainest terms – Gordy delivers Carl to Chief Russell, as the confessing killer. This gets Donald Zeterenk off the hook. Gordy then is given – and still has -- a nice paying job – at a Zeterenk-owned warehouse."

"To sum up what we believe is the truth, here are the key points:

1. Donald Zeterenk is the killer of Many Estevez.

2. Carl Hannaford was persuaded by his father, Gordy, that he was the killer. And he confessed. But our investigation leads us to believe that he is innocent.

3. The entire investigation by the Junction City Police Department –specifically Chief Russell – was a sham. Those extra hours I talked about before? We believe they were used by Russell, and probably Gus Zeterenk, to somehow seek out Gordy Hannaford, and get him to convince his dull-minded son, Carl, that *he* had killed Estevez. This task was made easier because we understand from the bartender that Carl was quite drunk."

"As you know, we believe a contract has been put out on Carl. A contract to kill Hannaford within one week. And to make it look like suicide."

"So, think about this, please. Here we have Carl Hannaford starting to remember things. Possibly including the name of the real killer."

"And right away, someone puts out a contract on him."

"To us, this looks like the people who framed Carl are now afraid their frame will come apart, as he remembers things. So, they have to get rid of him. To silence him. Hence, the contract to kill him."

"I want to thank you all for putting Carl into a safe location, as of this morning. I am convinced to have done otherwise, would lead to an attempt on his life."

"And, there is another new development that I'd like to tell you about."

"Last night, accompanied by my associate, she's a mother of three, and a grandmother of five, we went to Junction City, to pick up Melanie Hannaford, Carl's 12-year-old sister."

"We did so, at Melanie's request. She called me – I had left my card in their living room when I interviewed Gordy – she called me in almost a panic. She had locked herself in her room, because Gordy had tried to come in. According to Melanie, he had been assaulting her up until about a year ago. He stopped, then. But last night, he tried again, so Melanie called me. And Rose and I went to get her."

"I mention this for two reasons."

"First, I know I am in violation of some rule or other – by keeping Melanie – as regards the Department of Children and

Family Services. But I do not want to give her up, to them. Nor expose her to any further contact with her father."

"Second, and although I'd prefer she not be so directly involved, it does strike me, that Melanie probably knows a lot about what is going on, that involves her father and probably Chief Russell. I know that when I went to interview Gordy, she was nearby, in the hallway, and I am pretty certain she overheard our conversation. So, it may well be that she overheard other conversations involving her father and Chief Russell. At some point, therefore, she might be useful to the investigation."

"So, could you please put Melanie into protective custody, with Rose and me continuing to be responsible for her?"

I closed my notebook, took a deep breath and then looked directly at Baez, Johnson and Jose.

"Okay, Folks. You now have both of our files. Hannaford and Junction City corruption. We hope they both turn out to be successful investigations."

"Meanwhile, the only loose end from our side, is Melanie Hannaford."

Clarissa Johnson answered me.

"We'll work on that. As soon as this meeting is over."

"Thank you," I said.

Baez took the meeting back over.

"I'd say we've had a productive afternoon here," he said.

And then he added, "Let's get things moving!"

CHAPTER 47

Of course, once we made our presentations on both Hannaford and the corruption situation, Marty and I were pretty much confined to the sidelines, as the investigations went "official."

But the good folks did keep us in the loop, so we did have firsthand knowledge as to what was happening. We didn't have to rely on any "breaking news" screamers on television.

And what was happening was good.

Donald Zeterenk caved easily, as soon as he was confronted, and admitted to being the "white guy" in the UnaMas brawl, during which Manny Estevez was slain. Donald received the same sentence that Carl Hannaford had gotten – voluntary manslaughter – only with a heavier allotment of years attached to it – eighteen, to be exact.

Carl Hannaford was released shortly after Donald Zeterenk was arrested. Because of his limited mental capacity, the Court wanted to make sure that Carl could function safely in his daily life. Especially in view of what had happened. Marty, as Carl's lawyer, said he would handle the appropriate arrangements, and he found a suitable halfway house for Carl to live in. Also, when Fred, the bartender/owner of UnaMas, heard what the Court wanted, then Fred said he would employ Carl, full time, as a helper. This was acceptable to the Court, since Fred had already started expanding UnaMas into a family style restaurant. Marty also told the Court that he would continue to function as a sort of an unofficial guardian for Carl.

Gus Zeterenk, Chief Eli Russell and Mayor Anthony Crane were convicted on graft and corruption charges and were sentenced to terms ranging from five to twelve years. They also faced several criminal charges in connection with what they had done with Carl Hannaford and Donald Zeterenk – and for these, each of them was sentenced to 5 to 7 additional years – not concurrent – but in addition to the graft and corruption crimes.

As for Gordy Hannaford, I like to think that justice came to him in a different way.

A few days after the DA's task force started its work, two representatives went to the Hannaford home, to arrest Gordy. They had to enter on their own, since no one answered their knocks on the door.

When they got in, they found Gordy seated at the kitchen table – dead – from a gun- shot wound to the head. The coroner later ruled that Gordy had probably been passed out, from drinking, when he was shot.

And they found Hazel, his wife, sprawled nearby on the floor. Dead from what the coroner confirmed was a self-inflicted gunshot wound, also to the head.

Same gun responsible for both deaths.

Hazel had written a suicide note:

"You don't deserve to live. Nor do I. You abused our daughter and I didn't stop you.

You sold our son for money. And I didn't stop you. We deserve to die."

Rose and I tried to comfort Melanie about what had happened. And we were encouraged by how she took the news.

I think that, by this point in her life, Melanie had been so disappointed by the conduct of both of her parents that she really didn't have much emotional room left to grieve for them.

As for Rose, she just pulled the girl into her arms and began rocking with her – all the time humming something. I couldn't make out the words. What language it was.

But I decided that wasn't important.

What was important, was the love and tenderness that flowed from Rose to Melanie.

It seemed to help. I sure hope so.

One final point.

With both of her parents gone, Melanie became a ward of the State. So Rose immediately applied to become Melanie's guardian.

Family Services ruled that Rose was too old for that. Stupid. But there you have it.

The way around this bureaucratic idiocy? Lu and I joined

Rose as co-guardians. Seems we were young enough.

"See?" Lu said to me. "All your worries about getting old? The State of California doesn't think you're old.

MIND TRICKS

SAUL WARSHAW

CHAPTER 1

"Let me get this straight," I said to Captain George Klinger of the Los Angeles Police Department.

"You want me –Will Jonas Investigations -- and totally separate from the LAPD, to investigate your sister's claim that her husband was murdered. Even though the Department has already ruled it a suicide. And – the guy your sister is accusing of being the killer? Well…he's already dead."

I stared at Klinger.

"Did I get that right?"

The Captain squirmed uncomfortably. It was clear that this was one conversation he wished he wasn't having. Klinger was a do-it-by-the-book kind of cop, and our discussion went way beyond the covers of that book.

"Before I go any further, Will," the Captain said, "I need to be assured that this discussion will be confidential. Do I have your word on that?"

"Yes. You have my word."

I was surprised that Klinger and I were having this discussion.

Hell, I was surprised that we were even meeting. It was ten years since I'd retired from the Los Angeles Police Department, after spending thirty years on the Job, most of them as a homicide detective.

And in many of those thirty, Klinger and I had our problems. While he went by the book, that wasn't how my then-partner, Charlie Black and I, operated. We didn't mind bending the rule book, if it helped us put some deserving lowlifes into prison, where we knew they belonged.

So, Klinger and I had a history of run-ins. But it looked now, like he wanted to leave all of that behind.

I said to him, "Please tell me what's going on, Captain."

We were meeting in Jerry's Deli on Ventura Boulevard in Encino. That's in Los Angeles, in the San Fernando Valley, just north of downtown. I'd ordered the lox and eggs breakfast special and was just finishing it. Klinger had ordered eggs, which he'd hardly touched.

Klinger pushed his fork at the eggs, moving them from one side of the plate to the other. Obviously, not really wanting to answer. But, he finally stopped pushing and did answer.

"Maybe you remember, a couple of months ago, a businessman named Donald Corrington committed suicide by putting a .38 to his temple? It made the news because Carrington ran a fair sized importing business here in the Valley and Downtown. Corrington Imports."

"I read something about it. Don't remember the details,

2

though."

"Corrington was my brother-in-law."

"I'm sorry."

Klinger waved it off.

"Thanks. But frankly, I didn't like the man. However, Margaret – she's my sister – well – actually, my half-sister – it was her husband, so my feelings aren't important."

Klinger took a deep breath.

"Will, I'd like you to investigate Corrington's death."

"But the Department said it was a suicide, right? So what's to investigate? And why me? Why go outside the Department?"

"Yes, it was ruled a suicide. I know the detectives on the case. And their lieutenant. And I'm sure everything was done first rate. By the book."

"But…?" I prodded.

Klinger hit the table with his fist.

"It's this damned claim Margaret is making now! That her husband was murdered. That it wasn't a suicide."

"Anything to support that claim?"

"Nothing! And what makes it even stranger, is that during the investigation, Margaret never said anything about murder. She only came to me with that claim a couple of weeks ago. After the case was closed."

"How'd she explain the delay?"

"She told me she had always been suspicious about Donald having committed suicide. But she didn't say anything, because she felt everyone would think she was being foolish. She said she was hoping the police would uncover something during their investigation, to show that it wasn't suicide. When they didn't, she decided to talk to me about her suspicions."

"What did you do, when she told you?"

"I called John Lovelli, the detective in charge of the investigation. I told Lovelli what Margaret had said to me, and I asked him, as a favor, to check things out. To review the case, unofficially, of course."

"Did he?"

"Yes. He called me a few days ago. Said he had reviewed the file, talked to his investigating team, and it looked kosher to him. Strictly a suicide. I thanked him, and then I called you."

"But why?" I asked. "Looks like this one is okay. Suicide it is."

"I believe that," Klinger said. "Lovelli believes it. His team believes it."

Klinger hit the table again with his fist.

"But my sister won't accept that! She's...obsessed...with this idea that her husband was murdered. And she won't let it go!"

"You going to ask Lovelli to review the file again? To re-open the case?"

"Absolutely not. I can't do that. I stretched the line, asking him to review the case, the first time. I can't go back to him again. I can't go anywhere in the Department with this. And that's why I want you to take a look at it."

"But what can I do from the outside?"

"You can check things out and prove to Margaret that she's wrong."

Klinger leaned forward, the strain clear on his face and in his voice.

"I'm worried that if she persists in this, Margaret will end up looking foolish. Especially if she goes public with what she believes – and she's threatening to do just that."

The Captain nodded.

"And yes, I'm also afraid, personally, of being embarrassed within the Department – if she keeps this up. I'll admit to that."

I could sympathize with Klinger. For someone who lives his professional life by the rule book, having a sister who publicly embarrasses the Department – well, not good.

"Look," Klinger said, "If it's your fee you're concerned about, don't be. Margaret likes the idea of you investigating. And she says she'll pay your fee. And believe me, she can afford it."

Klinger sighed.

"Will – at times, Margaret can act like…well…like a nut case. She gets an idea in her head, and she won't let go of it. And this is one of those times! I'm convinced of it. What I'm hoping is that, when you present her with the results of your investigation, she'll let go, and put this obsession of hers to rest."

I thought about the whole deal. Sounded like a no-winner to me. I'd investigate. And come to the same conclusion as the Department – suicide. Would Margaret accept my conclusion?

Didn't sound like she would.

On the other hand, I'd had weirder cases back on the Job, and Charlie and I had solved them. So, who knows? This could be one of those.

Plus, and to use one of the bigger words in my vocabulary, there is the *pragmatism* of it. If I took this assignment, Klinger would owe me. And it never hurt to have a few favors on deposit with the Department.

"Okay," I told the Captain, "I'm in. I'll take it on."

"Good," Klinger said. "I owe you, Will."

See? Good decision on my part, right?

"Tell me about the guy Margaret is accusing of killing her husband. You said…he's dead?"

"George Palermo," Klinger answered. "Killed in an automobile accident. He went off the road up on Mulholland, and straight down a few hundred feet into a ravine. The car exploded and burned. There wasn't much left of George."

"Why does Margaret believe that Palermo killed her husband?"

"Palermo was a major investor in Corrington's company. As I understand it from Margaret, he put about a million dollars into the company a year ago, when Corrington was having some cash flow problems. Now, according to Margaret, Palermo was making threatening noises about wanting his money back. He and Donald were arguing about it, just about the time that Donald died."

Klinger shrugged.

"Will, now you know as much as I do. For more details, you have to talk to Margaret. I've told her all about you and your investigative agency, and she's anxious to talk. So please call her and set up an appointment—soon."

CHAPTER 2

Margaret Corrington put the telephone down on the night table next to her bed and smiled as she reviewed the talk she'd just had with George.

It's going to be all right, she thought.

Her brother had assured her that this Will Jonas would investigate her claim with the same thoroughness that had made him a standout LAPD homicide detective.

She looked forward to seeing Jonas, whom George had said would call her later in the day, to arrange a meeting.

Margaret wondered what Jonas was like. Her brother had said he was in his early 60's. Getting a bit up there, for this kind of work, she wondered? Not any more, she thought. What is it, the doctors and others were saying nowadays? The sixties were the new fifties? The seventies were the new sixties?

Well, when she meets the man, she'll check him out. Make sure he is up for the work that needs to be done. Make sure that her brother made the right selection. Not a guaranteed deal, since the two of them were so different from each other.

Not for the first time, Margaret wondered at the differences between her and her half-brother. Although they shared the same mother, the genes of their separate fathers seemed to have overwhelmed any potential similarities they might have been expected to have as brother and sister.

She thought back over their lives together, although "together" was a word that poorly described their relationship.

George was 18 years older. Born when their mother was just 19, in a marriage cut short a few years later, when George's father died of a heart attack.

When George was 16, his mother remarried, and Margaret was born two years later. By then, George was out of the house, having signed up for three years in the Marine Corps. And then, on to the Police Academy and his own marriage and family.

It wasn't surprising that they weren't close as brother and sister, given the age difference and the divergent paths of their lives. Too, they were so unlike in temperament.

George was the perfect middle of the road traveler. Do it by the book. Never take the chances that spice things up. That make things happen.

She was just the opposite. Indeed, it was one of the reasons she had married Donald.

Donald was almost her brother's age. Fifty-three years old, when he died, to her 38. Fifteen-year difference. When they married, she was 30, he was 45. Most women would have hesitated at such an age spread. After all, when Donald would be 60, and nearing an older, slower living pace, she would be in her prime, at 45.

But Margaret never worried about such long range things. Take advantage of the present, was her attitude. Have what you want, now. Worry about the future – in the future.

She knew that George had not approved of her marriage. Never said anything to her. But he thought it, she knew.

Margaret shrugged.

Well, he does it his way, and I do it mine, she thought. And just so long as he helps me out when I need it, I have no complaints.

Like now, with the ruling on Donald's death.

Have to get the ruling changed. Can't stay a suicide. Can't.

Margaret got out of bed. Although awake since 7:30, she hadn't yet showered or dressed, when George had called, after his breakfast with Jonas.

As was her usual practice when awakening, she had worked the daily puzzle in the L.A. Times. Margaret believed doing the puzzle first thing in the morning got her mind going at a higher speed. And that's how she liked to operate.

Walking over to the full length mirror affixed to the closet door, Margaret dropped her nightgown and began her daily, critical examination of her body.

Yes, there definitely was a dose of narcissism in this every-morning act, Margaret knew. But she also used the examination to rev up, to psych herself into pushing her body through the upcoming, daily rigorous exercise regimen she maintained.

Margaret believed in hard exercise. An hour every day in the home gym room adjacent to her bedroom.

What Margaret saw in the mirror generally pleased her. At 5 feet 6 inches, her figure still was slim. She knew that when she got on the scale before beginning her exercise regimen, it would register between 110 and 115 pounds. The breasts were still firm, her waist and abdomen flat. There were no folds of skin hanging from her upper arms, her legs were shapely, and her neck was free of the wrinkles that she knew were inevitably coming.

She shook her head and looked closely at her long dark hair. Another week, and it would be time to see Barbara for a hair coloring treatment. To keep those strands of gray out of sight.

Finished with her visual examination, Margaret put on her exercise clothes and walked from the bedroom into the gym.

As she began her workout, she reviewed in her mind the information she wanted to give Will Jonas.

So that he would draw the same conclusions she had, about her husband's death.

She had to make sure that her case was properly presented to Jonas.

CHAPTER 3

I didn't know it, of course, but at about the same time Margaret Corrington was physically beating herself up on her treadmill, I was beating myself up mentally, as I drove west on the 101 Freeway, toward my office in Warner Center in Woodland Hills.

Why did I agree to take on this crazy investigation?

Yeah, Klinger would owe me, I rationalized.

But what a mess. How the hell am I supposed to conduct a quiet, unofficial investigation, about a suicide that an LAPD captain's sister claims is actually a homicide – the murder of her husband? Only she didn't make that claim, until after the police had ruled the death a suicide. Plus, the guy she says did the killing? He's already dead.

I pushed the air conditioning up a notch. The early morning news had forecast another hot day in L.A. Must already be 80. It'd probably get to 90 plus by the afternoon.

At the Canoga Avenue off-ramp, I turned off the freeway. And to prove that I could do two things at once, I also rubbed my hand across my chin. New stubble. Too fast! But considering the alternative, I wasn't about to complain. And I couldn't complain about the rest of my body, either.

At 63, I still was 6 feet 4 inches. Hadn't lost any height, which usually started to happen just about now. My weight was a steady 210, and my hair, although thinning, still covered most of my head.

Driving north on Canoga, I reached Erwin, turned left, and then turned right, into the entrance for the office tower where I had a lease on a two room suite plus reception.

When I came into the office, Rose Shapiro, my all-purpose secretary-telephone operator-receptionist-bookkeeper-researcher-Jewish-mother-everything handed me several telephone messages.

Taking the messages, I realized once again how important Rose had become to my little operation, since she'd joined me, back in 1996, a year after I'd started Will Jonas Investigations.

At that time, I'd contacted an employment agency, asking to see some candidates for a receptionist/general assistant. So far, that afternoon, I'd seen five candidates, none of whom clicked with me. And I was tired of the whole process.

And then, in marched the last candidate. This short, round woman in her sixties, gray hair pulled back in a bun, wearing sensible lace-up shoes.

Just what I need, I thought to myself. Why isn't this one sitting in a retirement home, having tea and gossiping with the other old ladies?

Without bothering to introduce herself, the woman looked at

me and said, "You look like hell. Sit down. I'll make you a fresh cup of coffee."

Which she did. Which I drank. And it was the best coffee I'd had, in the five years since my wife, Vera, had died.

So, I hired Rose. Or maybe she hired me. I've never been clear on that point. All I do know, is that everything quickly was organized in the office.

Once Rose settled in, and at my prodding, she told me how she was widowed in her late fifties, had raised three children through college, and had returned to school to learn computer, secretarial and bookkeeping skills.

Now, as I looked through the messages Rose had given me, I brought her up to date.

"We've got a new assignment. I'm doing a favor for Captain Klinger. Looking into the suicide of his brother-in-law. Klinger's sister – the Suicide's wife – is claiming that the man was murdered. That he did not commit suicide."

"Nu? What does she base that on?"

"That's what Klinger wants me to find out."

I handed Rose a piece of paper with Margaret Corrington's phone number.

"Okay, here's what I need you to do, please. First, call Mrs. Corrington and set me up to see her any time tomorrow. She's expecting the call. Then, do a computer search and see what news coverage you can find on the suicide of a Donald Corrington, head of a company called Corrington Imports. This was a couple of months ago. Also see if you can find any background on Mrs. Corrington herself – aside from the news tied to her husband's death."

"All this is here in Los Angeles, right?" Rose asked.

"Yup. Here in the Valley."

Rose nodded toward the telephone messages I was holding.

"I think you should get back to Carl Makinowsky, first thing. He was very anxious to talk with you."

I went into my office and sat down at my desk.

Carl Makinowsky was the founder and CEO of Floragenics Laboratories, a startup biotech company. Makinowsky had founded the company a little over a year ago, hoping to exploit a patent he held for developing an additive that would spur growth in a variety of flowers. The company was funded by a venture capital group that planned to take Floragenics public in two or three years.

I was on retainer with Floragenics, to handle two ongoing assignments.

The first was to check out the backgrounds of applicants who were being interviewed for various high level positions in the fast-growing company.

And second, I provided general security services, with an emphasis on making sure the company's proprietary formulas did not land in the hands of rival firms. This was a constant concern of Carl Makinowsky.

I called Makinowsky's office and his secretary put me through.

When he came on the line, Makinowsky did not waste any "How are you, Will?" words.

Instead, he said, "One of my key scientists has been acting a little strange lately. And it's worrying me."

"What do you mean – 'strange?'"

"I don't have much to go on," Makinowsky admitted. "But my wife and Catlin's wife – that's my scientist, Eugene Catlin – they have mutual friends. And my wife heard that Catlin's been giving his wife some hard times. Coming home at odd hours. Stuff like that."

"Any changes in his work habits? His productivity?"

"No. Everything's fine. But this sort of behavior worries me. Catlin's involved in all of our top-secret work, so I need you to check him out."

"The guy's probably just having an affair," I told Makinowsky. "Harmless from the company's standpoint, no matter how much of a problem it may be to Catlin's wife. But I'll check it out. And to get me started, I'll need a copy of Catlin's personnel file and a recent photo."

"On your desk by tomorrow morning."

"I'll get back to you quickly," I said.

"Report back to me. And only me. No one else."

"Understood."

CHAPTER 4

I spent the next few hours returning most of the calls that had come in. Just needed to update various clients on the status of the work I was doing for them. No problems. Everything was going the way it was supposed to.

After my final call, Rose came in with several computer printout pages on the Corrington suicide.

"This should keep you busy for a while," she said. "Also, I've set your appointment with Mrs. Corrington. For tomorrow at 10:00 AM. Her home. In Calabasas Vista Estates."

Rose pointed at the computer printouts and to a picture of Mrs. Corrington.

"With a wife who looks that good, why would a man commit suicide?"

"Mrs. Corrington is attractive?" I teased.

"So you didn't notice?" Rose teased back. "And if she looks that good in a computer picture, then she must be a knockout in person."

"I'll let you know."

"Okay. But don't let Lu see the pictures. You never know what your wife might think."

I shook my head.

"Uh, uh, Rose. You can't get me worried on that score. Ain't no one as good looking to me, as Lu."

Rose patted my hand.

"Good man. So, is there anything else you need from me? I need to go home. I promised Melanie we could go shopping. She needs some school supplies."

I smiled as I thought about Melanie Hannaford and how Rose, Lu and I had ended up being Melanie's court appointed guardians.

I'd meet Melanie a year ago, when I was investigating her father as part of a murder and corruption case in Junction City, down at the southern end of Los Angeles County.

Gordy Hannaford was a poor excuse for a human being. He was an alcoholic with no desire to change. He was an abusive husband. He was part of a scheme that resulted in his son serving an unwarranted prison term. And he was sexually abusive to Melanie.

That sad family story ended when Melanie's mother shot and killed her husband, and then herself.

Legally, the next step for Melanie would have been to become a ward of the state of California.

But Rose, Lu and I decided Melanie deserved a chance at a better life. So we applied to become Melanie's guardians.

Our application was approved, and in the several months since then, it definitely was a better life for Melanie.

She lived with Rose, but also stayed part time with Lu and me. An arrangement that seemed to suit everyone.

"Kiss Melanie for me," I told Rose. "We'll be expecting her over the weekend."

After Rose left, I spread the computer printouts across the small conference table in my office, and went through them.

Didn't find any new information. Just more background on Donald Corrington and his company. Plus, information on Margaret Corrington.

There was one more item that I wanted to review before my meeting tomorrow with Mrs. Corrington – the police file that Klinger had given me.

I looked at my watch. Close to 7 PM.

I decided I'd take the police file home, and look at it, after Lu and I had dinner.

CHAPTER 5

Michael Palermo tossed the Corrington Imports second quarter financial report on his desk and swiveled his chair, so that he could look out the window. From his 11th floor office, he could see almost the entire length of Avenue of the Stars in Century City in Los Angeles.

But while his eyes registered the impressive view, his mind concentrated on something else. Or more correctly, on someone else.

Margaret Corrington. Damn Margaret Corrington. She was screwing things up. And he couldn't let that happen. No, he could not!

Palermo fidgeted with the knot of his tie. It was an old habit, part of his ongoing ritual to assure himself about his appearance.

He needn't have worried. Palermo could serve perfectly for Hollywood typecasting as a hard driving, powerful executive. His clothes fit just so. His hair looked like it was professionally tended every morning. And his skin had that smooth, health club tan.

Palermo turned back to his desk, picked up the financial report and looked again at the quarterly profit and loss statement. As a major investor in Corrington, Palermo received each quarter's P & L report from the CPA firm that kept the company's books.

And as each such statement over the past year had made clear to him, Corrington Imports was ripe for takeover, especially now that Donald Corrington was dead.

Taking over companies was what Michael Palermo did.

Not the big public companies, with their highly publicized, expensive takeover battles. Instead, Michael Palermo had become rich by finding small, privately held firms with cash flow problems, desperately in need of capital.

His modus operandi was simple. Find a company through one of his business or banking contacts. Approach the management with the offer of a reasonable loan. Put his brother George into the operation to keep an eye on things. And at the right time, abruptly demand his money back. In Corrington's case, that was one million one hundred and fifty thousand dollars.

Most of the companies were not able to meet the repayment demand. And that's when Michael let his rougher side appear. Threatening, bullying, nastily confronting the owners, he usually managed to beat them down, and to cut a deal that gave him control of the company.

Palermo sighed. That's how it was supposed to go with Corrington Imports. And that's how the first part of the plan *was* going. Until that stupid brother of his started getting greedy and careless.

Palermo shook his head. George had always been the family

idiot. Good looking. Attractive to women. But not very bright. The trouble was, that in the last few companies where Michael had placed George, including Corrington, his brother had started to do things on his own, rather than following orders.

This was not a situation Michael could continue to tolerate.

Well, the problem of George was now over. The nose dive down that Mulholland ravine had taken care of that.

But now, here was Margaret Corrington, with her claim that her husband was murdered, and that George was the killer.

Unacceptable.

Not that George wasn't capable. Michael knew what George could do.

Under the right circumstances.

But that wasn't the point. The point was, that with this claim of hers, Margaret was rocking the Carrington Imports boat. Putting the company under too much close-up scrutiny. Making it harder for him to push Margaret into selling out – and most important – doing so at his price.

He had started to raise the subject of selling the company, when she called him a couple of days ago, with her "George killed my brother" theory.

Margaret had told him she didn't want to talk about any sale. All that mattered now, was for the police to realize that her husband had been murdered by George.

"Wrong!" Palermo said aloud, as he thought about that phone talk with Margaret.

Now, he thought…it's time to make Margaret Corrington realize that he was going to own the damn company. Regardless of whatever she claims about Donald's death.

CHAPTER 6

When I opened the door to our condo in Tarzana, Lu came down the hall and kissed me, after which she handed me my usual drink – club soda on the rocks.

Yes. I'm a recovering alcoholic. Been 12 years since I stopped drinking. I still go to an occasional meeting – but otherwise, the disease is tamed. Never gone. But tamed.

I held Lu away from me and said, "You're definitely better looking than she is. Absolutely."

Lu smiled.

"Not going to thank you, until you tell me who you're comparing me to. With the strange people you deal with in your investigations, the 'compared to' is important. So?"

"The widow of a recently deceased man. And she is good looking. But you're much better."

Lu – full name, Sheila McClelland – is 46. Thanks to regular exercise and good eating – she looks ten years younger. She's got deep red hair, along with about 136 pounds distributed over a five feet nine inch frame, plus an angular face with a model's high cheek bones, and a perfect nose.

We'd met back in 2001 when I took a night class at Cal State Northridge on how to operate a computer. Lu, who is the head of computer programing for a bank headquartered in Glendale, was the instructor. I was having a hard time understanding even the basics of the damn computer, so Lu was spending a lot of time at my work station.

Well, it took a lot of nervous energy on my part – I really hadn't gone out much in the six years since my wife, Vera, had died. But I finally asked Lu out for coffee. We clicked, and we'd now been married for three years.

"And for dinner tonight, we have…?" I asked.

Some months ago, Lu decided it made no sense for us to go out to dinner almost every night. She decided we ought to eat at home more often.

"That's fine with me," I said to her at the time. "But there is one problem. Your ability in the kitchen is pretty much limited to making hard boiled eggs."

"I'll buy cookbooks. I'll take lessons. I'll become a first rate cook," she told me.

And that's exactly what Lu did. So that most weeknights – tonight included – dinner was great.

After dinner, while Lu did some office-related work of her own, I went into what I call my study. It's actually our second bedroom, where Melanie stays when she's with us.

I took out the police file that Klinger had given me, sat down on the bed, spread the papers out, and started going through the file.

Donald Corrington had ended his life with one shot from a .38 caliber Smith & Wesson. The weapon was registered to him, and kept in a locked drawer in his office desk.

The registration and the location of the weapon were reported to the investigating officers by both Carrington's secretary and his wife.

Corrington left a suicide note on the monitor of his desk. A copy also was in the "done" tray of a nearby printer. It read:

"It's too much for me to face. I'm sorry."

I wondered, what was too much to face?

I had my answer when I reviewed the coroner's autopsy report.

Corrington, the coroner noted, had cancer of the pancreas. Pancreatic cancer is fatal in about 90 per cent of the cases, with death usually occurring within a year of diagnosis, and with the diagnosis often not being made until the disease is in an advanced stage.

I thought Corrington probably knew what was going to happen to him, the pain he'd suffer, the heartache the illness would subject his wife to, so he decided to end it a few months early.

The investigating detectives had reached the same conclusion. Once they got the coroner's report, they questioned Corrington's personal physician. He told them that three months earlier, he had diagnosed the pancreatic cancer. And he had told Corrington that while he was suffering only mild symptoms at that point, the pain would increase and the disease was too far advanced to expect a cure.

Corrington had demanded to know all the facts, the doctor told the detectives, and had been informed that death probably would be in less than a year.

The doctor reported that Corrington had then refused any form of treatment, except for pain killers.

The doctor had last seen Corrington two weeks before the man shot himself. At that last visit, the doctor had increased Corrington's pain killer dosage, when the patient reported a higher level of discomfort. But Corrington had continued to refuse treatment, telling the doctor that since it was certain he was going to die anyway, why bother?

"Poor guy," I said aloud.

"Who's a poor guy?" Lu asked.

She was standing in the doorway.

"This guy I'm investigating. Donald Corrington, Klinger's late brother-in-law. Looks like he committed suicide, because he didn't want to suffer through the final stages of a terminal case of pancreatic cancer."

"How awful," Lu said, coming into the room and sitting down next to me. "Did he have a family? It must have been difficult for them."

"A wife. No children. And I don't know how difficult it was for her. What I do know, is that – now – she's claiming that her husband was murdered. That it wasn't suicide at all."

Lu nodded at the file spread out on the bed.

"Anything in there to support her claim?"

"Nothing I can see. But, maybe I'll learn more, when I see the widow tomorrow morning."

I smiled at Lu.

"She's the one I told you about, when I got home tonight? The one Rose says is very attractive. Hey – who knows? Maybe I'll get lucky. You know – grieving widow and all."

"I wouldn't even day dream about it," Lu threatened a mock warning. "Not if you want to come back here tomorrow night."

I put my arm around her and said, "Well, there is one way to make sure I can't do anything, even if the lady is attracted to me."

"What's that?" Lu asked.

"Make me happy tonight. And I won't be of any use to any woman tomorrow. Not at my advanced age."

Lu snuggled in close to me.

"Yeah, you're 63 and all washed up. That must be tough to handle."

I couldn't resist.

"Speaking of handling…"

CHAPTER 7

Over breakfast the next morning, I figured it would take about 30 to 40 minutes to get to Mrs. Corrington's home in Calabasas, an upscale community just west of the Los Angeles city line. The 101 Freeway wouldn't be too jammed. Most of the morning traffic would be heading in the opposite direction, toward West L.A. or Downtown.

Earlier, when I woke up, I was hit with an urge to attend an Alcoholics Anonymous meeting. Been about six months since I'd been to one. I don't go often. Don't feel I need to. But if or when my mind says go – I do.

I called the AA hot line and found a meeting just off the Parkway Calabasas exit of the 101, maybe ten minutes from Mrs. Corrington. That meeting was scheduled for 8:30. Perfect.

I didn't see anyone I knew at the meeting. The attendees reflected the upscale location of the meeting. Mainly business men and women, plus what looked like some retirees.

Most times, when I go to meetings, I'm not very active. Don't speak out much. But I get out of the meeting what I want – a reinforced sense of commitment to staying sober.

After the meeting, I headed south, toward Vista Estates, one of the many walled home developments in Calabasas. The idea behind these gated and guarded communities? People hoping to keep out the violence and crime that were in the central districts of most cities, including Los Angeles.

I reached Vista Estates and stopped at the guardhouse.

"Here to see Mrs. Margaret Corrington," I told the guard. "My name is Will Jonas."

The guard checked a list and nodded.

"You're expected. Go to the second street, turn right and go the third house, also on the right. Number 18854 Delta."

The gate opened and I drove through, following the guard's directions. As I did so, I couldn't help thinking – I bet these people have never experienced a drive- by shooting. I shook my head. Sometimes, Jonas – I said to myself – you do have the nuttiest thoughts.

Mrs. Corrington's house looked to be about five thousand square feet. It was set back from the street, fronted by a well-tended lawn and plenty of shrubs and flowers.

There was a 500 SL Mercedes coupe convertible parked in the circular driveway. I parked behind it, got out of my car, and started walking toward the double set of front doors.

One of the doors opened. A quick think back to the pictures Rose had given me. It was Mrs. Corrington.

"Hello," she greeted me. "I'm Margaret Corrington, and you

must be Will Jonas, the homicide detective my brother told me about. Please do come in."

"Ex-homicide detective," I corrected her, as I came into the house.

The inside was as impressive as the outside. All soft colors. Pale bare wood floors. Lots of marble.

And yes, I thought to myself, Rose was right. Mrs. Corrington was, as Rose had put it, "a beauty."

In the file Klinger had given me, Margaret Corrington was listed as being 38 years old, making her 15 years younger than her late husband. I decided she could pass for 30.

Mrs. Corrington led me into a den or family room, and not the more formal living room that I saw on my left as I followed her down the hallway.

"Would you like some coffee?" She asked, as she sat down on a couch. A China coffee urn, a pair of coffee cups and saucers, and a small plate of cookies were on a low table in front of the couch.

"No, thanks," I answered, sitting down in a chair facing the couch.

Mrs. Corrington poured herself some coffee and smiled at me.

"How do you want to do this?" she asked.

Not a bit nervous, I thought. One cool lady.

I said, "Your brother told me the situation in general, and he gave me a copy of the police report. Now, I'd like to start by asking you three questions," Mrs. Corrington.

"I'm ready. And please call me, Margaret."

"And you please call me Will."

"Agreed."

"Okay, now those three questions. First, why do you think your husband was killed, especially when the police are certain it was a suicide? Second, why didn't you say anything to the police during the investigation, rather than waiting until now? And third, why do you believe George Palermo was the killer?"

Margaret took a sip of her coffee. Well, she thought to herself, he certainly is a no-nonsense type. Keep it simple, Girl.

She put her cup down and looked directly at Will.

"I know it's hard to understand my actions, but please let me try and explain them to you."

She reached over to a file folder lying on the low table in front of the couch, and took out several pieces of paper.

"Two weeks ago," she said, "I was going through my husband's desk here at home. Cleaning things out. And I found a computer disk in one of the drawers. There was a label on the disk, but nothing on the label."

"I couldn't imagine why the disk was in the drawer by itself – Donald usually was very meticulous about filing things. I wondered if there was anything on the disk. So, I booted it up. And I found some disturbing memos, from Donald to George Palermo."

"Concerned, I went to Donald's office, looked in the incoming correspondence file, and found the memos Palermo had written to my husband on the same subject."

She handed me the papers.

"These copies are for you."

I took the papers, and while Mrs. Corrington sat quietly, waiting, sipping, I read through them.

In the first memo, Palermo told Corrington he wanted to take out his one million, one hundred and fifty-thousand-dollar investment.

In a memo back to Palermo, Corrington said he could not meet the demand so quickly, and certainly not in the one lump sum payment that Palermo wanted.

Next, Palermo wrote a memo back, pointing out to Corrington that, according to the terms of their investment agreement, he could demand his capital in one immediate payment. He told Corrington he wanted his money – now – and he further said that "it will create a very difficult set of circumstances if the funds are not forthcoming within ten days."

In a memo back, Corrington wrote Palermo that "there is no possibility of meeting this unreasonable demand. I know what our original agreement called for, but I simply cannot do it. The effect on our cash flow will be too severe, and a bank loan will be difficult to obtain, given our current debt ratio."

There was one final memo in the file. It was the response from Palermo to Corrington, and it was short and specific.

"I will get my money back, according to the terms of our agreement," Palermo had written, "Or you will be very sorry."

The hardnosed tone of this memo was clear, I thought. But as the basis for her claim that Palermo killed her husband? I doubted it, and I told this to Margaret.

"Look, this is a pretty intense exchange of correspondence. But it's a big jump, to conclude that George Palermo killed your husband."

"Don't you think the memos are threatening?" Margaret countered. "Especially the part about ... 'or you will be very sorry'".

"Those words could mean a lot of things," I answered. "Such as the threat of a law suit. To me, that's a more likely possibility. These were two businessmen, involved in a financial dispute. And that usually is a situation where both sides turn to their lawyers. The language they both were using? Sounds to me like the set-up for getting their lawyers involved."

"Well...there's more," Mrs. Corrington said.

"What?" I asked.

"Palermo threatened Donald. He telephoned him. Here. At home.

Several times. I heard the threats. Donald wanted me to listen in. Will, my husband was afraid, because of those threats. And so was I."

"What kind of threats? Did Palermo ever specifically say he'd kill your husband, if he didn't get his money back? Kill him, like you now are claiming he did?"

"No. Nothing as blatant as that. He was too smart for that."

Her hands became fists.

"But they were definite threats! He said things like, 'you will be personally sorry if I don't get that money.' And, 'you keep saying you are certain you cannot afford to repay the loan now. Well, let me tell you something – there are only two things that are certain. One of them is taxes. And you know what the other is!'"

"Why didn't your husband go to the police, then? Or at least, contact your brother. Just like you've done now?"

Mrs. Corrington took a deep breath.

"Because...well...it just was so difficult. I mean...we felt threatened. But what could we say to the police? *You* just told me the memos weren't that threatening. And Palermo certainly could have denied that he made threats during the phone calls."

She shook her head.

"We...just weren't sure what to do. And Donald...he kept hoping he could talk some reason into Palermo."

Verging on the edge of crying, Margaret continued.

"But he couldn't. And I tell you, George Palermo killed my husband!"

She bit her lip, then reached down and picked up her coffee cup. She took a long sip.

"I...I'm sorry. I...didn't mean to get worked up like this."

"It's okay," I assured her.

Then I took another look at the memos between Palermo and Corrington, and something jumped out at me.

"I just realized," I said to Mrs. Corrington, "that all of these memos are on Corrington Imports letterhead. I'd expect that, on the memos your husband sent to Palermo. But Palermo's memos also are on Corrington letterhead."

"Yes," Margaret explained, "There's a reason for that. You see, even though George was primarily an investor, he also was active in one part of the company, so he was in the office for a few hours at least two or three days a week. It would have been perfectly natural for him to use Corrington letterhead, especially on a company matter."

"How was he active?"

"He was involved in a division that I started about two years ago. The Individual Desires Division. Donald had the idea and helped me set up the division. A great idea. Just what the name said it was – the importing of specific, very high end items, tailored to the individual desires and dreams of wealthy clients. One of a kind gifts, artifacts, art, sculpture. But Donald didn't have the time to develop the division, so he asked me to. And George had experience in that sort of thing, so he was working with me."

"But you didn't know this correspondence was going on, between your husband and Palermo?"

"No. I had no idea. It was before the phone calls started coming. And even then, Donald never mentioned the memos to me."

I shifted to another question.

"The gun...that killed your husband. It was registered to him, right?"

"Yes."

"According to statements from you and your husband's secretary, the weapon was kept in a locked drawer in your husband's desk. Who had the key to that drawer?"

"As far as I know, Donald had the only key."

"Another thing I wonder about. Your husband had pancreatic cancer. Terminal, according to his doctor. Don't you think that could have been reason enough for your husband to commit suicide?"

Margaret shook her head.

"To you, that sounds logical, I'm sure. But you didn't know Donald. He was a strong person. It just was not in his nature to...commit suicide. It wasn't something he would do. Under any circumstances, including having cancer."

Margaret looked steadily at me, and I could see her working to control her emotions.

"I just know I am right, Will. I...just...know...it!"

I figured I'd gone about as far as I could, this time around.

So I told her, "Okay, I think I have everything I need for now. Next, I'd like your permission to go through your husband's office. And later, through his study here at home. I know, of course, that the police have done all that. But still, I want to do it myself."

"Of course," Margaret said. "I'll call Mary Chase. She is...she was...Donald's secretary. And make the arrangements."

"One more question. What are you planning to do with the

company? Run it? Sell it? Or what?"

"It's a good business," Margaret answered. "Not big, but successful. We did just over $3 million in sales last year. I'll have to see."

"I'll want to get over to the office tomorrow," I said.

"I'll call Mary today and arrange it," Margaret assured me.

CHAPTER 8

When he hung up the phone, Benjamin Hahn was worried. Very worried.

A call from Michael Palermo always did that to him. God, he thought, Michael is even worse than George…his sonofabitch dead brother.

Hahn was in the small office at the rear of his antiques store, one of several such retail outlets, located on a few blocks of Sherman Way in Reseda.

In his mind, Hahn played back the phone call with Palermo.

"Hahn?" Palermo had said, "Listen carefully to me. Okay?"

Not even realizing he was doing so, Hahn had nodded, but not said anything.

"Hahn, are you there?" Palermo demanded. "Are you listening to me?"

"Yes. Yes. Of course," Hahn managed to say, his stomach beginning to lurch.

Palermo said, "There's a private investigator, named Will Jonas. He's probably going to contact you, because he's investigating the suicide of Donald Corrington of Corrington Imports."

"What's that got to do with me?" Hahn protested.

Palermo answered, "All I know is what Margaret Corrington told me. That he's ex-LAPD and that she's employing him to investigate her husband's suicide, so he's talking to people who were involved in the company. And that includes the Individual Desires division, so he'll want to talk to you."

"What is he going to ask me?"

"I would imagine, just some general stuff about the Individual Desires division. So he has a more complete picture of Corrington."

"Nothing about the...the other things...George and...and I...were doing."

Palermo spoke soothingly.

"No, nothing about what you and George were doing. Hell, Margaret doesn't know anything about that. So she couldn't have mentioned anything to this Jonas. No questions from him, on that stuff."

"You're...you're sure about this?"

"I'm sure about this," Palermo told Hahn. "Stay calm. Just a few general questions, and he'll be out of there."

But after hanging up, and as he thought about the conversation, the last thing Hahn felt, was sure about anything.

He took a deep breath, trying to ease the tightness in his chest. But the tension wouldn't go away.

This is a terrible price I'm paying, he thought, for dealing with people like the Palermo's. A terrible price.

CHAPTER 9

The drive from Margaret Corrington's home to my office took about 15 minutes. East on the 101, off at Canoga, and north to my office building.

When I came in to the office, Rose gave me the personnel file on Eugene Catlin that Makinowsky had sent over.

"Okay," I said to her, "I want to take a look at this, so hold my calls."

"Held they will be," Rose promised.

I went into my office, sat down at my desk, and started in on the file. Everything was pretty standard. Catlin had been recruited by Makinowsky, shortly after he founded Floragenics. He lured the scientist away from one of the big drug companies with an annual salary of $150,000, a $10,000 expense account allowance, and an attractive stock option plan. It was the stock option plan that was the convincer for Catlin, I suspected. The plan would make him, if not super rich, certainly plenty comfortable when Floragenics went public in a few years.

I didn't see anything in the file that made me think Catlin was selling Floragenics' trade secrets. He was well paid and had plenty of responsibility and authority on the technical side of the company.

If this guy is keeping odd hours, I thought, then my money is on what I told Makinowsky on the phone yesterday. Catlin is having an affair.

I looked in the file at his personal history.

Married for eighteen years. Right out of college.

Probably no sexual experience, except with his wife?

And now, here he was, making a lot of money.

And pretty high up on the corporate ladder.

Under those conditions, plenty of guys are perfect candidates to be bitten by the marital cheating bug. Its elements include -- a growing sense of importance, and a self-entitlement attitude because, hey, I'm an important person.

"Why are you grinning?" Rose asked as she came into my office.

I waived the Catlin file at her.

"Are you a sporting woman, Rose?"

"You shouldn't ask me a question like that. I'm a grandmother."

"What I mean is, do you want to make a bet?"

"On what?"

"On an affair of the heart."

"Nu…as long as it is not my heart."

I waived the file again.

"Makinowsky's worried that one of his scientists might be

selling proprietary information to a competitor. Seems the scientist has been giving his wife a hard time lately, with an odd pattern of when he comes home, and when he doesn't. Well, I say there's no industrial espionage going on here. Just an itchy scientist looking for some fresh sexual experiences. Care to bet on it?"

"I'll pass," Rose said. "What I came in to tell you, is that a Mary Chase just called, from Corrington Imports, to say that whenever you want to come to the office is fine. And she wanted to know if she should prepare anything special for you to look at."

"Call her back and tell her I'll be there at 9:30 tomorrow morning. I may want to review some specific items, once I've taken a first look around, but it's too early for me to tell."

The telephone rang and Rose answered it. She listened, and then handed me the phone.

"It's Captain Klinger," she told me, and she left my office, to call Mary Chase.

"Hello, Captain," I said. "I guess you're calling to find out how my meeting went with your sister?"

"From her standpoint, it went okay," Klinger said. "That's what she told me. What do you think?"

"Yeah, it went okay. I was surprised, though, about some memos she showed me – between Donald Corrington and George Palermo. Did you know about those?"

"Not until she told me about them, in our phone call. I've asked her to make copies for me. In the meantime, though, they seem completely circumstantial. And not very strong. You saw them. What do you think?"

"Same reaction as yours. Yes, circumstantial. Not anything that shouts out at me – about a possible homicide. But Margaret is pretty strong on feeling that they are very much threats of homicide, so I'm going to have to convince her, otherwise."

"Now, switching subjects," I said, "I want to let you know that I'll be over at Corrington Imports tomorrow morning. I'll call you, if I come up with anything."

After talking with Klinger, I went back to the Catlin file, and decided there were two things I had to do.

First, of course, I had to make sure Catlin *wasn't* selling company secrets. I was pretty sure that was the case, but I'd have to check it out.

And second, it would help if I could definitely find out if Catlin *was* having an affair. While that wasn't the kind of "good news" Makinowsky wanted to hear, it most likely would explain why Catlin was keeping erratic home hours. What Makinowsky would want to do with that information was not my concern.

I looked at my watch and decided I might as well start my surveillance of Catlin tonight. Pick up the trail when he left work.

CHAPTER 10

"I'm not interested in selling the company right now, Michael. I thought I made that clear when we spoke on the phone," Margaret Corrington said to Michael Palermo. They were sitting in the same family room, in Margaret's home, where she and Will had met.

Palermo took Margaret's rejection in stride. He had expected this answer. And anyway, the sale of Corrington Imports actually was not on Michael's discussion agenda. He had only used that topic as a cover, to set up the meeting. There were other, more pressing reasons Michael wanted to see Margaret.

In particular, he needed to find out if she knew anything about the deals between his brother, George, and the antiques dealer, Benjamin Hahn, in connection with Corrington's Individual Desires division.

And second, he wanted to know more about *why* Margaret was accusing his brother of having killed her husband. When Margaret first made the accusation, Michael admitted to himself that George certainly was capable of murder, but he truly doubted that his brother had done anything of the sort to Donald Corrington. It made no sense.

Aloud, he addressed Margaret, a smile accompanying his words as he tried to ease the tension between them.

"I just thought with all of the responsibility you now have to run the company, you…might be seeking some future alternatives. For example, I know how deeply involved you were in the Individual Desires division. Certainly, it could be a term of any sale of the company, that you could have carte blanche to run the Division. That's how it was before. You and George pretty much ran that division."

"Well," Margaret replied, "When Donald first set up the division, yes, the idea was that I would run and develop it. And it did start out that way. But then, I have to admit, that when you and George invested, I eased up a lot, because George was so insistent about participating actively in the division. So for the last six months, George did most of the running of the division."

That George had taken control from Margaret, was not news to Michael. That was what he had instructed George to do. It was part of his plan to get Margaret out of the way, so that George and Hahn could do their business without the Corrington's suspecting anything.

Perfect! George concluded. She doesn't know anything about what George and Hahn were doing.

But to double-check his conclusion, Michael decided to take his questions one step further.

He asked Margaret, "Did that mean George worked with the

customers and their product requests? Or did he concentrate on the suppliers...the dealers? I sort of got the impression from George that he did more of the dealer side than the customer side."

"Actually," Margaret answered, "In the last several months, George worked both sides – customers and dealers. He was far more active than me."

Again, an answer that pleased Michael. It reinforced the conclusion that Margaret knew nothing of the deals Hahn and George were making within the Division.

But now, Michael knew, he had to bring up a very sensitive subject with Margaret. She was not going to be happy – but it was a discussion that was necessary. Because it might help him understand why Margaret was accusing his brother of having killed Donald. And it would certainly affect his takeover strategy for Corrington Imports.

"Margaret," he began, speaking in as neutral a tone as he could, "please understand that what I am about to say, I only do so out of a sense of confusion...and concern...for you."

He paused deliberately, and then continued.

"I imagine you must know...that I know...George and you were...having an affair. Of course, I make no judgement about this. Whatever you do...you do. But what confuses me is this. How can you accuse a man with whom you are...having relations...of killing your husband? I mean, would not an obvious conclusion to that be, that he killed your husband...on your behalf?"

Margaret glared at Michael.

"You bastard!" she said angrily.

Then she took a deep breath and worked to regain her composure.

"No, I won't deny that I had an affair with your brother."

She laughed, almost sneered.

"But have George kill Donald on my behalf? As part of a…a plan? That's ridiculous!"

Margaret shook her head.

"No. Sorry to disappoint you, but it wasn't anything like that."

Then she asked, "Are you done with your questions? Because I've got some of my own to ask."

"Please…" George invited.

Margaret studied Michael carefully, almost to the point where he became uncomfortable.

Then she asked, "Did you know that your brother was pressuring Donald? Was demanding that Corrington Imports immediately pay back the money you loaned us?"

Michael Palermo was surprised. What Margaret was saying couldn't possibly be true. Yes, what she described was the key to the takeover strategy he planned for Corrington Imports. But when George died, he – Michael -- hadn't yet implemented the plan. Hadn't even started to talk to Donald about wanting his money back.

"I don't know what you mean?" Michael protested. "I didn't

make any such demand of Donald!"

"Maybe you didn't," Margaret answered, "But your brother did. And doesn't that amount to the same thing?"

"No it doesn't," Michael protested. He had to convince Margaret on this point. Had to if ever he was going to have a chance at taking over the company.

"Look," he said to Margaret, "I don't know what proof you have to support what you're claiming, but believe me, I did not...I repeat...I did not have any discussions whatsoever with Donald about wanting the loan repaid."

Margaret smiled at him, but it wasn't a friendly smile.

"I have the proof, Michael."

She handed Palermo the file of memos between George and Donald.

"I have these memos that George wrote to Donald, demanding repayment. That's what I have."

Michael looked at the memos, shook his head and cursed his brother.

"The idiot! The damned, stupid idiot!"

CHAPTER 11

Floragenics Laboratories was headquartered in one of the many industrial parks clustered in Chatsworth, a community located in the northwestern corner of the San Fernando Valley.

One of the things I like about the Valley is how easy it is to travel around. Sure, things have gotten much more crowded in the last twenty or so years, with the Valley's population now topping one million people. But getting from here to there still beats trying to do the same thing in downtown Los Angeles, Westwood or West L.A.

Before leaving my office, I had Rose call Floragenics and ask for Eugene Catlin – just to check and see if he was still there, since it was 4:30 PM. Rose did get through to Catlin, but of course, she hung up, as soon as he answered.

About twenty-five minutes after I left my office, I reached the parking lot in front of the one story Floragenics building. I pulled into a vacant visitor's parking slot and started watching the building's glass-fronted double doors. I knew what Catlin looked like, having seen his employee picture in his personnel file.

After a short wait, I saw Catlin come out the front entrance and walk to his car, in one of the spaces reserved for senior executives.

Catlin was a thin man, with poor posture that accentuated the start of a pot belly. He had sandy colored hair that lay flat against his head. He was wearing a pair of rim glasses, and he was dressed in a plain, dark grey single breasted suit that looked ready for the cleaners.

Catlin got into his car, started it up and drove out of the parking lot. I let him get half way down the block, before following him. Lucky for me, it was quitting time at other businesses in the neighborhood, so I didn't have any trouble keeping three or four cars between Catlin and me.

Catlin drove south, across Tampa, turned right on Victory Boulevard, left at Canoga, and then left again, into the entranceway for the Hilton Hotel.

Damn! I thought to myself, if he's planning what this looks like, it's going to be a long evening.

Catlin drove past the hotel's valet station and into the self-parking garage. I followed, and pulled into a space down the line from where he parked.

The scientist got out of his car and walked toward the pathway that led up to the lobby. I followed, staying far enough back to make sure he didn't spot me – although the way he was walking – fast – I got the feeling he was only intent on getting *to* where he wanted to be – which I figured was the woman I was almost certain he'd be meeting.

Catlin went straight across the lobby and into the crowded cocktail lounge, me following.

He looked around and then he walked to a booth occupied by an attractive blond woman. Couldn't see her up close, of course, but at a distance, she looked to be in her early thirties.

I went to the bar and sat down, angled so that I could keep Catlin and the woman in sight.

The bartender gave me the usual smile and greeting.

"What'll you have?"

"Diet Coke," I told him. "I'm a friend of Bill's."

"Good for you," the bartender smiled. He filled the glass and put it down on the counter.

"Compliments of the house," he said.

"Thanks."

I looked over at Catlin and his companion. Well that was quick!

Catlin and the woman were standing up. They joined hands and walked out of the bar, me following, of course.

Didn't take much imagination to figure out where they were headed – and there they were – at the elevator bank. Standing close – very close – arms around each other.

I thought about following them. See what floor they went to. Then decided that didn't make any sense. I already knew what they were going to do. And where they were going to do it. Didn't need the room number to verify the anticipated sequence of things.

I considered leaving, now that I had the answer for Catlin's erratic behavior. Hey, I thought to myself – Catlin is being erratic, because he's erotic.

Ugh! Enough with the rhyming.

I decided to stay. Why? Because I wanted to know more about the lady with Catlin.

She was very attractive. Catlin was very plain. To put it bluntly, I figured she could do a lot better than getting into the sack with the scientist.

So, why was she involved with him? A good question. And I wanted an answer, which started with the need for me to find out who she was.

I thought about trying to get her name from the registration desk clerk, but they are trained not to give up that kind of information. Also, she might not have rented the room. Catlin might have taken care of that detail.

No way around it, I realized. Just have to stay, and when they come down to the lobby, follow her to her car, and get the license number. Then, too, I can try and follow her home, and get an address. Armed with that data, Rose can attack the Internet and come up with some information on the lady.

I looked around the lobby. There were a few groupings of chairs, couches and tables. I sat down in one of the chairs, off to the side of the lobby – not in a direct sight line with the elevator bank, but with a clear view of it.

For cover, I'd carried a small brief case in with me. I opened it up now, took out a few sheets of a file, and started looking at the pages. Hoped I looked like an executive hard at work.

Decided to use the time to call my wife, Lu. See what I was missing for dinner. Took out my cell phone and dialed her. Lu answered on the second ring.

"Boy, are you going to be disappointed when you don't get home in time for dinner," she said, without any preamble. "You're missing my finest Italian dish – veal parmigiana. Preceded by a hearty bowl of minestrone soup, and then to clear the palate for the veal, there is a Caesar salad. Sound good, Will?"

"Are you really making all of that?" I asked.

"Nah! Just wanted to tease you. If you aren't coming home for dinner, then a couple of eggs with toast will be my dinner."

"Well, I wish it were otherwise, but I'm stuck in the lobby of the Hilton in Woodland Hills, while the guy I'm following enjoys himself with some lady, other than his wife."

"Gee, I thought you were long past that kind of investigating."

"So did I. But sometimes…"

"Yeah…sometimes," Lu agreed.

I ended my call with Lu and settled down, prepared for a long wait, which didn't turn out to be that long. About an hour and a half was all – until I saw Catlin and his companion come out of one of the elevators and walk through the lobby, toward the pathway, leading to the parking garage.

I put my papers away and followed them into the garage. They walked up to a car that was parked on the same level where both Catlin's' car and mine were parked.

Catlin and the woman kissed and embraced in a serious way, giving me plenty of time to note her license plate number, and then to get into my car, ready to follow her.

The woman gave Catlin a final kiss and sat down in her car. She backed out of her parking slot, then turned and headed for the exit. After several seconds, I followed.

This time, it was a little trickier. No so many cars on the road as before. But I managed okay. At least I think I did. The woman didn't do anything that made me think otherwise.

I followed her over to nearby Northridge, where she drove up to one of the condo complexes dotting the area around Corbin. She parked on the street and walked to the front entrance of one of the units.

Okay, now I had her car license and her home address. Tomorrow, I'd give this information to Rose. And she, in ways that I didn't want to know about, would attack her computer and hopefully come up with a name for the woman, and some history on her.

Time to go home.

CHAPTER 12

The next morning, before I left the condo for my appointment at Corrington Imports, I called Rose and gave her what I had on the woman with Catlin – her car license plate number and home address.

"Work your computer magic," I told Rose. "Let's see what you can find out about the lady. Maybe have something for me, by the time I get to the office?"

"And when might that be?"

"Not certain yet. But probably by about noon or so."

"Nu? I'll see," was Roses' only commitment. But I knew she'd be attacking that computer just as soon as I hung up. So I did.

Corrington Imports was located in an industrial area in Canoga Park. It had its own two story building that included space both for offices and for warehousing the products the company imported.

Parking was in front of the building, with visitor spaces just to the right of the entrance. I drove my car into one of the visitor spaces, went into the building, gave the receptionist my name and told her I was there to see Mary Chase.

A couple of minutes later, out comes a very nice looking lady, probably in her late 50's.

We recognize each other.

"You were at the AA meeting yesterday morning," she said.

"Stuck out like a sore thumb, huh?"

"Not at all," she assured me, "but it's usually the same people at that meeting, so a new face does stand out."

She went on to tell me that she attended that AA meeting two or three times a week, noting that she lived in Thousand Oaks, a community west of Calabasas. The meeting site was convenient for her, as she drove to work east on the 101 Freeway.

While she talked, Mary, as she had told me to call her, walked me down the corridor and into an office at the end of the hall.

"This is…was…Donald's office," Mary said.

She pointed to a stack of papers on a conference table at one end of the office.

"I put together some background material on the company for you, information on operations, financial reports, profit and loss statements, employee benefits, product data. And of course, I'll be happy to provide you with anything further."

"I appreciate it," I told her, "but before I get started on that pile, can we talk?"

"Of course. Any way I can be of help…"

I walked over to the conference table, sat down and motioned for Mary to join me.

Once she did, I asked, "Do you know why I'm here?"

"Yes, and I'm afraid I don't understand. Mrs. Corrington said you are investigating whether George Palermo killed Mr. Corrington. I thought the police had already decided it was suicide."

"You're right…about what the police have decided. But Mrs. Corrington feels differently, and I've been asked to look into it."

Looking at Mary, I could see she was dubious about Margaret's claim. I asked her about it.

"Do I get the feeling you don't think George Palermo could have killed Donald Corrington?"

"I find it hard to believe."

"Why?"

"Because…well…I…I never saw them arguing. Or disagreeing about anything. They seemed to get along well."

Mary paused.

"Of course, as I think about it, Mr. Palermo didn't have that much to do with Mr. Corrington. Mr. Palermo actually worked more closely with Mrs. Corrington, on the Individual Desires Division."

Then, for just an instant, I spotted what seemed to be a look of disapproval on Mary's face. Needed to find out, why.

"Mary, I get the feeling you're holding back on something here. Come on. You and I know the drill from AA. We have to be honest with ourselves, and with each other. So, what is it? What's bothering you?"

Mary shook her head.

"You're not shy about pushing all the hot buttons," she said.

"I'm just trying to get to the bottom of things. And I think you've got something to tell me, that can help me get there."

Mary was quiet for a few seconds. Looked like she was working something out in her mind. I kept quiet, too. Then Mary made up her mind.

"I…I can't be absolutely sure, but…I think Mrs. Corrington and Mr. Palermo were having an affair."

Well! That came out of nowhere, I had to admit.

I said, "Big news there, Mary. What do you base it on?"

"Their out of town travel schedules. Not too long after Mr. Palermo started working here, they went out of town several times – together – to sales conventions, major client meetings…"

"How do you know? Did you book their travel?"

"No. Each of them booked their own trips through the travel agency we use. But I don't think either of them realized that the travel agent always checked everything through me. It was something the agent and I had gotten in the habit of doing over the years."

"So," I asked, "neither of them was likely to realize that you knew they were out there together?"

"That's right."

"But just being in the same city, doesn't necessarily mean they were having an affair."

"I saw copies of all the hotel, travel and restaurant expenses.

It…it was pretty conclusive."

"Did Mr. Corrington know anything about this?" I asked.

Mary shook her head.

"No, I don't think he suspected. And I don't think he ever would have suspected, either."

"Why is that?"

"Because, despite whatever she might have been doing with Mr. Palermo, I must say…Mrs. Carrington was always good to Mr. Carrington. It was a second marriage for him, you know. He was a widower when he met her. And from his standpoint, I don't think he could have been happier."

"You cared for him very much, didn't you?"

"Yes. He…he was a fine person."

Mary looked at Will and sighed.

"I've been sober now for eleven years. And I've been Mr. Carrington's secretary for almost that entire time. When I first was trying to get back to work, in those early days at AA, I was having a hard time finding a job. No one wanted to take a chance on a middle aged woman who had been a drunk. But Mr. Corrington, he was different. He listened to what I had to say. And…I'll never forget it…he listened, then he opened his desk drawer, took out a pad and pencil, handed them to me, and asked if I could take shorthand."

Mary dabbed a small handkerchief at her eyes.

"I'm sorry. I didn't want to do this. I promised myself I wouldn't do this."

"It's okay," I assured her. "Do you think you can answer a few more questions now? I could put it off…"

"No. It's all right. Please. Let's continue."

I started my questioning again.

"I get the feeling that you didn't care for George Palermo. Why? Was it because he was having the affair with Mrs. Corrington?"

Mary shook her head.

"Yes, I'm sure that colors my feelings. But, aside from that, I just didn't like the man. He was…very opportunistic. Always looking for…other…easier ways to do things."

Mary shook her head in exasperation.

"I'm not expressing myself very well!"

"Maybe what you mean," I suggested to her, "is that he was always looking for an angle?"

"Yes! That's it, exactly."

I made a mental note to ask Captain Klinger to check and see if there was anything in the police files on both Palermo's. Then I asked Mary another question.

"You say Palermo and Mrs. Corrington worked closely together in the Individual Desires Division?"

"Yes."

"Could I see the files for that Division? Is the information with the material here on the table?"

"I did put a brochure in there on the Division. But perhaps the best source of information I could give you, would be a copy of the computer disk files. Both Mrs. Corrington and Mr. Palermo were heavy computer users, so most everything on the Division's activities – sales, customer lists, pricing and the like – is on those disks."

"That'll work for me," I said, figuring Rose would be able to look at the disks for me. Hell, if I tried, with my barely basic computer capability, I'd probably screw things up. And if Rose needed help, then I'd ask Lu to work on it. As chief computer programmer at her bank, she certainly had the knowledge to do so.

With my next question, I changed subjects.

"I'm sorry to have to ask you this…but the gun Mr. Corrington…used…I understand it was in a locked drawer in his desk?"

"That's right."

"And he had the only key to that drawer?"

"No, that's not so. There was a second key. In my desk."

"Also in a locked drawer?"

"No. In the unlocked center drawer. The key was in there. And the drawer was unlocked…on purpose."

"Why was that?"

"Because Mr. Corrington wanted whoever might stay late in the office, to have access to the gun. He only bought the gun after there were some burglaries in other buildings in the area."

"So, Mr. Corrington bought the gun for protection?"

"Yes, and he told all of us about it. And where it was. And about the second key in my desk, so any one of us could go in and get the gun…if we were working late and we thought someone might be trying to break into our building."

I remembered that Margaret had told me that her husband had the only key. But here was Mary, saying that everyone knew about the second key in her desk.

So I asked Mary, "Did Mrs. Corrington know about the second key in your desk drawer?"

Mary thought for a moment before answering.

"I'm not sure. She may have. But then again, Mr. Corrington bought the gun before Mrs. Corrington started coming in regularly, to work on the Individual Desires Division. So she may not have known, unless Mr. Corrington told her himself. I know I never mentioned anything to her."

"Mary, did you know that Mr. Corrington had pancreatic cancer?"

"I knew something was wrong. It was becoming obvious that he was sick with…something. But whenever I asked him – and I did, a few times – he'd only say that it wasn't anything worth talking about."

"Why do you think he was so secretive about his illness?"

"I'm not surprised. Even though he could be very outgoing and charming in business – and he was – when it came to personal things, Mr. Corrington never liked to talk about himself. And he didn't like people fussing over him."

"Final question. I'm going to want to talk to Mr. Corrington's lawyer, his accountant, and his doctor. Can you please give me their names, addresses and phone numbers?"

"Of course."

"Mary, thank you very much. I appreciate your help."

I turned to the files on the conference table.

CHAPTER 13

I finished up at Corrington Imports about noon.

Didn't learn anything new from my review of the files.

So, where'd this leave me?

Suicide, as the police had ruled?

Or, murder, as Margaret Corrington was claiming?

I was tilting toward suicide, but not ready yet to make a final decision. I needed more information. And that's why, when I got back to the office, I asked Rose to call Captain Klinger.

"There are some things I'd appreciate your checking out," I said to the Captain, after Rose connected us.

"What do you need?"

"When I was at Corrington Imports this morning, I talked with Donald Corrington's secretary. Turns out she's no fan of the Palermo's —both the deceased George and the alive Michael. She's a pretty sensible lady, and if she has bad feelings about them — especially George, whom she got to know up close when he worked at the company —then I'd like to know more about these guys."

"We didn't run anything on either of them," Klinger said. "No need to. The death was ruled a suicide. No indication of foul play, so no digging into the backgrounds of any other people."

"Can you run backgrounds on both Palermo's, now? Police records, of course, if they have them. But also, any good general background. I'd be interested in knowing how they made their money. They invested a million dollars in Corrington. And I bet they have other holdings, too. How did they get to where they are?"

"Okay. I can get that."

"And one more thing. I'd like a copy of the file on George Palermo's auto accident."

"You think there's something there?"

"It probably *was* an accident, but I'd like to know the details. Just to make sure."

When I was finished talking to Klinger, Rose came into my office and handed me several computer printout pages.

"Everything there is to know about the Femme Fatale," she announced. "Otherwise known as Maria Fletcher. Here are the goods on her."

"The goods?" I mimicked her. "What do you think we're running here? A private eye operation? Next, you'll ask me if I want to put a tail on the lady."

"But you did. Last night."

"That was not a tail. That was a…surveillance operation."

"Surveillance, schmurveillance," Rose shot back. "You

followed Catlin to the hotel. You saw him meet the lady. Saw them go up to the room. Then you followed the lady home. I know what I call that. You got a better name for it?"

"Not another word, leave me the file and depart," I said. And then I grinned at Rose. "Okay, you win this round."

"Put it in my paycheck," Rose laughed, as she left.

I went through the file Rose had given me. She'd managed to pull together a solid amount of information on this Maria Fletcher. Most of it was routine, until I came to a page that Rose had highlighted. It showed Fletcher's work record, and I could see why Rose had highlighted it.

The file showed that Fletcher never stayed on a job very long. According to what I read, she changed jobs about every six months.

What also caught my attention were the companies where Fletcher worked. Over the last three years, there had been six of them, all in the biotech field, like Floragenics.

And then, there was Fletcher's educational background to consider. She had undergraduate and graduate degrees in chemistry.

But despite those degrees, she always worked as a secretary.

Strange career path, I thought. Staying at the bottom of the ladder, when she could have gone a lot higher.

So, why? Why did she do that?

The answer looked pretty clear to me. I'd put money on it. Maria Fletcher was an industrial spy.

Putting things together, I thought I could see how she operated.

Fletcher would go to work for a target company where, for whatever the reason, she thought their proprietary information might be of interest to another, competing company.

Working at that target company, she'd become friendly with a key scientist. Not hard for someone as attractive as she. She'd develop an affair with the guy. He would never suspect how much she really understood about his work, because he wouldn't be aware of her educational background.

Then, through "pillow talk" – and most likely, opportunities to go through his brief case – she'd gather useful information for selling to a rival company.

Once she got all of the information she could, Fletcher would break off the relationship, sell her information to a competitor company, and move on to her next target company.

It looked like Carl Makinowsky was right to be worried. Catlin, via this Fletcher woman, probably was already giving up proprietary information, or soon would – and most likely, without even realizing it.

It was time to bring Makinowsky up to date on the investigation. I called, and after his secretary put me through, I told Carl, "Okay, I believe Catlin is involved in some industrial espionage, although he may not even be aware of it."

"Shit!" was Makinowsky's first reaction. And then, "what have you got?"

I gave Makinowsky the details and then told him what I recommended as our next steps.

"I want to confront Catlin with what I know about his relationship with this Maria Fletcher. I suspect he will break down pretty fast. If so, then I want to use him to trap Fletcher into a specific act of stealing Floragenics proprietary information. We can bring the police in on this, if things progress the way we hope."

Makinowsky was silent for a few seconds.

"My first priority is to shut Catlin down. Stop him from giving Fletcher any more proprietary information."

"If we do it the way I'm proposing, that's how I see it playing out."

"Okay, so what's the next step?"

"I want to meet with Catlin – alone – tomorrow. At your place. Like I said before, I think I can break him down. And if I do, then I want you to join us, and please bring along your in-house counsel – Paul Reeverson. The purpose of that meeting will be to work out the details of how Catlin is going to help us nail Fletcher."

"Suppose he doesn't want to cooperate?" Makinowsky challenged me. "What then?"

"Well, you've still accomplished the main objective of the investigation, which is to get rid of the industrial espionage problem. And carefully stated, I bet you can get some word out to your rivals about this Maria Fletcher, so that no one else hires her."

Makinowsky was satisfied.

He asked, "When do you want to have that meeting with Catlin?"

"Make it for ten tomorrow morning. Have your secretary tell him you want to see him in the conference room, rather than your office, because there are some large, screen-sized graphics you want to go over with him."

I ended my call with Makinowsky and then I called Lu, at her office, at the bank headquarters in Glendale. We didn't usually talk much during the day, but I needed to ask if she could do something for me that evening, at home. With her experience as the bank's chief computer programmer, it was something I knew she could handle.

"Am I a suspect in some investigation of yours?" Lu asked, when we connected. "I'm sure you didn't call, just to tell me how much you love me."

"Ah, but I do love you."

"How nice to hear." Lu laughed. "Okay, now that I've gotten you to admit that, what is it you *really* called me about?"

"I've got some disks that cover the operations of the division of a company that I'm investigating. If I bring the disks home – there are just two of them – can you print them out, and then help me analyze them –meaning, looking for some patterns of operation that may be unusual? Frankly, I'm not sure what I'm looking for. And we may find nothing – but I need to know."

"Sure, I can help," Lu said. "How much I can get done,

though, is a matter of how much information there is to analyze."

"It's just two disks."

Lu laughed.

"I love you, Will – but despite my best efforts, you're still a computer Neanderthal. You see, each disk is capable of holding large quantities of information. Or limited amounts. Just depends on what the user wanted to put on the disk."

"Okay, I guess we'll just have to see."

. . . .

After my call with Lu, Rose came into my office.

"Will, we have to talk about Melanie. There is a problem we have to discuss."

My stomach tightened. My protective mode, getting ready to help Melanie overcome whatever problem Rose was talking about. That kid had been through so much. Can't let her suffer anymore. Couldn't. Wouldn't.

Rose explained, "This morning, when you were out, I got a call from one of the other ladies who does the car pool with me, for Melanie and the other children in our school car pool arrangement.

"This lady told me that her daughter – who is a friend to Melanie – has told her that a group of girls at the school are giving our Melanie a hard time."

"What kind of hard time?"

"What Amy – that's the mother's name -- is telling me is, that these girls pick on Melanie, because of her background. You know – her coming from Junction City. And…and what happened with her parents – God knows how they found out about that."

"Has Melanie said anything to you about this?"

"No. But you know Melanie. She is one strong young person. God help us, she has learned the hard way. But still, this…this abuse has to be hurting. And we have got to get it… stopped."

"You bet we do!"

"So, I've arranged for Lu, you and me to meet with the director of the school – along with the parents of the girl who is the leader of the group of girls bothering Melanie. The meeting is for tomorrow afternoon…at five o'clock."

"No sooner?"

"It's the soonest it could be done. The girl's parents had other things on their calendars earlier in the day."

"Screw their calendars! This is Melanie we're talking about. That girl has already had enough hard knocks for anyone's lifetime. We need to get this straightened out! Fast!"

"Will…Will…please calm down. I feel like you do. But if we are going to do right by Melanie, then we need to approach this calmly. And if that means the meeting can't be until tomorrow afternoon…well…so be it."

I took a deep breath and then exhaled.

"You're right, of course. I just go a little crazy, when it comes to trying to make sure Melanie has the best possible experiences in her life. She deserves that."

"We all want that for her. You, Lu and me. She'll have it."

CHAPTER 14

That evening, Lu and I spent our dinnertime discussing the next day's meeting at Melanie's school.

It was clear that Lu and Rose had talked. Lu knew what kind of a mood I was in.

"Will," she cautioned, "promise me you won't lose your temper and play 'bad cop' at that meeting tomorrow."

"Just so long as that girl's parents promise to straighten her out. As long as they do that, I'll be a sweet pussycat."

"Promise me you'll be reasonable, no matter what happens at the meeting. This is not a showdown meeting. It is a meeting to work things out."

"I'll be fine," I told Lu. "I'll be fine."

Time to switch subjects.

"Now, how about you taking a look at those two Corrington disks? Let's see…what we can see."

About an hour later, Lu came out of her home office with some computer printed sheets.

She said, "When you gave me these disks, you told me to look for patterns, for anything unusual in the Individual Desires division's activities. You said that this George Palermo may have been doing something not quite kosher."

"And…" I prompted.

"And I didn't find anything specifically *wrong* so far, but I did find a pattern that might mean something. Palermo did most of his business with just a few antiques and collectibles dealers around the country. That's in contrast to how Margaret Corrington worked in the division. She did a lot less business, but it was much more spread out among a larger number of dealers."

I thought about the pattern Lu had described.

"You know, if Palermo was into some questionable deals, it'd make sense that he'd do those with a few, carefully selected dealers. People he could work out…arrangements…with."

I carried this thought forward to the next stage.

"And, if this meant some illegal stuff – and Richard Corrington somehow found out – well, I can see a possible motive for murder here. Palermo killing Corrington – just like Margaret is claiming. Mind you, nothing certain here, but sure worth some more checking."

"Makes sense to me," Lu agreed.

I asked, "Any of those dealers local?"

"One. A Benjamin Hahn. He's got a store in Reseda."

Lu handed me a note.

"Here's his name, address and telephone number."

"Okay. I'll give him a call tomorrow morning, before I go to Floragenics."

CHAPTER 15

And that's what I did – call Benjamin Hahn the next morning— before leaving my office for my meeting with Eugene Catlin at Floragenics.

My call was answered on the third ring.

"Hahn Imports,"

"Mr. Hahn, please."

"This is Benjamin Hahn."

"Mr. Hahn, my name is Will Jonas. I'm a private investigator, and I wonder if I could have a few minutes of your time, let's say, tomorrow morning?"

I didn't know it, of course, but at his end of the line, Hahn gripped the telephone, as he struggled to stay calm.

"What...why do you want to see me? I don't know you...do I?"

"No. But I believe you knew George Palermo, right?"

It was a few seconds before Hahn answered me, and he sounded nervous.

"Yes…but…I still don't understand what you want with me…?"

"It's just routine," I assured him. "I've been hired by the widow of Donald Corrington to check into some of the facts about Mr. Corrington's death. And your name came up, in connection with the Individual Desires Division. If you can spare me a few minutes, that's all it will take."

Again, there was a pause before Hahn answered.

"I…I really don't see what I can tell you…"

I was not going to let this guy off the hook. I didn't know what I might learn from a meeting with him – but *because* he didn't *want* to meet – that did it for me. I had to meet him, whether or not he liked it.

"How about 10:00 tomorrow morning?" I pushed.

"Tomorrow…tomorrow morning is not…good for me…"

I came back at him. "Any time that's good for you, is good for me. You pick the day and the time."

Then, I waited… silently. I figured I'd be able to outlast him with that tactic…and I was right. Hahn finally replied.

"The day after tomorrow. In the morning. Before I open. At …at 8:30."

"Good," I confirmed. "See you, then."

…………………………………………..

After the call from that Will Jonas person, Hahn began pacing about his small office at the rear of the store. Although the building's air conditioning was working, he began to sweat. He pawed at his stomach, which was starting to ache. He wondered if he was going to throw up.

He sighed, as he thought back over the last several months, during which he and George Palermo had started their operations together.

At first, it had gone just as Palermo had said. Easy deals. Easy money. And not just with Palermo and the Individual Desires Division. Palermo also had arranged for other people to place orders with Hahn. People like Palermo, who had clients with the same needs and desires.

Yes, he had been frightened right from the start. But he had managed to keep that feeling in check. At first. After all, it seemed the chances of being discovered were so slim. And the benefits so large.

But not now. Now, there was the fear. The nervousness. The tightness in his stomach and chest.

He didn't know how much longer he could go on with the Palermos of the world. It had gotten bad enough with George Palermo. But now, Michael Palermo was even worse. More frightening.

Sure...Palermo could tell him to stay calm. And to instruct him in what he should say to the private investigator.

But Hahn knew he might not be capable of following through the way Palermo had scripted it.

And what, then?

CHAPTER 16

Makinowsky had instructed the Floragenics receptionist to pass me into the conference room, when I arrived at the company – and she did. Once in the room, I set it up, for my meeting with Eugene Catlin.

With its exterior window glass wall exposed to the outdoors, the room was bright and cheerful. Not the mood I wanted, so I pushed the button and down came the drape.

Next, from my briefcase, I took out a manila file folder containing Catlin's personnel file. On the cover of the file, using a broad, felt-tipped black ink pen, I had written: Catlin/Fletcher Report. I laid this file on the table, next to my seat, positioning it so that Catlin would read what I had written, as soon as he sat down.

Then I took out a small recorder from my briefcase and put it in the center of the conference table, between where Catlin and I would be sitting.

Okay, I was ready for the guy.

I looked at the wall clock. It was one-minute shy of ten

o'clock. I figured that Catlin – no doubt being a precise kind of scientific guy – would be coming in, very soon.

And I was right. As the clock hit ten, the conference room door opened and Catlin did start to come in. But he stopped in the doorway.

"Oh, I thought I was meeting here with Carl Makinowsky."

"You *are* meeting here," I told him, keeping my voice low -- and I hoped, a bit menacing. "But with me, not Carl."

"Who...who are you?"

"I'm Will Jonas. I'm an internal security consultant to Makinowsky and Floragenics. Sit down."

"I don't understand..." Catlin began.

"Carl knows we're meeting," I interrupted him. "He'll be joining us later. But we need to talk first."

I pointed to the chair opposite mine, on the other side of the conference table.

Catlin was puzzled – not concerned yet. But when he did sit down, and he saw the Catlin/Fletcher file folder, he was jolted, just as I figured he'd be. The concern was clear on his face.

Good. Just what I was hoping.

When I was planning for this meeting, I sensed that the way to crack Catlin would be to come down on him, hard and fast. And that's how I started.

"Catlin, we know that you've been passing Floragenics proprietary information to Maria Fletcher."

"No..." Catlin tried to interrupt.

I road right over his attempt, and stretching the truth, I said to him, "We have your meetings with Fletcher on videotape, including the last one at the Hilton. I was there. I saw you two go up to the hotel room."

Catlin, shaken, was silent.

I pushed him.

"You're screwing Fletcher and paying for it by giving her Floragenics proprietary information."

Catlin swallowed hard. His body began to sag.

I picked up the Catlin/Fletcher file folder, leaned across the table and held the file close to Catlin's face.

"It's all in here, Catlin. Everything."

I stopped talking and just kept holding the file folder up in front of Catlin. I kept looking at him, and I saw him start to break.

Time to change tactics a bit. Show him how Fletcher had played him for the fool. Of course, I didn't have the actual information I was about to give Catlin, but my objective was to bang him into submission – and then to get his cooperation in nailing Fletcher. So I spun a story for Catlin.

"Let me tell you about this lady you've been screwing. In the last three years, Maria Fletcher has had six secretarial jobs at different biotech companies. She always works as a secretary – despite the fact that she has Bachelor's and Master's degrees in chemistry."

The information clearly surprised Catlin.

I kept going.

"Now, why do you suppose she hid her academic credits? Maybe so that you wouldn't realize how much information she was pumping out of you? How much she really understood of what you were telling her, whenever she asked those seemingly innocent questions of hers?"

Okay, time for the killer, I decided. Time to crush the man all the way down, so we can get him to work with us, in catching Fletcher and prosecuting her.

"Here's something else for you to wonder about, Catlin."

"Do you think, in those six jobs over the last three years, that maybe, just maybe, you weren't the first corporate scientist Maria Fletcher screwed, in order to get proprietary information? Maybe she told you differently – but you were far from the first."

That did it. Catlin crumbled all the way.

"Oh, God. Oh, my God," was all he could manage.

He bent forward in his chair, his head in his hands, and he cried.

For an instant, I felt sorry for the guy. And yes, I wasn't too happy with myself, and how I'd acted. But the man did bring it on himself, didn't he? And my job was to investigate and find out. Not to be a therapist.

I let Catlin stew for a moment, and then I changed tactics again – this time speaking in a soft and reasoning voice.

"Mr. Catlin, I know things look bad for you now, but I can help, if you'll let me. Will you let me help you, Mr. Catlin? Will you let me help you?"

"How...how can you help me? It's such a mess. Such a terrible mess."

I assured him, "Look, we realize you're a victim here. This Maria Fletcher is a very smooth operator. Who can blame you for going to bed with her? You'd have to be a saint to walk away from someone as good looking as she is."

"I was a fool," Catlin cried. "A damned fool."

"But now you can be smart. You can be smart. You can get even. And most important, you can help yourself in the process. Isn't that the best thing to do?"

Catlin looked imploringly at Will.

"My wife. This will ruin our marriage. I...I've never done anything like this before!"

I didn't like what I was about to say in response...what I was about to promise. But...it made sense...as a way to get Catlin's cooperation in nailing Fletcher – which is what Makinowsky wanted to do.

I assured Catlin. "You know, there's no reason for your wife to know about this. Ever. We don't plan on telling her –if you'll help us. Your wife doesn't have to know. And you can save your marriage."

Catlin grabbed at the life preserver I was tossing him.

"What...how can I help? What...do I have to do?"

I reached over and put my finger on the START button of the recorder.

"First thing," I told Catlin, "I have to get the details recorded."

"Do...do you have to record everything?"

"Yes," I answered. "To stop Fletcher. You do want to help us, right?"

Catlin nodded.

I pushed the START button, identified myself and stated the date, and where the recording was being done. Then, I had Catlin identify himself and state the date.

Then, I asked Catlin several questions that established how the scientist and Fletcher had met, the extent of their affair, and the types of information Catlin had given Fletcher.

From the answers Catlin gave, it was clear to me that the scientist had not yet passed any documents to Fletcher, and had only generally described some of the projects going on at Floragenics. It looked to me as if Catlin hadn't even realized he was giving proprietary information to Fletcher. It was probably all just pillow talk.

Clearly, Catlin's affair with Fletcher was in its early stages. They had met only a few weeks ago – not enough time, evidently, for Fletcher to have gotten Catlin to the point of knowingly cooperating and passing Floragenics information and documents on to her.

When I had what I wanted, I stood and walked to a door at the end of the conference room. The door connected with Makinowsky's office.

I opened the door. Makinowsky and Reeverson were waiting.

"Come in" I said. "I believe Mr. Catlin is ready for you."

Watching Makinowsky as the Floragenics chairman entered the conference room and glared at Catlin, I felt sorry for the scientist. Makinowsky's normally florid face was several shades redder than usual, and his fire plug body was tightly coiled and ready to spring out at Catlin.

Not going to be much of a life for Catlin, from this point on, I thought to myself. I sure hope Fletcher was good to him in bed.

CHAPTER 17

At five o'clock in the afternoon, Rose, Lu and I were sitting in a semi-circle, facing the director of the Denton Academy, Dr. Susan Rice, in her office in Encino. We were ready to discuss Melanie and the girl who was bothering her, Jennifer Karp.

But as Dr. Rice had just explained to us, "Jim and Vivien Karp are running a bit late. They should be here momentarily."

"Any particular reason why they couldn't get here on time?" I asked, not bothering to hide my irritation. I was still stewing about what Rose had said to me – that our meeting with the Karps could not be set any earlier than at 5 this afternoon, because their calendars were filled up. Hey, as far as I'm concerned, calendars don't mean a damn thing, when your kid is having a problem.

Lu, who knew my feelings, because I'd shared them with her last night, shot me a warning look and shook her head, as if to say, "Cool it."

The door to Dr. Rice's office opened and the Karps came in, Jim Karp in the lead, and talking.

"Had to wrap up an audit," Karp said, as he walked to one of the empty chairs facing Dr. Rice and sat down.

His wife followed, and sat in the other chair.

Karp shook his head, then continued talking.

"Busy. It's that time of the year for CPA's. And with the kinds of clients my firm has, these are companies that need a lot of tender, loving care, from the headman. And yup, that's me."

No apology for being late, I noticed. And of course, he had to let us know how important he was.

This time, Rose was the one who gave me a warning look, as Dr. Rice started the meeting.

"Good to see you, Vivien and Jim. I'd like you to meet Rose Shapiro and Lu and Will Jonas. They are Melanie Hannaford's guardians."

We nodded to each other, as Karp asked, "Guardians? Not parents?"

"Melanie is an orphan," I explained. "All three of us are close to her, so we share the guardianship."

"What about the parents?" Karp pushed. "What happened to them?"

I didn't like his probing. I sensed that the guy was looking for an angle -- for an advantage – for today's meeting. Maybe he was thinking...what...no parents? Just guardians? *There's* the problem. Nothing to do with Jennifer. It's the other kid who is screwed up.

I was about to ream him out – but Dr. Rice took over the meeting.

"Please...I'd like to get to the purpose of our meeting here today, which is to discuss this situation wherein you – Mrs. Shapiro – have been told by one of the mothers in your carpool, that Jennifer – to put it in the vernacular – is giving Melanie a hard time. I think it would be useful, if you could tell us whatever details you have."

"Yes. Of course," Rose replied. "A few days ago, one of the mothers in our car pool – her daughter is friendly with Melanie – well, her daughter told her that Jennifer and a few of her friends, are taunting Melanie about coming here from Junction City. Calling it a 'trailer trash' place...making it sound terrible. And that Jennifer and her friends confront Melanie with the fact that she is an orphan because her mother killed her father, and then killed herself. And they also taunt Melanie about her brother who was in prison. My friend says this kind of...of abuse...goes on all the time."

"Has Melanie talked to you about this, Rose?" Dr. Rice asked. "Or with you, Lu and Will?"

"We all three sat down with Melanie last night," Lu answered. "We talked with her about this. She told us she could – to use her words – 'handle it'. And that there is no need for us to be worried."

"But we are worried," I said. "Melanie has had a rough life. Fortunately, it's left her very mature and strong. But still, this is not the kind of abuse we want her to face. It has to stop."

Dr. Rice turned to the Karps.

"Vivien and Jim, since our telephone discussion, have you spoken with Jennifer about this situation?"

"Well...no...not really..." Vivien said uncertainly. "We felt it would be best to get all the facts...before we had that discussion."

"And besides," Jim added, "I'm not sure there is a need to discuss anything with Jennifer. Based on what I can see, I think we're blowing this out of proportion. I mean, kids are always picking on other kids. It's the way it is. And besides which, your Melanie told you there was no reason for you to get involved. So, I don't think there is anything much we can...or should... do about this."

This was too much for me. I leaned forward in my chair, staring directly at Karp.

"There is damn well much that can be done about it!" I said, "You have to talk to your daughter. And you have to get her and her buddies, to back off. To leave Melanie alone. That...has...got...to...happen!"

I stared at Karp and he stared back. Nothing. No give on his part.

Dr. Rice broke the silence.

"Mr. Karp, will you and Vivien at least agree that you will talk to Jennifer about this?"

Karp shrugged.

"Yeah. Even though, like I said, I don't think this is any big deal."

I was about to argue the point with Karp, but Dr. Rice, whose job it was, to try and keep peace among the parents, moved to wrap up the meeting. I guess from her standpoint, things were at least okay, for right now.

She had brought both parties together, in a meeting.

The Karps had agreed to talk to their daughter.

And Rose, Lu and I had a chance to voice our concerns.

But I sure wasn't satisfied. I wanted to see what Karp did, about talking to his daughter. And let's see if Jennifer does back off from Melanie.

If she doesn't?

I've got some ideas...

CHAPTER 18

"I did some more analyzing of those two Individual Desires disks," Lu said to me, after dinner that evening. "And I agree with Corrington's secretary. Margaret Corrington and George Palermo were definitely having an affair."

"Yeah, I've pretty much come to that same conclusion," I said. "And it's leading me toward some interesting questions."

"Such as…?"

"Well, if they were lovers, then did they plot Donald Corrington's murder together? That is, if it *was* murder."

"Which the police said it wasn't," Lu pointed out. "They ruled it a suicide."

"That they did," I agreed. "But now, we have Mrs. Corrington claiming it *was* murder."

"But why would she make that claim? Doesn't it draw attention to her and to George Palermo?" Lu asked.

"Not to her," I pointed out. "Remember, she's claiming that George Palermo is the killer. She doesn't associate herself with the killing, in any way. And a dead man sure can't deny doing it."

"Okay," Lu conceded. "Then, here's something else I saw on

the disks.   There were plenty of back and forth letters, memos, notes on telephone calls, invoices.   The Division catered to some wild – and expensive –tastes by their customers.   Things like a pair of live llamas delivered to a farm in Michigan.   Or the importing of an Irish country cottage – dismantled in Ireland, shipped to the U.S. and then reassembled on an estate in Pennsylvania."

"What's your point?" I asked.

"My point is," Lu answered, "that I found plenty of sales records for transactions like these.   But, then, there was another whole sales category that was unusual.   That had its own definite – and odd –pattern of business."

Using her fingers, Lu began ticking off what she had found.

"First, there would be a letter by Palermo to a customer.   Just a basic, almost a form letter, saying he's pleased to write and let that person know he has been able to locate the item he was asking about."

"Second, Palermo would suggest in the same letter that they meet on such and such a date, in a particular city."

"Third, there would be, at a later date, after each such meeting, an invoice sent by the Division to the customer.   And a check received from the customer – but – both the invoice and the payment would only be for a small amount.   Usually between $100 and $200.   And *that* struck me as odd."

I picked up on what Lu was thinking.

"All that correspondence?   And travel? And a meeting? For $100 or $200?"

"Right," Lu said, picking up the thread again. "Next, the invoice itself would be odd. There was no mention of the product involved in the sale. Just something like, 'For completion of order,' or 'Due on delivery.'"

Lu shrugged.

"That's what I found, Will. Something was going on here."

We both were quiet for a moment. And then I spoke.

"I think those small payments were a cover. To explain what couldn't be avoided – the necessary airline travel, hotels, restaurant meetings, the letters – the business paper trail. And those small invoices were issued to cover that trail."

"But – and here's the key – at those meetings, the real business was done. For cash. Large amounts of cash. Sales off the books. For illegal collectibles."

"If this was so," Lu said, "then it looks like it was only George Palermo doing it. The records show these were one-person trips. Not the trips he and Margaret Corrington took together."

"Uh, uh," I objected. "Just because she didn't go with him on the trips, that doesn't necessarily mean she wasn't involved."

I thought about something else.

"You know, if this illegal stuff was going on – and Donald Corrington found out about it, that strengthens what we were thinking about before. That there's a motive here for murder."

"For George Palermo to kill Donald Corrington."

"And for Margaret Corrington being involved."

CHAPTER 19

"It's easy enough for you to tell me to be calm," Benjamin Hahn whined at Michael Palermo, "but he knows something! Why else would he want to talk to me?"

"I already explained that to you," Palermo told Hahn. "So let me explain it again. This private investigator doesn't know anything. He wasn't hired to investigate what we're doing. He was hired by Margaret Corrington, strictly to look into Donald Corrington's death. She is claiming murder, not suicide. This Jonas is only interested in things that are tied to Corrington's death. And you are not connected in any way to that death, right?"

Hahn nodded in agreement.

"So," Palermo continued, "Why would this investigator be interested in your business dealings? No reason. No reason at all, I tell you. He's just being super careful and checking out anything and everything."

"You really think so?" Hahn asked, his voice a little less doubtful.

"I really think so," Palermo assured him.

The two men were silent for a few seconds. Hahn's body

became a bit less tense, and the pain in his stomach eased up a bit. It was going to be all right, he thought to himself.

"It's going to be all right," he said aloud, to Palermo. "Nothing to worry about," he reassured himself.

Hahn took out a crumpled handkerchief and wiped away the gloss of sweat that was on his forehead.

"Nothing to worry about," he said again.

Watching Hahn, Palermo thought, there's *everything* to worry about.

Aloud, he said to Hahn, "Yeah, you'll be fine. You'll be just fine."

CHAPTER 20

As I'd asked him to do, Captain Klinger had run files on George and Michael Palermo. And when Rose gave me the two files the next morning, I told her to hold my calls, so I could go through them.

Right away, I could see why the Palermo's had invested in Corrington Imports. The company was tailor-made for them.

According to the files, the Palermo's had been in the importing business for many years, either in their own firm, or as investors or senior level executives in other firms.

Their specialty was the importing of rare artifacts, sculptures and antiquities that were wanted by wealthy individual collectors. Exactly the kind of people George Palermo was dealing with in the Individual Desires division.

The files showed that the Palermo's had police records. During the last 8 years, they were under investigation three times – never charged – but suspected of smuggling national artifacts out of host countries and into the United States for illegal sale to individual collectors.

That's exactly what Lu and I figured was the reason George

Palermo had taken all those out of town trips. The Corrington Imports setup was perfect for the Palermo's.

Still, I warned myself, everything I have is all theory and smoke. No hard facts. Have to do more digging. About George Palermo's possible illegal importing. And about the idea that he and Margaret Corrington had killed Donald Corrington.

Time to see Margaret Corrington again. To ask some questions, and rattle her cage.

I buzzed Rose on the intercom.

"Please call Margaret Corrington and ask if I can see her at home this afternoon. Tell her I want to look over her husband's study. She said I could, the last time we met."

"Will do," Rose said. "And are you ready to take calls now? Captain Klinger has called twice. And you've also gotten two calls from Carl Makinowsky."

"Did Makinowsky say what he wanted?"

"To talk to you as soon as possible. That is all that he would tell me."

"Okay, I'll call Makinowsky back."

"What about Klinger?"

"Have to wait."

I looked through my note pad. "I also want you to make two other appointments for me. One is with Corrington's lawyer. His name is Elliott Goodrich. The other is Corrington's doctor, a Hal Watlow.

Mary Chase had given me the phone numbers for both, and I

gave them to Rose.

Then, I called Makinowksy.

"What's up?" I asked him.

For once, when he spoke, the Floragenics CEO wasn't abrupt.

"I need your advice."

"What kind of advice?"

"It's about Catlin. What I'm wondering is, do you think we have enough to go after Maria Fletcher? To get her arrested, for what she was doing with Catlin?"

"Well, on our side of it, we do know that Catlin will cooperate with anything we decide to do. He knows we want to go after Fletcher. And we do have his confession on tape."

"That's the easy part of it. But trying to get Fletcher arrested? Right now, our case is kind of thin."

"How so?"

"The main reason is…according to Catlin… Fletcher hasn't asked him for any Floragenics proprietary information. So all she and Catlin have done up to now, is pillow talk. And while she did hide her educational background from him, that's certainly not a crime in and of itself."

"No, right now, I'd say there's not enough to get Fletcher arrested."

"I didn't think so," Makinowsky admitted. "But I don't want to give up on this. I want to nail Maria Fletcher! So we got to figure out some way to do it."

I asked, "How does Catlin feel about your wanting to go after

Fletcher? When I left him, he was pretty shaky. Very worried about how this is all going to go down with his wife. His marriage."

"He *is* shaky. But I've put the screws to him. I told him that if he cooperates, he still has a future at Floragenics."

"Does he?"

"What? You don't believe me, Will? Okay. Let me put it this way. He'll have a job. I do recognize that he is an old-fashioned, simple kind of a guy, who didn't stand a chance with Fletcher, once she'd targeted him. So he'll have a job. Not his present position. But something."

"And the effect on his marriage? On his family?"

"What are you Will, some kind of spiritual advisor? "Makinowsky was getting irritated. "Look, I don't run a marriage counseling service. If all of this gets his marriage in trouble? Go find a counselor. Or a minister, a priest, a rabbi."

"He's got a simple choice here. He cooperates...he has a job. The rest is up to him."

I could see I'd pushed Makinowsky as far as I could.

"Fair enough," I said. "The job's a good thing. And he'll just have to work on the marriage."

"So, Will, what can we do?" Makinowsky persisted.

"Well, let's see if I can get the police interested at this point. They may not agree. They may feel we don't have enough for them to get involved, yet. But on the other hand, they might like the idea of taking over early—and building their own case."

"Can you start things going on this? And when?"

"Yes, I can set it up. Give me a few hours to get back to you. In the meantime, it's important that Fletcher not suspect anything. Have you and Catlin talked about what he does? If Fletcher calls him and wants to get together tonight, for example?"

"Catlin told me he never sees Fletcher two nights in a row. That would be too obvious at home, he says."

"Good. That gives us some breathing room."

I hung up and called Captain Klinger. I explained the situation at Floragenics. Klinger said he'd call someone at LAPD who was involved in industrial espionage cases.

Klinger also started to ask me about his sister's investigation, but I told him I was seeing Margaret later in the day, and would talk to him after that.

A couple of hours later, I got a call from Detective Waldo Wilson. I gave Wilson the details on Floragenics.

"Okay," he said after listening to me outline the case, "I'm going to call Makinowsky directly, to set up a meeting. Can you be there, too? It would be good, if you can."

"Depends on the timing," I told him. "I can do it this afternoon, any time after 4 o'clock. Or tomorrow. I'll be out this afternoon, but if you call Rose with the information, I'll be there."

"I'll try for this afternoon."

After Wilson hung up, Rose came into my office.

"You are seeing Mrs. Corrington at 1:30 this afternoon. The other two appointments? I am still working on those."

CHAPTER 21

Just like the last time I went to Margaret Corrington's home, I had to pass through a guarded gatehouse at Calabasas Vista Estates in—where else? – Calabasas. And it set me to wondering about our current style of living, with the rich folks feeling safer if they live behind high walls and armed guards.

It reminded me of my history courses in high school, where the feudal lords barricaded themselves behind their castle walls and a surrounding moat.

Of course, the problem then, as now, was that every once in a while, the lords had to come out of their castles. And when they did, they often got the shit kicked out of them by the tougher lords and common folk who roamed the countryside.

Damn, I thought to myself, I am getting philosophical in my old age!

I arrived at the Corrington home, parked in the driveway leading up to the house, got out of the car and walked toward the front door. When I reached it, Margaret opened the door and let me in.

"Hello, Will."

"Margaret. Thanks for letting me come back again."

"Of course. You said you wanted to see Donald's study?"

"Right. Just want to go through it. See if there is anything there of any use to our investigation."

"I can't imagine what," Margaret said, as she closed the front door and began walking down the central hallway of the house, me following.

When we reached the study, Margaret opened the door and stepped aside,

"All yours to examine. I'll wait for you in the living room."

"Good. Thanks. Shouldn't be too long."

Margaret shrugged and started walking back toward the front of the house. I turned and went into the study.

Judging by the few Corrington Imports files I found in the study, it looked like Donald Corrington did most of his work at the company's office, not at home.

So, no surprise when – about a half hour later – I finished my search of the room – and I hadn't found anything useful.

I went back to the living room, where Margaret was waiting for me.

"Find anything helpful?" she asked.

"Not really," I said.

"All right, then. I believe it's time for you to bring me up to date on your investigation. Specifically, what progress are you making toward what I hired you to do? Find evidence that George

Palermo killed my husband"

Critical point, here.

While it is true that the lady is, technically, my client, my employer on this particular investigation, I sure wasn't going to tell her that my "progress" included putting her on a list of suspects for the possible homicide of her husband.

So what did I do? I ducked.

"I've still got a lot of ground to cover," I said. 'I need more time."

Margaret wasn't going to be put off.

"My brother tells me you asked the police for files on both Palermo's, and it turns out that they were under suspicion for smuggling antiques out of other countries and into the U.S. I must say, I am surprised. And I wonder if perhaps George was doing this at our company, and Donald found out, and that's why Palermo murdered him."

Neat, I thought. Thanks to her brother, she knows what I know, and she's using it to back up her claim, that her husband had been murdered by George Palermo.

I decided to push her a bit on the smuggling angle.

"If Palermo was smuggling, wouldn't you have known about it? I mean, didn't you two work closely together?"

My question surprised Margaret, caught her off guard. She was fast on the recovery, though.

"Obviously, if I had known about it, I certainly would have told Donald, don't you think?" She paused, and then added, "And frankly, I'm surprised at your question. It's rather accusatory."

"I gave her one of my "high sincerity" smiles.

"Not meant to be," I lied. "Please appreciate the fact that when I investigate, I investigate. Your brother told me that's what you wanted, and that's what I'm doing."

We stared at each other for a moment, and then Margaret eased up a bit and went on to another question.

"My brother also tells me you asked for the files on George Palermo's auto accident. You must suspect something, if you want to see those files, right?"

I decided to dodge her question and move on, with my own questions. After all, my objective in setting up this meeting was to get Margaret Corrington worried and on the defensive. And she sure wasn't there, yet.

"As I say," I countered, "it really is too soon to tell you anything specific. I'm still turning up a number of puzzling things. For instance, you told me that your husband had the only key to the drawer in his desk, where the gun was kept."

"Yes. So?"

"According to Mary Chase," I answered, "there was a second key. In a drawer. In her desk. A drawer that was kept unlocked on purpose, so that anyone could have access to the gun."

"Mary said everyone in the office knew about the key, because your husband wanted them to have the comfort of knowing they could get to the gun, if they were working late, and they became concerned about something. Evidently, there had been some break-ins in the area."

Margaret shrugged.

"Perhaps others knew about the key, but I didn't"

She thought for a moment.

"It seems to me, that again points to George Palermo. That's how he must have gotten the gun. He knew about the second key."

"The point is," I said, looking closely at Margaret, "everyone in the office knew about the key. So anyone could have gotten the gun and killed Donald, if it wasn't suicide, as the police have ruled."

"Except me, of course," Margaret reminded me, matching my stare. "As I said, I didn't know about the key."

Well, I had to admit to myself, Mary Chase had said that although she thought Margaret Corrington knew about the second key, she couldn't be sure.

I decided to go on to another point, and to confront Margaret about her suspected affair with George Palermo.

"Something else concerns me," I said, and then I deliberately stopped. I wanted her to worry about what that "something else" might be.

She wasn't long in taking the bait.

"What's that?"

"Well…it's a bit awkward," I said, hoping my voice gave off that meaning, "but I have reason to believe that…you and George Palermo were…having an affair."

Margaret was jolted – but only for a second. She quickly got back her composure, stared at me and allowed herself a small smile.

"You *are* every bit as good a detective as my brother said you were." She went silent for a few seconds, and then replied.

"I don't imagine it would do much good to deny it?"

I had to admire her. The lady certainly was one to stay cool under pressure.

"It wouldn't do much good," I agreed.

Margaret nodded.

"You're right. George and I did have an affair."

She shook her head.

"It didn't last long. And it didn't change my feelings toward Donald. And most important, it doesn't alter my belief that George Palermo killed Donald."

I asked, "Was the affair over by the time your husband died?" I asked.

"Do you mean, is my accusation of George...how would one of those grocery checkout magazines put it...'the act of a jilted lover?' You can banish that thought from your mind. I do not operate that way."

"Still, it is puzzling to me," I pressed her, "when someone accuses a lover of murdering a spouse."

"I can't help what's puzzling to you!" Margaret snapped back at me. Then she reigned in her anger. "I'd like to explain things, if I may?"

"Of course."

"I loved Donald. I know you may find that hard to believe, but it's true. I loved him. And I cared for him. But…Donald was much older than me. That didn't make any difference when we first married, but in the last few years, his…interests…changed. He didn't love me any less. I know his love for me was constant. But…physically…he wasn't so…active…anymore."

"So you had an affair with Palermo."

I guess there was a tone of judgement in my voice, because Margaret snapped back at me.

"Don't be so damned judgmental! I…had my needs. George was an attractive man. And we were discreet. Or so I thought."

She shook her head dismissively.

"The entire thing didn't last very long. Just a few months. And it was over well before Donald died."

She looked challengingly at me.

"My brother doesn't have to know anything about this. I see no reason for you to tell him. Agreed?"

"I'll try not to. If it doesn't affect anything about my investigation, we'll just leave it out of things."

Time to shift to another subject.

"You told your brother that you had hoped the police would find something suspicious when they investigated your husband's death. You said you didn't want to come forward at that time, because you thought you would look foolish."

"That's right."

"I wonder, though, if the real reason you didn't come forward then, was because Palermo was still alive, and you were afraid to name him, because then, the knowledge about your affair might come out."

"No! That's simply not true! Yes, I was suspicious about Donald's death. And yes, I did think, maybe, just maybe George might have had something to do with it. But I didn't have anything to go on. Other than those phone calls and a general feeling.

"Remember, it wasn't until after the case was closed, that I found those memos between Donald and George. When I found those memos, that's when my suspicions became stronger, because I felt I had something concrete to base them on."

I decided this was about as far as I wanted to go, today, with our conversation. All it seemed to be doing, was giving Margaret Corrington a soap box to stand on, to argue her claim that George had done Donald in. And that was a discussion I wanted to have at a later point, when I had more of the kind of facts that I felt I still needed.

So, I said my goodbyes and after Margaret let me out the front door, I headed for my car. I happened to look back, and I saw her standing in her front doorway, looking after me.

Well, I had to admit to myself, I wasn't sure how useful this visit had been. It left me with several concerns.

First, there was no way to prove, or disprove, whether Margaret knew about the second key.

Next, while she admitted having an affair with George Palermo, Margaret also provided, if not a morally acceptable reason for the liaison, one that was at least understandable.

Then, she had an explanation – maybe not very strong, but still, an explanation – as to why she accused George Palermo *after* the police had closed their investigation.

Pretty good lineup of points for the other side.

So, what did I think? I thought, either she's telling the truth, or Margaret Corrington is one accomplished and quick-thinking liar.

Standing in the doorway, watching Will walk to his car, Margaret reviewed her meeting with him. She didn't like it. Not one bit. Didn't like his line of questioning, and his suspicions. Needed to figure out how to get him looking only at the killing of Donald Corrington by George Palermo. That's the outcome she wanted from Will Jonas's investigation.

CHAPTER 22

Leaving Calabasas Vista Estates, I drove out of the hills, down toward the 101 Freeway. When I reached Calabasas Road, I stopped for the traffic light.

I guess by force of habit, going back 40 years to when I was a patrolman and drove a black and white, I checked the surrounding area. You know, to make sure everything was okay.

Only it wasn't!

There was a building on my right. L-shaped, two floors, stores on the street level, and offices on the second.

And what I saw at that building definitely was not good.

There was an ATM station at the point where the two wings of the building came together

And a woman was being escorted toward that ATM, by a couple of beat-up-jeans-and-tee-shirt low-lifes.

The men were on each side of the woman. Boxing her in, as they walked in tandem.

I watched them for a couple of seconds, just to make sure I was seeing what I *thought* I was seeing.

And yes, it did look to me like I was watching an ATM

robbery about to happen.

So, what to do?

I picked up my car phone and dialed 911. It was busy.

If I were still a cop, I'd be on my radio now, calling for backup, and deciding if I should wait for the backup, or try to do this on my own.

I looked around the area. No one on the street. I looked again at the woman and the two men. They were getting close to the ATM.

I had my answer.

I wasn't so much concerned about the money the perps could get – probably a max of two or three hundred – but with what might happen after the money was withdrawn.

The woman was well dressed and attractive.

And I suspected that these dumbasses might want to take her away with them, for some rough stuff.

So, I didn't have much choice, did I?

I opened the glove compartment in my car, took out my Glock 19 and loaded it.

I opened my car door, and in a crouch, I ran into the parking lot, toward the ATM, which was about 150 feet away. I stayed in close to the building, which was on my right, hoping to get near the ATM before the perps spotted me.

I was hoping they didn't have weapons. Maybe a knife would be all. They sure didn't need a gun to control the woman.

I got to about 50 feet of the ATM, when it coughed up the

money.

One of the men grabbed it. And then, with the woman pinned between them, they turned away from the machine.

And that's when they saw me.

The jerk to the right of the woman had a gun in his right hand. For a second, we were all motionless. Then the man with the gun made a mistake.

He'd been holding the woman with his left hand. Now, he let go of the woman, stepped forward, and started to bring his left hand up, to his right hand, for a two-handed shooting stance.

I really didn't want to fire my weapon at 50 feet. Too much of a chance that I'd hit the woman.

But since the perp was about to fire at me, I didn't have much choice.

I aimed for the man's chest, and fired. My aim wasn't that good, but I did hit him.

The bullet exploded into the guy's right shoulder.

He screamed, dropped his weapon, and fell down, twisting in pain.

I looked at the other man. He was all tensed up, breathing hard. He was holding the woman with his right hand. She was screaming.

This perp didn't have any weapon. I started to move in on him.

"Police," I shouted. "Let her go. Drop your gun. And get on the ground!"

The man hesitated. He looked toward his partner, and then at his weapon, which was about 10 feet away from him.

I saw where he was looking and I knew what he was thinking.

"Don't do it," I shouted. "Give it up. Now. You haven't got a chance."

But the man started sliding over toward where the gun was. He pulled the woman with him, holding her in front of him, like a shield.

She was screaming, and in response, he tightened his hold across her neck, choking off her air supply, which only succeeded in further panicking the woman.

I kept moving toward them. I was now about 25 feet from them, and I weighed my chances of taking a shot at the man, without endangering the woman.

Not close enough.

I kept moving forward.

The woman was twisting in an effort to loosen the man's choke hold on her neck, and somehow, she managed to partially free herself from his forearm grip. In a combination of fear – and yes, anger – she bit into his forearm.

Now it was the man's turn to scream, and he involuntarily pushed the woman and her teeth away from him.

The woman fell off to one side.

The man dove for the gun, scooped it up and started to aim it at me.

By now, I was only about 8 or ten feet away from him.

I steadied myself. Took a deep breath, and shot the guy squarely in his chest.

CHAPTER 23

"You okay?" Los Angeles Sheriff Department Deputy Tony Vargas asked me.

"I'm fine," I told him.

And I *was* fine – even though it was only about an hour since my meet-up with the two guys who were robbing the lady at the ATM.

Vargas and several other deputies had gotten to the scene within a minute or two after the shootout. That's because people on the second floor in the office building had seen what was happening, and they'd called it in, even while the action was still taking place.

Of course, as soon as Vargas and his guys showed up, I put my weapon on the ground, held my hands up in the air, and identified myself as LAPD. Sure, this was no longer true, but at that moment I really wasn't too concerned with the finer points of an accurate ID of me. There were several deputies swarming into the parking lot of the building, weapons drawn, and I just wanted to make sure everyone knew I was the solution – not the problem.

The deputies sorted everything out within a few minutes, as they talked to the woman and to me. Although badly shaken, the lady confirmed my version of the incident, as did the office and store onlookers who had now come to the fringes of the parking lot, where they were held back by a line of deputies.

Both wounded perps, very much alive, were on their way to a hospital via ambulance and under police guard.

"Goes to show, you can't keep a good cop off the job, even when he turns dishonest and becomes a PI," Vargas joked

I shook my head.

"Believe me, this was the last thing I needed. I'm too old for this. I finished my thirty some 12 years ago."

"Well, you made the right move here," Vargas said. "Those guys are real bad-asses. The money they took from the lady probably wasn't all they wanted from her."

"You know them?"

"The Shane brothers. Members of one of the most miserable families living, unfortunately, in our jurisdiction. The pack of them are over in Topanga Canyon, in a couple of those grungy trailers the good folks never see as they drive between the Valley and Malibu. There's the parents, the two brothers you shot, another two boys, and two girls. And every damn one of them's got a record."

"Fun Family of the Year," I said.

Vargas turned serious.

"Will, these are crap-hole, get-even kinds of people. And

stupid. So there's a chance they might try and get back at you. Especially when they find out you're not really a cop, anymore."

"Just what I need."

"Sorry, but I figured I'd better mention it."

"Understood. And appreciated."

I switched subjects.

"What about the victim? Who is she?"

The woman had been put into an ambulance and taken to the hospital, to be checked out. She'd suffered some bruises around her neck, from the choke hold one of the brothers had on her.

Before she left, the lady had thanked Will for saving her, but he hadn't learned her name.

Vargas checked his note pad.

"Name's Mrs. Barbara Emmons. She told me she came here, to go to the cleaners. But when she got out of her car, the Shanes intercepted her and forced her over to the ATM."

"She live around here?"

"Up in the hills. In one of those gated communities."

I remembered what I'd thought when I was on my way to Margaret Corrington's house. About the feudal lords being safe behind the walls and the moat. But being wacked, when they came out and mingled with the common folk.

Need I say more?

CHAPTER 24

Before the ATM incident, I'd been on my way to Floragenics, to meet with Makinowsky, Catlin and LAPD Detective Waldo Wilson.

On the way over, I called Lu at her office in Glendale, and Rose in my office in Woodland Hills, to tell them what had happened at the ATM. There were television news trucks at the scene, so I wanted to make sure that Lu and Rose got the facts from me, and not from a "breaking news," hyped up story on television or radio.

After assuring them I was okay, I promised more details that evening, when we were having dinner, with Melanie, at our condo in Tarzana.

When I got to Floragenics, I was shown into Makinowsky's office, where he and Catlin were waiting.

I started our meeting by asking some questions.

"You do realize, that once this police process starts, it'll be difficult to stop it?"

"Don't want to stop it," Makinowsky replied strongly. "Want to nail her ass."

I looked at Catlin, and I didn't like what I saw

Catlin clearly was under a tremendous strain.

I asked him, "Are you ready for the role you'll be playing with Maria Fletcher? And if this goes all the way, then to the publicity and attention you – and your family – are going to get?"

Catlin hesitated.

Makinowsky gave him a hard stare.

"Yes," Catlin answered.

I looked from Catlin to Makinowsky. The Floragenics CEO looked defiantly back at me.

I thought about challenging him as to the wisdom of the whole operation. I mean, at what price, to Catlin? The man looked like he was nearing his personal breaking point.

But then I thought, what the hell alternative does he have? I knew

Makinowsky had told Catlin that he had to cooperate, or he'd be out on his ass. Lose his job, benefits, stock options, everything.

So, Catlin was cooperating.

I thought, in this operation, Catlin is going to be the ultimate loser. Hell, he's lost already. I just hope he keeps his sanity.

Detective Waldo Wilson arrived at that point. And after the introductions, he questioned everyone in detail. Then he summed up for us.

"What I want to make sure everyone understands is – that we are a long way from making any arrest in this situation. The suspect – Maria Fletcher – has not specifically asked you, Mr.

Catlin, for any proprietary Floragenics information. Correct?"

"Correct."

"Nor to the best of your knowledge, has she actually stolen any documents from you?"

"Yes. Correct."

Makinowsky interrupted.

"Hey, we know what she's doing here. And why she seduced Eugene!"

"We don't know anything," Wilson corrected him. "We suspect all of that. But we don't really know – because Fletcher hasn't done anything yet."

Everyone was quiet for a moment, until Makinowsky spoke.

"So, where does this leave us? I mean, what can we do?"

"What we can do," Wilson answered, "is be alert to – if and when—she tries anything specific with Mr. Catlin here."

"Hell, that could be a long time from now," Makinowsky complained.

"Could be," Wilson agreed. "But probably not. If she is true to pattern, she will want to score soon and then take off."

Wilson stood up, signaling that his part of the meeting was over.

"So, as soon as anyone at this end has some more of what we've been discussing, you should immediately get in touch with me."

I walked Wilson out of the meeting.

"Thanks for explaining everything to them – especially to

Makinowsky," I told Wilson. "I've tried to slow him down, but he isn't a waiting type."

"Yeah, I could see that. But listen, the person in there who is worrisome is that Catlin. He looks like he's about ready to go off the deep end."

"Yes," I agreed. "And the last thing he needs right now, is more pressure. But Makinowsky is determined to nail Fletcher. And Catlin is the key to that."

"Unfortunately," Wilson agreed.

He stuck his hand out and we shook.

"Okay, Will. Keep me up to date, and let me know when you think I should get back into this."

He held up the Fletcher file I'd given him at the meeting.

"Thanks for the file. I'll be building on it. We'll now start doing our own checking on the lady."

CHAPTER 25

"Here's to our hero," Lu said, lifting up her coffee cup in a mock toast. "Our Guardian of the ATM, you might say."

This was at the end of dinner that evening at our condo in Tarzana. Rose and Melanie had joined Lu and me.

Lu continued.

"Will, what you did today was very brave. But dangerous. Please don't do something like that again."

"Hey, I didn't even want to do it, today." I said. "But what was happening…I just couldn't let it happen to that lady."

"Do you always have a gun with you?" Melanie asked.

"Yes," I said. "Melanie, when you've done something for most of your life…it's hard to stop doing it. I was with the LAPD for thirty years. And I've been a private investigator for twelve years. That's forty-two years I've kept my gun with me."

"Well," Rose cut in, "We know one thing for sure. You won't be carrying a gun 42 years from now."

I decided it was time for some serious talk.

"Melanie, so what's going on at school now? Are those girls still bothering you?"

Melanie hesitated.

Rose encouraged her.

"Come on, Darling. I checked with my friend today. She says her daughter tells her nothing has changed. Is that so?"

"They…don't bother me that much…"

"They're not supposed to bother you at all!" I said, getting angry – not with Melanie, but with the situation, which evidently still was going on. I figured this meant that Karp either hadn't talked to his daughter, Jennifer. Or if he had talked to her, then he needed to do so again.

Aloud, I said… "I'm going to have to talk to Karp!"

"Will," Lu warned me "You can't go after Karp like he's about to rob an ATM."

"No," I corrected her, "This is worse than robbing an ATM. What he's doing, by not controlling his daughter, is robbing our Melanie of what should be some of the happiest days of her life. And that is not going to continue!"

"What are you going to do?" Melanie asked, her concern obvious.

"I'm going to talk to Karp. Convince him that he needs to control his daughter. That's what I'm going to do."

I checked my watch. It was 8:30. I got up from the table

"Still early enough tonight. I'm going to call him now."

I left the dining room and went into my small office-at-home. In my files there, I had a copy of the parents' directory for Denton Academy, which included a listing of home addresses and telephone numbers.

I found Karp's phone number and dialed it. It was answered after a couple of rings.

"Hello?"

A man. Probably Jim Karp? It tried it out.

"May I talk with Jim Karp, please?"

"This is Jim Karp. Who's calling?"

"This is Will Jonas, Mr. Karp."

"Oh. What's up?"

"What's up, is that I wanted to ask if you had spoken to your daughter...to Jennifer...about her treatment of Melanie."

"Yeah. I said I would. And I did."

"But...did you tell her to leave Melanie alone? Because I've just been with Melanie, and evidently, right up through today, nothing has changed. Your daughter is still giving Melanie a hard time."

"Look, Jonas. Like I said at the meeting, I think you're blowing this out of proportion. Kids are always picking on other kids. It's the way it is."

Just what I didn't want to hear from this guy. Time for him to understand me. I spoke slowly and distinctly.

"Look, Karp. You have to talk – seriously – to Jennifer. She has to leave Melanie alone. Starting like...right now. Do you understand me?"

"Hey," Karp came back at me, "You don't give me orders on what I need to do. Yeah, I know you're some kind of a hotshot today. With that ATM robbery and all. But *you* don't tell *me* how to do anything."

"But I *am* telling you. And I expect you to listen."

I waited for a response, didn't get any, so I continued.

"Karp," I said, "I'm making a simple request. Control your daughter. It would be much better…if you did so."

"Are you threatening me?"

"Threatening you? No. Just telling you. Just telling you."

And I hung up.

Karp wasn't going to talk to his daughter. That was clear to me.

So be it, I thought. Time to get things going.

Earlier in the day, suspecting that any conversation I had with Karp would end up where it did, I'd called my old LAPD partner, Charlie Black. Charlie was still on the job – a couple of years short of his retirement.

I explained the situation to Charlie, and then I told him what I wanted to do. And asked him if he thought he could organize it.

"Not a problem," he answered. "Especially not right now – when you're the poster child of the week, with that ATM shootout. I mean, you got two of them. With a handgun. Not many of us could do that -- even with an assault rifle."

"Pure luck, Charlie. Plus, two very dumb perps."

"Regardless, you did it, Will. And everyone's walking proud because of it. So we can definitely trade on your accomplishment, to get in motion, what you want."

"Any idea when?"

"A couple of days, at most. I'll let you know when we're going to start."

CHAPTER 26

The next morning, I steered my car into one of the parking spots assigned to "Hahn Imports" at the rear of Benjamin Hahn's store on Sherman Way in Reseda.

A late model Mercedes 300 E was parked in one of the other Hahn spaces. Hahn's car?

I checked my watch. It was 8:31…time for my appointment.

Hahn had told me to ring the bell at the back door and he would let me in. So I got out of my car and walked up to the door. There was a sign on it, announcing that the premises were electronically guarded. Probably a pretty good security system, I thought, what with the kind of inventory Hahn carried.

There was a bell to the left of the door. I pushed it, and I heard the ringing inside.

I waited for Hahn to open the door. Nothing happened. So I pushed the bell again -- this time, keeping it depressed, so the ringing didn't stop.

Still, nothing.

I looked over at the Mercedes.

Could that be Hahn's car, I wondered?

Or is the guy just plain late?

I checked my watch again. Now, it was 8:20.

I looked up and down the service road backing Hahn's store and the other stores in the block. No sign of any approaching cars, and there weren't any other cars parked behind the line of stores. Not surprising. I knew from shopping trips with Lu, that none of the stores opened before ten in the morning because they were open until at least 9:00 PM. Pity the long hours of the retailer.

I looked again at the Mercedes. And now, I wondered why it was parked in Hahn's spot, if it wasn't Hahn's.

I walked over to the Mercedes and looked in.

It was Benjamin Hahn's car, all right. And Hahn was in it. I could see that. And I also could see that he was sprawled across the blood soaked front seat, motionless, dead eyes open, and a large hole in his chest.

CHAPTER 27

"What the hell is going on? And what does it have to do with my sister?" Captain Klinger demanded.

He and I were in Denny's, a coffee shop on Topanga at Roscoe, a couple of miles away from Hahn's store on Sherman Way. It was just under two hours since I'd discovered Hahn's body in his car.

After finding the dead man – at least, I assumed he was dead because he sure looked like it -- I'd made two calls.

The first was to the LAPD West Valley station on Vanowen, to report what I'd found.

And the second was to Klinger, who was still at home. I wanted to fill the captain in, as soon as possible, given what I considered the strong possibility that any examination of Hahn's business records would turn up a connection between Hahn Imports and Corrington Imports, and this could lead to Margaret Corrington, the captain's sister.

I also knew that the detectives assigned to the case would ask me why I had an appointment with Benjamin Hahn. And I'd have to tell them I was investigating Margaret Corrington's claim that Donald Corrington had been murdered – even though the LAPD had already classified it as a suicide and had closed the file. Of course, chances were good that the detectives would track Margaret as Hahn's sister, and I wanted the Captain to be aware of this.

When I called him, I told Klinger I'd discovered Hahn's body, and that Hahn had business dealings with the Individual Desires division.

Now, in the coffee shop, Klinger sounded an optimistic note.

"It looks to me like you can still keep my name out of this loop," he said. "After all, it's Margaret who hired you – not me."

"I wouldn't count on it. If the authorities find a link between Hahn Imports and the Corrington Individual Desires division, Margaret's name is likely to come up. And it's not much of a step from there, to tracking Margaret as your sister."

"Well, maybe it'll happen. Or maybe it won't. I'm just going to hope," the Captain said.

"You might luck out," I conceded. "But there's more I have to tell you. More that could come out – if not now – then at some point."

"Like what?"

"I can't prove it yet," I answered, "but I think George Palermo was using Individual Desires as a base for illegally smuggling newly discovered antiques. artifacts, sculpture, things like that – out of their countries of origin and into the United States. And then, selling these items for unreported cash to private buyers."

"And it looks, too, like this activity was running through Hahn Imports."

"And your sister may have been involved. Or at the least, she may have known what Palermo was doing, and she didn't do anything to try and stop him."

Klinger slumped in his seat.

"Shit!"

Then he looked at me, and he read my expression.

"There's more?"

"There's more. Turns out that Margaret was having an affair with George Palermo. And I'm not guessing about that. She's admitted it to me."

"While Donald was still alive?" Klinger asked.

"She says it was over *before* Corrington died."

Klinger sat quietly. He sighed. Then he spoke.

"Do we have a situation here, where my sister could be…responsible for her husband's death? Let alone the illegal importing of antiques?"

I measured my words carefully. I knew how straight arrow Klinger was. How duty bound he would feel, if the facts warranted it, to report to the Department, what I'd just told him.

"Look," I said, "as far as I'm concerned almost all of what I've told you is theory. I don't have any facts yet. I just figured I had to tell you."

I paused, and leaned forward for emphasis.

"But right now, I don't feel you have to tell anyone about this. Don't have to do a damn thing about it, until and unless I come up with some hard facts."

Klinger grabbed at the life raft I'd thrown him.

"You think that's the way to go?"

"Yes. I had to tell you what I did tell you. You had to know. But until we have more facts, there's nothing I'm going to do about reporting this. And I don't think you should, either."

Klinger thought for a moment. He looked at me, and I could see the guilt reflected on his face.

"If these things that you're telling me…do turn out to be true…then I have to report all of it to the Department. In fact, I'm uncomfortable about not reporting what you've already told me."

"I don't think you need to do that," I said. "I recommend that we wait, until I have more facts, not just theories."

Klinger nodded in agreement, then shifted subjects.

"What do you know about this Hahn killing? Do you think it has anything to do with Palermo and the Individual Desires division?"

"I don't know. I never had a chance to talk to the guy. So, your guess is as good as mine."

CHAPTER 28

After meeting with Captain Klinger, I headed back to my office, where I was met by Rose and two piles of invoices. The higher stack, unfortunately, contained invoices *to* us, while the smaller pile had those invoices *from* us. Ah well, some months are better than others, I told myself. And on balance, in the twelve years I'd had my agency, the invoices-going-out pile did beat out the other pile most of the time.

After signing off on both piles, it was time for me to go to Century City for an appointment with Donald Corrington's lawyer – Elliott Goodrich, Esq., senior partner in Goodrich, Young and Delson, a mid-size firm representing corporations and wealthy individuals.

Goodrich, Young had the usual impress-the-clients offices, located on the ninth floor of one of the high rises on Avenue of the Stars.

I gave my name to the receptionist, and didn't even have time to sit down, before an efficient Ms. Hendrickson – that's what her nameplate said -- arrived to guide me down a corridor to the large corner office of Elliott Goodrich, where he was waiting for me.

After exchanging introductions, Goodrich was all business.

"After your secretary called," he said to me, "I of course checked with Margaret, and she told me you were investigating her husband's death. I don't understand. I thought that investigation by the police was over and done with."

"I'll explain in just a minute," I said, "but first, I'd like to make sure I have my facts straight. I understand you're legal counsel to Corrington Imports? Also Mrs. Corrington's personal attorney? And you were Mr. Corrington's personal attorney?"

"Correct on all points," Goodrich verified.

"Thank you. Now, did Mrs. Corrington tell you why I'm investigating her husband's death?"

"She said you would explain."

So I did.

"Mrs. Corrington is convinced her husband did not commit suicide. But instead...he was murdered. And, she's accusing George Palermo of being the killer."

For an instant, Goodrich lost his lawyerly reserve and was startled. But then he regained his composure.

"I really find that hard to believe. And didn't the police rule that Donald committed suicide?"

"They did."

I went on, to give Goodrich the details of Margaret's claim.

Goodrich shook his head.

"I am as certain as one can be in these circumstances, that Donald Corrington took his own life."

"What makes you so certain?"

Goodrich took his time answering.

"There are certain client confidentiality considerations I must observe. But Margaret did ask me to cooperate, so I'll tell you what I can, and then some. But I must ask that you respect the confidentiality of the information."

"Whatever you tell me," I said, "I'll share only with Mrs. Corrington," I assured him. I didn't think it was necessary to mention Klinger, although I was sure I would tell the captain, if Goodrich gave me anything worthwhile to pass on.

Goodrich continued.

"Perhaps you already know this?" Goodrich asked, "but were you aware that, when he died, Donald had an advanced case of incurable pancreatic cancer?"

"I did know that," I told him, "but did you know about it *before* the autopsy? Because as far as I can tell, Mr. Corrington had kept that information as confidential between he and his doctor. Not even Margaret Corrington knew about it, she told me."

"Yes, I did know about it, before the autopsy," Goodrich said. "Donald told me shortly after he learned of the condition from his doctor. He also informed me that he was not telling anyone else, including Margaret, and he instructed me to keep the information confidential."

I said, "Mary Chase told me that was Donald Corrington's style. He didn't like to get into his personal life with anyone. Do you agree?"

"Yes. That was Donald's – style – as you put it. The only reason he told me, was because there were a number of legal matters to resolve before his death. Wills, insurance, trusts, real estate and the like. He was a thorough man, in that regard."

"Was Corrington's terminal cancer the only reason you believe he committed suicide?"

Goodrich took some time to think about my question. Then he replied.

"I believe his incurable pancreatic cancer was the main reason he did commit suicide. However, I do believe there was an…overlay…of business problems that definitely had him down."

"Can you elaborate?"

"Donald was very depressed about Corrington Imports. While sales volume was fair, the profits had been dropping sharply the last few years, and the banks were getting edgy about their lines of credit to the company."

"In a word, Donald had cash flow problems, and they were getting worse."

"Is that why Corrington brought Michael Palermo in as a major investor?" I asked.

"You know about that, I see," Goodrich said. "Yes. Donald allowed Michael Palermo to buy in because he needed Palermo's capital infusion."

"Were you aware that – recently-- Palermo wanted to get out, as an investor? That George Palermo was demanding their money back?"

Goodrich was puzzled.

"That's the first I've heard. About them wanting their investment back. And did you say – George – not – Michael – was doing the demanding? That's surprising, because Michael always was the key person. Not George. Not by a long shot."

I said, "Margaret Corrington showed me a series of memos exchanged between Donald Corrington and George Palermo, with Palermo demanding the money, and Corrington saying he just couldn't do it. Not enough cash flow. Are you aware of these memos? Did you ever see them?"

"No, to both questions. I was not aware of them. So of course, I never saw them."

I was puzzled – that Goodrich, so close to Donald Corrington on all parts of his business, would not be aware of the memos. That Donald had not told him about them. Strange.

I asked Goodrich another question.

"What's your opinion of Michael Palermo?"

Goodrich shook his head.

"Not the kind of businessman I like to be associated with. His business practices leave much to be desired. Of course, Donald knew this before Palermo invested in Corrington Imports, because Donald had asked me to check Palermo out. But, unfortunately, Donald needed the money that Palermo could provide. Needed it badly – at a time when the banks were considering pulling Corrington's lines of credit."

"Can you tell me more about Palermo's business practices?"

"Michael Palermo describes himself as a businessman. An investor. And he is that. But from what I learned, his method of investing, while legal, is in my opinion beyond the line of being moral or ethical."

"He specializes in finding smaller, usually privately or closely held companies, often undercapitalized, and experiencing cash flow problems."

"He comes in with financing, and then, after a period of time, he works to get control of the company – usually with threatening and bullying tactics. Not illegal, but harassing and very difficult for the original ownership and management to deal with. Then, once he has control, he liquidates the company, thus getting his investment back, plus a profit from the liquidation proceedings."

"Could that strategy be what he and his brother were trying to pull on Donald Corrington?" I asked, thinking again of the exchange of memos between George Palermo and Donald Corrington.

"No," Goodrich answered. "At least, not yet. I had warned Donald about the modus operandi of the Palermo's. And we talked about it periodically. If Palermo had made any such move at Corrington Imports, I would have known about it. Donald would have immediately consulted me."

Again, I was puzzled how Goodrich could be so certain on this point, given the memos from Palermo to Corrington. Of course, I reminded myself, until I just now mentioned them, Goodrich didn't know about the memos.

I had another question for Goodrich.

"Do you think George Palermo was capable of killing Donald Corrington, as Margaret believes?"

Goodrich thought it over, then shrugged.

"Who knows what anybody is capable of nowadays? George Palermo, and his brother Michael, are unsavory characters. I do believe that. But murder?" He shook his head. "I wouldn't want to venture a guess."

Goodrich glanced at his watch, obviously his way of saying that the meeting was over.

I decided a summary of the meeting might be a good idea, given the fact that I was dealing here with a lawyer, a dot the "I" and cross the "t" type of person.

"Just to make sure I have the correct information," I said, "you knew Donald Corrington had incurable cancer and was dying. And that Carrington Imports was having serious business problems. For those reasons, you agree with the LAPD finding that Donald Corrington did commit suicide."

Typical of a lawyer, Goodrich couldn't resist a summation, and he gave me this one.

"I realize we are dealing with intangibles here, but I knew

Donald Corrington for the better part of 20 years. And I saw that his illness, and his business problems, were getting him down."

"I had never seen him as depressed as he was in the last few weeks before his death. In his own guarded way, I'm sure Donald did not allow others to see this side of him. But I did. And frankly, I think it all simply became overwhelming to him."

"But what about Margaret's murder claim?" I pressed.

"I don't know why Margaret feels as she does. But I believe she is wrong."

CHAPTER 29

"Don't want to take any calls for a while," I said to Rose, when I got back to my office, after meeting with Elliott Goodrich."

"Time for your afternoon nap?" she teased.

"How I wish," I teased back. "You know how grouchy I get when I'm sleep deprived."

"It comes with aging," Rose said. "You are at that point."

"Then you better get away from me, before I throw a tantrum," I warned.

"God forbid," Rose said, as she started to leave my office. "But in between napping, you might want to look at the file that Captain Klinger sent over. The one on George Palermo's auto accident."

"I'll try. No promises," I said. I could have saved this last supposedly clever comment of mine, because Rose missed it, having already left my office and closed the door behind her.

So, I turned to what I had intended to do –even before Rose and I had our conversation. I reviewed the death-by-auto-accident file on George Palermo.

The police report was straightforward. The accident occurred at 8:37 PM on a Tuesday evening. It was drizzling, after a dry spell, and the roads in Los Angeles were a bit slick with the usual film of automotive oil buildup during the preceding dry days.

Palermo was going west on Mulholland Drive, the winding, one-lane-in-each-direction road that cuts across the Santa Monica Mountains, separating the San Fernando Valley region of Los Angeles from the rest of the City.

He was on that stretch of Mulholland that extends from the University of Judaism, goes over the 101 Freeway, and on to Encino.

At one of the sharp curves, near a Los Angeles Fire Department sub-station, tire skid marks seemed to indicate that Palermo lost control of the car.

The vehicle skidded across the right shoulder of the road, hit the low metal fence barrier, flipped over it, and tumbled down a deep ravine. When it hit the bottom of the ravine, the car exploded and burned.

There wasn't much left of Palermo. He was identified by his dental records, and his ownership of the car was confirmed by the still readable VIN – Vehicle Identification Number.

The police concluded that Palermo may have been traveling too fast for the road, citing the tire skid marks as their support for this conclusion.

They did rule out a DUI, driving under the influence, because the autopsy showed no presence of alcohol in Palermo's body.

I tossed the file on my desk. Nothing in it of any help, I decided.

Just like the rest of this case. Nothing definite. Nothing certain. Nothing clear.

And nothing to support Margaret Corrington's claim.

I thought back to my planned meeting with the antiques dealer – Benjamin Hahn. And I figured, there had to be some connection between him and my investigation about Corrington's death. The police ruled Donald's death a suicide. Margaret claims it's murder. Where did Hahn play in all of this? *Did* he play at all?

He must have, I reasoned. Why else did someone kill him? Who was afraid about what I might learn…if I met with Hahn?

Again, nothing definite. Nothing certain. Nothing clear.

Right now, I was a long way from believing that Donald Corrington had been killed at all. Right now, I shared the view of the LAPD, of Klinger, of Elliott Goodrich, that Donald Corrington had committed suicide.

So why the hell does Margaret Corrington keep insisting that her husband was murdered. What's the motive? The reason?

I thought about this for a while, looking at things from as many different angles as I could figure out.

And the outline of a possible explanation started to show itself. It went something like this.

That Donald Corrington *was* murdered, despite the LAPD's suicide finding.

That Margaret Corrington was somehow involved in the

killing.

That now, Margaret, for some reason, was afraid of being discovered.

That she was taking the offensive by pointing her finger at George Palermo.

That Palermo couldn't deny any such allegation -- from the grave.

All of these "maybe's" and "what-if's" and "perhaps." They all came together in one pile. And they didn't show anything.

So, I made the best decision I could, under the circumstances.

I decided to go home. Hopefully, Lu was cooking up one of her big-time, chef-worthy dinners. What'd she call them? "Comfort foods?"

Yeah, that's what I needed about now – some great comfort food.

CHAPTER 30

It was going to be a busy day, Jim Karp predicted to himself, as he wolfed down two slices of toast and a cup of coffee. And a productive one, too – with a couple of new clients about to sign retainers. They weren't in yet, but the meetings he would have with the two prospects later in the day, should just about do it.

Karp finished his breakfast and checked his watch. Six forty. Early enough to beat the morning traffic on the 101 Freeway. It usually stayed light until the Balboa exit, which is where he got off.

That put him in the office by about 7 o'clock. He was always the first one in. The way he liked it to be. No hitches. No surprises. Everything nice and calm.

He went into the hall and picked up his briefcase. He turned off the alarm. No need to re-arm the device. Both Vivien and Jennifer would be getting up in a few minutes.

Karp went back through the kitchen and let himself into the three-car garage via a doorway in the far wall of the kitchen. He settled himself into his 500 SL Mercedes, started it, pushed the garage door opener and backed out, on to the street.

He turned the wheel and guided his car down the block, toward the nearby intersection. When he reached it, Karp did what he did every day. He ignored the stop sign and kept going. A required stop at that intersection was stupid, Karp had decided, a day or two after moving in to their present house. He couldn't remember the last time he'd seen a competing car at that corner.

So, just a light touch on the brake pedal, a quick look around, and as he did each day, Karp sailed past the stop sign.

Only to then hear a police siren behind him.

Karp looked in his rear view mirror, and saw the car, roof lights flashing.

"Where the hell did he come from?" Karp muttered.

Annoyed at the interruption to what had started out as a nice morning, Karp steered his car over to the curb, parked and watched, via his side mirror, as the cop driving the patrol car got out and approached him.

Karp lowered his window and addressed the policeman when he approached.

"Good morning, Officer. Sorry I missed the stop. I live right up the block. I drive this way every day. Don't know why I didn't stop today. Must have been thinking about something. Won't happen again, Officer."

"Driver's license and car registration, please," was the only response Karp got.

"Of course," Karp said, seeing the cop's lack of interest in small talk.

But he didn't want to get a ticket, so he kept up his line of what he hoped would be useful chatter.

"Sure hope you can give me a break on this one, Officer. Haven't gotten a ticket in years. Actually, never, I think. Could you...maybe...just give me a warning, or something?"

The officer looked at him -- at first, not saying anything. But then, when he did address Karp, what he said was a complete surprise.

"You have a daughter, right?" he asked.

"What?"

"I said, you have a daughter, right?"

"Yes..."

"And she goes to Denton Academy?"

Karp didn't know what to make of the cop's line of questioning, but it concerned him.

He answered, "Yes." Then he asked, "Why are you asking me about my daughter?"

Before answering, the officer bent down and leaned in close to Karp's window.

"One of my good friends...Will Jonas...his ward – Melanie Hannaford -- also goes to Denton. Maybe your daughter knows her? Maybe she ought to be nicer to her? As I say, Will is a good friend of mine. And what matters to him, matters to me."

The officer leaned in closer to the open window and stared at

Karp.

"Just wanted you to know that, Karp."

He paused, then spoke again.

"Okay, you can go. But do yourself a favor...and remember...about Denton. And how your daughter treats Melanie."

The policeman stared at Karp for a few seconds longer, then turned and walked away.

Karp found himself breathing hard. Everything had happened so quickly. And he still didn't understand how come the cop had mentioned his daughter, and Melanie, and the school.

But then – he did understand. What he'd gotten, just now, was a warning. A warning about how his daughter was treating Melanie.

Thinking about what the cop said, Karp grew angry. So, big deal. So Jonas knew a cop who was willing to hassle him.

Well, that sure wasn't going to change anything.

If Jonas thinks he can turn loose a cop buddy of his like this – no way is that going to do anything.

And with that thought it mind, Karp continued down the street, toward Ventura Boulevard, where he would turn right and take the Boulevard to Winnetka and the on-ramp for the 101.

Karp looked at his watch. The stop back there had cost him some time. Put him behind his own schedule. Needed to get caught up.

So, when he reached Ventura Boulevard and turned on to it,

going east, he speeded up, easy enough to do, on that long slope of a hill that was the Boulevard at that point.

And that's when he heard the siren behind him.

Almost automatically, Karp checked his rear and side view mirrors, to see where he could pull off, so that the fire department engine could go through.

But Karp didn't see any fire engine. Instead, there was a police patrol car behind him. Not the same one as before. Another one.

With an extra blip of his siren, the cop driving the car signaled for Karp to pull over to the side of the boulevard.

What the hell! Karp thought.

He drove over to the curb and stopped. He watched the LAPD cruiser pull in behind him, and the officer get out and walk toward him. Karp rolled his window down.

The officer said, "License and registration, please."

Karp handed both over. His concern was growing. Another cop who was a friend of Will Jonas? Unbelievable. But here it was…happening.

The officer looked at Karp's license and registration. Then he spoke, his voice almost a low growl.

"You have a daughter, right?"

Karp didn't want to believe what he was hearing.

"What?"

"I said, you have a daughter, right?"

"Yes…"

"And she goes to Denton Academy?"

"Yes…"

The cop leaned down, close to Karp.

"I got a very good friend. His name is Will Jonas. His Melanie also goes to Denton. I hear your daughter…her name's Jennifer, right? I hear she's giving Melanie a hard time. And that's not good. What would be good is if Jennifer would stop giving Melanie a hard time, and be nicer to her."

The officer handed Karp his license and registration.

"Remember what I said. Will Jonas is a very good friend of mine. If he's not happy, then I'm not. And not only me…but a lot of other cops. Here in the city. And sheriff's deputies in the county. And even the California Highway Patrol Officers around the Los Angeles area."

The policeman was silent for a few seconds.

Then he added, "Do yourself a favor, Mr. Karp. Listen to what I'm saying."

Then he turned and left.

Karp understood what the cop had just told him. And he didn't like it. Even thought for a few seconds about how he could fight back.

But he liked even less the prospect of ongoing hassling from the police. Hell, who am I going to fight? Every damn cop that this guy, Jonas knows? Or can get connected to?

No. That'd be stupid. There were too many of them…ready to hound him.

Okay. He'd talk to Jennifer. Tonight. Make sure that she leaves that…what was her name…that Melanie…alone.

CHAPTER 31

I'd asked Rose to set a meeting with Michael Palermo. And the next day, when it came time for that meeting, I retraced the route from my office in Woodland Hills, to Century City, because Palermo, like Elliott Goodrich, had his office in that same complex.

Strange, I thought, as I drove down the 101. These two people – Goodrich and Palermo – seemingly at opposite ends of the legal, moral and ethical spectrum. Yet, their offices were just about next door to each other. Yes, in different high-rises, but both on Avenue of the Stars.

I wondered, does this mean that the great equalizer in business has nothing to do with morals, ethics or whatever? But everything to do with how much rent per square foot you're willing to pay?

Okay, enough rental rates philosophy, and on to business.

Palermo's offices were not quite as – we're-rich-and-you-better-believe-it –as Goodrich's offices – but they were well appointed. The southwestern décor was in a tasteful blend of brown and tan and black. The wall behind the receptionist desk displayed large gold letters, stating "Palermo Investments."

After I'd announced myself to the receptionist, it took only a few seconds for an attractive woman, probably in her 40's, to come out, identify herself as Palermo's assistant, and take me to his large, corner office.

Palermo rose to greet me. We shook hands and he guided me to a couch and coffee table setup on one side of his office.

We sat down. Palermo seemed completely at ease to me. If there was anything worrying him about this meeting, he was doing a good job of hiding it.

He started by saying, "I'm aware of your investigation on behalf of Margaret Corrington, because she told me she had hired you. What I don't understand is, what you hope to find. Donald's death was, after all, a suicide."

"You're sure of that?" I challenged him.

"What I'm sure of, isn't really important," Palermo countered. "To me, what *is* important is that the police ruled the death a suicide."

"True enough, But Mrs. Corrington is convinced her husband was murdered." I paused for emphasis. "And that the killer was your brother."

Palermo smiled and shook his head.

"Yes, Margaret told me that, too. And I'll repeat to you what I said to her. Nonsense. Complete nonsense. I mean, why would George want to kill Donald? We were in business with the man. It was a good relationship."

"If the relationship was so good," I asked him, "then why were you trying to get out of it? To get back your investment capital?"

"I don't understand what you mean."

"What I mean is, that your brother wrote several memos to Donald Corrington, saying he had other uses for the capital, and asking that the whole million plus be returned at once."

"Yes, I know about those memos. Margaret showed them to me."

Palermo shook his head.

"I don't know what my brother was thinking, when he had that exchange with Donald. Until Margaret showed the memos to me, I had no idea he'd had that correspondence going."

Palermo leaned forward for emphasis.

"Look, my brother did not, I repeat, he did not, make the business decisions in this company. I make them. George did what I told him to do."

"So," I asked, "how do you explain the memos?"

"I really can't explain them. All I can tell you, is that I had no knowledge of them."

Palermo shrugged.

"Every once in a while, George had a tendency to forget who ran things. This must have been one of those times. Why he did it, I don't know. But it wasn't with my knowledge."

I figured I'd gotten about as far as I would with Palermo, about the memos, so I shifted subjects.

"What do you know about your brother's dealings with a

Benjamin Hahn, an antiques dealer in Reseda?"

Palermo thought about it.

"I think George may have mentioned the name to me a few times. But nothing more. You have to understand, I'm not at all active at the operating level of Corrington Industries. I just keep my eye on what's happening overall, to protect our investment. I don't know anything about the day to day operations."

I continued.

"From some things I've been able to piece together, I think your brother may have been illegally importing antiques that were smuggled out of other countries, and using the Individual Desires division of Corrington, and Hahn Imports, as his conduits for doing so. It also looks like he was selling the stuff to wealthy collectors, for unreported cash."

"Got anything to back that up?" Palermo asked, without showing any signs of anxiety.

"Not yet, but I'm getting close," I bluffed.

"Well, as I said before, I have nothing to do with the day to day operations, so I wouldn't know anything about this. But offering my opinion, I don't think you'll find anything along those lines, no matter how much investigating you do. It doesn't make any sense."

"Why is that?"

"Because doing what you just described would involve criminal activities. And that certainly would be a poor way to protect our investment in Corrington, now wouldn't it?"

I thought – he's toying with me. He has all the right answers, and I'm getting nowhere.

I tried a different question.

"Can you think of any reason why Margaret Corrington is now claiming that your brother killed her husband?"

Palermo sighed.

"Margaret Corrington is a very bright person. And that makes it all the more puzzling to me, as to why she would make such a ridiculous accusation. It makes no sense at all."

"You don't seem to be upset by it," I said.

Palermo smiled.

"I'm a businessman, Mr. Jonas. I have a major investment to protect in Corrington Industries. Margaret Corrington is the company's controlling stockholder. Her accusation is baseless. And it really can't go anywhere, anyway, because George is dead. So, what's to get upset about? I'm sure your investigation won't turn up anything. And then Margaret will come to her senses. And at that point, she and I will get along just fine."

Palermo sat back and looked at me. I saw the challenge in his look. It said – you can't touch me.

And he was right.

And it angered me.

Nothing we had talked about had hit him in any negative way.

I decided to cover one more subject with Palermo.

"I'm sorry about your brother," I said. "I mean, about his accident."

"George always was a reckless driver," Palermo said.

He offered nothing more. The pause between us dragged on, and I couldn't see any reason to keep going. So I said my goodbyes and left.

My take on Michael Palermo?

He was smart, smooth and controlled. And I figured him to be someone who could rob a blind man, and get the victim to believe he was doing him a favor.

There was one point, though, where I had to admit I was beginning to agree with Palermo. That is – that Donald Corrington had definitely committed suicide. No murder involved in his death, despite Margaret Corrington's claims.

I wasn't quite there yet. Not definite in my conclusion. Still had some people to see. Things to check out. But I was leaning in that direction.

CHAPTER 32

After Will Jonas left, Michael Palermo, as he always did when he wanted to think something over, swiveled his desk chair around to the large picture window behind him, and looked out over Century City.

He retraced the key points of his discussion with Jonas, and as he did, Palermo allowed himself a thin smile, satisfied as to how he'd been able to answer or brush off every question he'd been asked.

He realized, though, that Jonas could not be put off so easily over the long term. When Margaret Corrington had told him that she'd hired Jonas, Palermo did some checking. And what he found out, was that the ex-LAPD homicide detective had a reputation for being a bulldog on any investigation he conducted. He also was described as being very smart and intuitive, in working with whatever facts he collected.

Yes, today he had successfully answered Jonas's inquiries. But the questions the man asked, made it clear to Palermo, that Jonas had already figured out, or suspected several things.

Especially the illegal imports scheme.

Well, at least the weak link in that chain is no longer of any concern. If Jonas had been able to talk to Benjamin Hahn, the guy would have caved, and would have given away the whole deal, Palermo was sure.

Thinking back to the discussion with Jonas, there was one subject that irritated Palermo. Those memos that George had written to Donald Corrington.

Damn George! Every once in a while, the idiot thought he had brains, and tried to make business decisions on his own, rather than following orders. This must have been one of those times. Though why the hell George would send Corrington memos demanding the return of the capital, Palermo could not understand. There was no reason for that kind of pressure. At least not yet. Not the right squeeze-their-balls timing.

Well, business idiots like George don't need good reasons for the stupid things they do. And anyway, what with the nosedive off of Mulholland, George couldn't create any more problems.

Just keep the lid on, Palermo cautioned himself. Don't do anything rash at Corrington Industries. Hold off pressuring Margaret to sell out to me.

And everything will work out.

CHAPTER 33

"So, a call came in from Jim Karp," Rose said, when I got back to the office. "And since you weren't here, he talked to me,"

She stopped and smiled.

I knew what she wanted. For me to beg.

"Are you going to tell me what Karp said?"

"Odd things. He said odd things. Maybe you'll understand. He said... 'Okay, tell Jonas he can call off his cop buddies. I'll talk to Jennifer tonight. Alright? Tonight.' And then he hung up."

I smiled. What I'd asked Charlie Black to set up, had definitely come through.

"Nu? So what he was talking about?" Rose asked.

I filled her in, on what I'd asked Charlie to do. Evidently, the cop caper had worked beautifully, if Karp was going to talk to his daughter tonight.

With Rose on the line, I called Charlie at the Chatsworth Station.

"Thanks, Charlie," I said. "Rose is on the line with me, and we both want to thank you for getting that Karp guy straightened out. He called, to say he was going to talk to his daughter tonight."

Charlie laughed.

"You know what? I'm not surprised. The two officers I asked to work on this – they're both wannabe actors who get small parts in movies. As guess what? Tough cops. And they're damn good in those roles. Frank Gruber, especially. He's the second guy who stopped Karp. Gruber can come across as such a hard case, that even knowing who he is, I'd still get scared if he pulled me over."

"Charlie, we are so grateful," Rose said. "Things should be much better, now, for our Melanie."

"Glad it worked out Rose," Charlie said.

After we finished talking with Charlie, Rose handed me a pile of phone messages. Flipping through, I decided most of them could wait. There were two, though, that I did want to return, soonest.

One was from Phil Gleason, the detective assigned to the Hahn case. He wanted me to come in to the Station, for my formal statement.

I called Gleason back, and arranged to come to the Station at noon tomorrow, which worked out well, with my other meetings that day.

The other call was from Detective Waldo Wilson. I called him back. He picked up on the third ring, identifying himself as "Detective Wilson."

"Will Jonas," I said. "Returning your call. How's it going?"

"Right now, it's not going, and that's why I called you. We got a problem. Maybe you can help."

"What kind of problem?"

"A Eugene Catlin problem."

"Isn't he cooperating?" I asked.

"I'm not sure that Catlin, at this point, is capable of cooperating, or of even functioning," Wilson said. "He's damn near a basket case, and it's a basket that Carl Makinowsky is shaking hard and fast."

"You mean, Makinowsky's pushing, and Catlin is having a hard time with the whole thing?" I asked.

"Exactly," Wilson agreed.

"I was afraid that might happen," I said. "I've never been sure Catlin had the stomach to see this thing through, what with the effect on his wife, and the publicity. But Makinowsky's told him that he stays on the payroll, and on the stock option gravy train, and his life insurance, only if he cooperates. If he doesn't, he's out. Poor bastard. It must be hell on him."

"You're figuring that right," Wilson said. "So, why I called you is this. Makinowsky has to slow down a little. Not push Catlin so hard."

"Easy to say, hard to do," I said. "Makinowsky would like to see Maria Fletcher not only arrested by now, but tied to the stake and burned. When he gets a bug up his ass, everyone gets stung."

"I can see that," Wilson answered. Then he continued, "I understand Makinowsky tends to listen to you. Can you talk to him? Make him ease up the pressure on Catlin? Otherwise, the poor slob is going to flip out."

"And by the way, Catlin's madder than hell at you. Blames you for all his problems. Because you followed him and found him out. That kind of reasoning give you an idea of how screwed up his state of mind is right now?"

"His pecker is what he has to blame," I said. "He went looking for some new hunting grounds, and that's what got him into trouble."

I stopped and thought for a few seconds.

"Tell you what," I said to Wilson, "I'll get out to see Makinowsky tomorrow afternoon. This isn't something I can do on the phone. If I want to convince Carl about anything, I've got to stare him down."

"I'll wait to hear from you," Wilson said.

"Call you right after the meeting," I promised.

CHAPTER 34

"Not now," I groaned, when the telephone rang as Lu and I were eating dinner that night.

And some meal it was. One of my favorites – meat loaf. Plenty of seasoning. Crusty and brown on the outside. And just a bit dry on the inside. Perfection.

"You could let it ring, and the answering machine will pick it up," Lu teased me, not believing for one second that I'd let the call go that way. She knew that because of all my years with the LAPD, it was built in to me, that I *had* to answer that call.

Pushing my chair back from the kitchen table, I reached for the phone on the nearby counter.

"Will Jonas," I announced.

"This is Margaret Corrington," the response came back. "I hope I haven't called at a bad time."

Damn! I didn't really want to talk to Margaret, until after I had a chance to bring Klinger up to date. I wanted to let the Captain know that I was leaning toward agreeing with the LAPD that Donald Corrington's death was a suicide. I had tried to reach

Klinger late in the afternoon, but the Captain had not returned my call.

Well, I thought, no avoiding getting at it now. Aloud, I said to Margaret, "No. Not a bad time. What can I do for you?"

"I'd like an update on your investigation. Can we meet tomorrow?"

In my mind, I reviewed the next day's schedule. Dr. Watlow in the morning. Detective Gleason at noon. And Makinowsky in the afternoon. And I *did* want to talk to Klinger before sitting down with Margaret Corrington.

"How about the day after tomorrow?" I suggested. "I'm kind of jammed up tomorrow."

There was a short silence at the other end. Mrs. Corrington was not happy.

"Well, if that's the best you can manage…"

"I wish I could juggle things around, but these aren't appointments I can change," I lied.

Margaret turned the conversation in another direction.

"Since we can't meet until the day after tomorrow, I'd like you to give me an idea – now – of how your investigation is going. What are you learning?"

"I think it would be better if we discussed it in person," I said, trying to put things off. But she was all over me.

"But at least, can't you give me some idea of what is happening? What are you learning about George Palermo and his killing of my Donald?"

Well, the Lady was insistent, right? So I decided I'd give her, as they say…the bottom line.

"I have to tell you, Margaret, that although I haven't yet finished my investigation – I still have a few people I need to talk to – I'm not finding anything to support your claim that George Palermo killed your husband."

"But that is simply unacceptable!" Margaret snapped. "How could you possibly reach that kind of conclusion?"

"Based on the facts I've been finding…" I started to answer, but she interrupted me.

"What about those memos to Donald from George? What about those? *They* certainly were life threatening."

"They were…harsh," I said, "but we can't say for certain that they were life threatening."

"And the calls?" Margaret went on. "The calls from George to Donald, that I told you about? What about those?"

"Same thing," I answered. "Rough, yes. But that's about it. And on those, we don't even have any hard evidence. Nothing physical. Just your say-so."

There was a long silence at the other end.

"I'm not at all happy," Margaret finally said. "Not at all happy."

Hoping to bring some reason into our discussion, I said, "I'll be able to explain everything in greater detail when we meet."

"Yes," was all that I got back, followed by a hum on the line as she hung up.

I put the phone down and turned back to my beloved meat loaf.

"That is one angry lady," I said to Lu.

I shook my head.

"This whole case beats the hell out of me. The guy clearly committed suicide. And yet, she keeps insisting he was murdered. I just don't get it."

"Eat your meat loaf before it gets any colder," was Lu's practical advice to me. "Margaret Corrington's thought processes, you can't hope to control. Enjoying your dinner is something you can control."

And enjoy it, I did. And guess what? I'd just finished eating, when the phone rang again. This time, it was Captain Klinger, returning my afternoon call.

I told the Captain about my discussion with Margaret, and we agreed to meet tomorrow afternoon, so I could give him detailed chapter and verse on the investigation. We also agreed that the Captain would join me at my meeting with his sister.

Then, I brought Klinger up to date on the Benjamin Hahn investigation.

"I'm seeing Detective Gleason tomorrow at noon, to give him my statement," I told Klinger. The Captain knew Gleason.

I said, "I'm thinking, that I should tell Gleason pretty much everything. And I especially want to clue him in on Michael Palermo, because I think Palermo may have something to do with Hahn's death."

I figured that Klinger would be uncomfortable about telling Gleason everything, but that he'd agree. It was the only way the Captain knew. The straight and the narrow.

I wasn't surprised. Klinger did agree.

"You're right, of course," he said. "I don't much like it, but there's no avoiding it. Especially if you have something to offer Gleason in the way of a suspect."

Klinger paused, then added, "So you think this Michael Palermo might have some tie to the Hahn killing?"

"Yes, I do," I said. "Listen, this guy is as smooth as a baby's behind. But not nearly so innocent. I'll fill you in on the details when we meet."

CHAPTER 35

The office of Dr. Hal Watlow, Donald Corrington's personal physician, was on Clark Street in Tarzana, adjacent to the Encino-Tarzana Regional Medical Center, one of the largest hospitals in the San Fernando Valley.

I arrived at the office promptly, for my ten o'clock appointment. However, I had to wait about a half hour until the doctor had a break in his patient schedule.

Watlow was a soft spoken guy in his late 50's. Having been contacted by Mary Chase and asked to cooperate, he was receptive to my questioning him. So, I began.

"I wonder, Dr. Watlow, if you know that Donald Corrington kept the information about his having cancer, from his wife – and from just about everyone else?"

"Yes, I knew that. I didn't agree with his decision, but that's what Donald wanted. And since he was terminal, I wasn't going to deny what he wanted, as long as it didn't affect my medical treatments – or ethics."

"Why do you suppose Corrington wanted it that way? I mean, I would think he'd at least want his wife to know."

"You may have already heard this elsewhere, but the fact is, Donald was a very private person. Charming and outgoing in business, I understand, but not at all willing to share confidences about himself."

"When we found the pancreatic cancer, I urged Donald to tell his wife, if no one else. But he chose not to. And despite my personal feelings, I had to honor his decision. I do understand, though, that his lawyer knew about the cancer. Donald told me he was telling his lawyer. It had to do with the need to work out wills, family trusts, life insurance...things of that nature."

I confirmed, "Goodrich told me all that, too. But he also told me something else. He said he thought Donald was very depressed in the immediate weeks leading up to his suicide. Were you treating him for depression?"

"Not in a clinical sense. That is, I wasn't giving him any antidepressants."

The doctor thought for a moment, and then continued.

"Please understand...Donald certainly wasn't happy. He made me spell out for him exactly what was going to happen over the course of the cancer. So he was grim about the future, but he was not in a classic clinical depression."

"What about toward the end. Was he in a lot of pain? Could that have contributed to his deciding to commit suicide?"

The doctor looked at Corrington's file.

"In the last two weeks, before he committed suicide, Donald was in considerable…and growing… pain. To the extent that it was becoming increasingly difficult for him to hide it. I had him heavily into the pain killers. Still within acceptable medical practice, but definitely at a high dosage level that was needed to control the ever-worsening pain."

The doctor shrugged.

"Of course, I can't draw any definitive conclusion about it – but I think Donald may have ended his life a few months sooner than he had anticipated, because the pain was so bad. And he didn't want to inflict any of the accompanying emotional trauma on his wife and others."

"Sounds like he was one strong individual," I said.

"That he was," Dr. Watlow agreed. "I believe he made a rational decision to take his own life, at a time of his own choosing, deciding it was the best way to handle a terrible situation."

CHAPTER 36

After leaving Dr. Watlow in Tarzana, I headed north on Reseda Boulevard, to Vanowen, and then west on Vanowen to the West Valley Division of LAPD in Reseda. I knew the station house, having served a couple of tours there, at different times in my thirty.

I got to the station a little early for my appointment with Phil Gleason, so I schmoozed with some of the cops that I knew. Near noon, Gleason arrived, and we went into one of the interrogation rooms.

We weren't close friends, but I did know Gleason when I was on the Job, so we spent a few minutes catching up on the who-what-where and when of things. Then Gleason turned on the video, stated the date and the time, identified both of us, and started the formal part of our meeting.

"Looks like the victim died maybe a half hour before you found him," Gleason told me. "So, did you see anything or anyone, when you came into the alley and up to the rear of the store?"

"Nothing," I answered. "No cars. No people. You know, of

course, that most of those places don't open until about ten in the morning."

"Yeah," Gleason answered. And then he asked, "What were you doing back there, so early?" He checked his file. "At the scene, you told me you had an 8:30 meeting with this Benjamin Hahn. What was that about?"

I smiled.

"You won't believe the first part of what I'm going to tell you," I said.

"Try me."

"You know Captain George Klinger?"

"Yes."

"Well, a few days ago, Klinger asked me to investigate a claim his sister was making about her husband being murdered."

I paused for emphasis.

"Even though the Department had already ruled the death a suicide."

Gleason was surprised.

"Why'd he come to you? Why'd he do that?"

"Because he was embarrassed. And because he didn't want to embarrass the Department. Like I said, the husband's death had already been investigated, and ruled a suicide. And now, after the fact, here was the Captain's sister, making this wild-ass claim about murder."

"Klinger told me he had already asked the original investigating officers to re-check the case. They did. Nothing changed, of course. And now, he was caught between that rock and a hard place."

"Meaning...?"

"Meaning, he knew the suicide ruling was right. He didn't doubt it. But he had to do something to convince his sister that she was wrong. Especially since she was threatening to go public with her claim. Klinger figured that would look like hell for the Department. You know...'Captain's sister claims her husband was murdered, even though cops ruled it a suicide'. Real tabloid stuff, right?"

"Not to mention embarrassing Klinger personally," Gleason said.

"Yeah, there is that, too. Look, we both know Klinger pays a lot of attention to the image side of things. But he is a good cop."

"Agreed," Gleason said. "So what was the plan Klinger came up with, for you to carry out?"

"Klinger thought that if I did an independent investigation, and I came to the same conclusion as the LAPD – and he figured I would, for sure – then he and I, together, could convince his sister to drop her claim."

I shrugged.

"At least, that was our plan, and Klinger's hope. He told me that his sister has always –even as a kid – been someone who – if she wants something – she fantasizes about it, even if that 'something' really wasn't there. In this instance, although he couldn't figure out why, Klinger thought his sister had latched on to this belief that her husband had been murdered. And despite proof to the contrary, she had attached herself to this murder theory."

Gleason said, "I looked at the file. Donald Corrington shot himself in the head, in his office, at Corrington Imports, over in Canoga Park, right?"

"Right."

"And it was ruled a suicide, right from the start. No hint of it being a homicide, right?"

"Right. The investigating team is sure of it. Klinger is. And so am I."

I had a favor to ask Gleason.

"Listen, about what I just told you -- the close-up stuff about Klinger and his sister – can you keep it in the background of your investigation on the Hahn homicide?"

"Sure. Can't promise, but I'll try."

"Thanks."

"But I do need to know why you had an appointment with Hahn. Why were you meeting with him?"

"The guy Margaret Corrington is accusing of having killed her husband is one George Palermo. He was a major investor in Corrington Imports, and active in one of the company's divisions, called the Individual Desires division. That division catered to wealthy people who wanted special things imported – like cottages taken apart in Ireland, shipped here and rebuilt, piece by piece."

"Yeah, I've heard of things like that," Gleason said.

I said, "In checking over the records of the Individual Desires division, I got a hunch this Palermo wasn't legit. That he was using the division to import antiques that had been illegally smuggled out of other countries."

"Then he brought them into this country, again illegally, and sold them, for unreported cash, to willing and wealthy citizens for their personal collections."

"Palermo had a rap sheet, too. No convictions. But three or four suspected, along the same lines I just described."

"From the division's records, it looked to me like Palermo was using Hahn's company as the cover, to bring the stuff in, and to sell it. I was going to meet with Hahn, to talk to him about all of this, because I was trying to get a better line on Palermo, since he's the one Margaret Corrington is accusing of killing her husband."

Gleason asked, "Do you think Palermo found out about the meeting? And it worried him enough, so maybe he decided to shut Hahn up? Permanently?"

I laughed, then explained.

"Would have been a hell of a trick for him to do so. Palermo died a couple of months ago. Had a car accident up on Mulholland. Burned to death when his car went off the Drive and down one of the ravines."

Gleason looked at Will, an unbelieving expression on his face.

"Are you telling me, that the guy Klinger's sister is accusing of murdering her husband, was already dead by the time she made the accusation?"

"Yes."

"So, obviously, you don't think there's anything to what she's claiming, do you?"

"There's nothing. Nada."

"So what the hell is she doing? Why is she making the claim?"

"Neither Klinger nor I can figure that one out. And maybe we never will. We just know, she's wrong. And hopefully, tomorrow night, we'll finally convince her of that."

"Well," Gleason began thinking aloud, "if Palermo was already dead when you were going to see Hahn, then there's no motive for homicide there, of course."

It was, I decided, time to bring up the matter of Michael Palermo.

I smiled and then said to Gleason, "Depends on which Palermo we're talking about."

Gleason looked at me, and then he sighed.

"Okay, Will. Stop with the games. What the hell are you saying?"

I turned serious.

"Listen, Phil, I'm just working on hunches now, okay? I'll tell you what I think. What might be *possible*. But I haven't got a fact to back it up."

Gleason nodded.

"Understood."

"In my investigation, I found out there was a *Michael*

Palermo, in addition to George. And that Michael had the brains in the family. Michael invested the capital in Corrington Imports. And then he put his brother, George, into the company to keep an eye on things."

"And from what I understand, George didn't make a move without direction from Michael. So, if George *was* doing this illegal importing, I can't believe Michael didn't know about it. And probably planned it – although he denies everything, of course."

"You've gone to see him about this?" Gleason asked me, an edge to his voice. "You got into the middle of my investigation of Hahn's homicide?"

"Whoa! No way," I assured him. "I saw Michael Palermo *before* I scheduled my meeting with Hahn. Before Hahn was killed."

Gleason relaxed, thought about something, and then spoke.

"So, if Michael Palermo knew you might be figuring out this illegal importing deal, and then Hahn told him about his upcoming meeting with you – maybe Palermo got worried, and decided to kill Hahn off – since he was the only link that might tie him to the illegal imports."

"That's what I'm thinking," I agreed. "Got any other suspects right now?"

Gleason shook his head.

"We're still in the early stages. Still checking all of Hahn's business records. But nothing's turned up, so far."

Gleason made a note in his pad.

"And, we're going to check out this Michael Palermo, of course. Thanks for the tip."

Gleason looked at his notes again.

"Anything else you can tell me?"

I thought, then shook my head.

"No. I'm pretty much wrapped up with my investigation. If I come across anything new, I'll let you know. But I doubt I will."

CHAPTER 37

After my meeting with Gleason, I had almost an hour until I was due to see Carl Makinowsky at Floragenics out in Northridge. Getting there would take about 20 minutes, I figured, so I had about a half hour plus to kill.

Okay, I felt guilty about it, but I decided to stop at a Wendy's and order the double-everything-hold-nothing-back cheeseburger they were pushing this week.

Yeah, Lu and Rose would give me hell, if they knew what I was ordering. But that was the point, wasn't it? They *didn't and wouldn't* know.

So, I enjoyed my juicy artery blocker, even the assorted relishes that dribbled on to my chin during one especially satisfying bite.

A half hour later, I was in Carl Makinowsky's office, trying to persuade him to ease the pressure he was putting on Eugene Catlin. Makinowsky was friendly but firm in rejecting my warning that he was pushing Catlin too hard.

"Hell, Catlin should be grateful I'm even giving him a second chance," Makinowsky said. "I mean, how many industrial spies get that kind of a break?"

"He's not an industrial spy," I said. "He's just a frustrated laboratory nerd who let his penis lead him, and I bet it's the first time he ever cheated on his wife. Come on, Carl, ease up on him."

"Look," Makinowsky said, "I promised Catlin he'd keep his job here, if he cooperated in catching that Fletcher woman. I'm keeping my end of the bargain, and he's got to keep his."

I answered, "Like I told you, Detective Wilson is worried that Catlin might crack, if he has to take any further part in the investigation, by meeting and sleeping with Maria Fletcher."

"But without Catlin doing what he has to do, nothing is going to be accomplished."

"So maybe," I suggested, "this has to be one of those times when nothing is accomplished, even if the bad guy gets away."

"Sorry, but I don't operate that way," Makinowsky shot back. "People like Maria Fletcher have got to be stopped. And I need Catlin for that."

I could see that nothing was going to change Makinowsky's mind. But maybe I could get him to make things a bit easier for Catlin?

I said to him, "At least do me one favor."

"What's that?"

"Make sure, just about every day, to call Catlin in, and massage him a bit. Make him feel better."

"Come on, Will," Makinowsky said, clearly annoyed, "I'm not

a baby sitter."

"In this instance," I countered, "you're probably a lot closer to being one than you think. From what Detective Wilson tells me, Catlin needs some heavy duty support. I recommend you provide it."

Makinowsky thought about it.

"Okay. Whatever it takes. I'll make it a point to see the guy every day, for some stroking. Satisfied?"

It was the best I could hope for. "Satisfied," I told him.

I left Makinowsky and walked out to the company parking lot. As I was about to get into my car, I spotted Catlin driving in. I waved a friendly greeting at him, but when he drove by me, all I got was a glare.

He looks terrible, I thought. Makinowsky better damn well give him that daily stroking.

CHAPTER 38

I had one more meeting to squeeze in, before I figured my investigation was complete. It was with Irving Balter, the CPA – certified public accountant – for Corrington Imports.

Rose had set the meeting up for me, after Elliott Goodrich – Corrington's lawyer – had suggested it. This was when I started asking Goodrich about the finances at Corrington.

Balter's office was in Sherman Oaks, in one of the hi-rises at the intersection of Ventura and Sepulveda boulevards.

Balter turned out to be a friendly type. He came out to greet me in the reception room of his office, no suit jacket, his tie pulled loose, and a smile.

"I'm Irving Balter. Come on in," he said, turning and leading me into his large office, which seemed a lot smaller than it was, thanks to the stacks of file folders piled almost everywhere."

Balter smiled as he noticed me looking around the room.

"An accountant's life, Mr. Jonas, is made up of files, files and more files. Believe it or not, though, there is a system to this seemingly unorganized mess."

"For your sake, I sure hope so," I said.

Balter laughed, as he sat down behind his desk. I sat down in a chair that was in front of the desk.

"What can I do for you?" Balter asked. "I've spoken to Elliott Goodrich and Mary Chase, and they both said I should cooperate as much as I can with you. So, fire away, with your questions."

"Thanks. Getting right to it, I understand that Corrington Imports was having some financial problems when Donald Corrington died. Is that so?"

"Was having problems, and continues to have them now," Balter answered. "The fact of the matter is, that Corrington Imports, while certainly not insolvent, is a company in trouble."

"Can you be more specific," I asked.

"Profits are down. Cash flow is a problem. And the banks are concerned about the stated value of the company's inventory, because the inventory is the collateral for any bank loans."

"Added to these factors, Donald's personal finances were in terrible shape because he kept pouring his own money into the business."

I thought about the large house in Calabasas, where Margaret Corrington was living.

"Where does this leave Margaret Corrington?" I asked.

"Not in a very enviable position," Balter answered. "A lot depends on how much the company ends up being worth, either if another company acquires Corrington. Or if we liquidate."

"How is she going to come out of all this? In what kind of

financial shape?"

"Not very well," Balter said. "Oh, she's not going to starve. But things will be a lot tighter than they've been up to now."

"How long did you know Donald Corrington?" I asked Balter.

"For almost 16 years. That's how long we've represented Corrington Imports."

"Did you sense that Donald Corrington might be in a depressed state – in the weeks before he died?"

Balter thought for a while about my question.

"I don't think I can answer that," he said. "You see, Donald was a very private person. Hard to tell what he was thinking. Or how he was feeling. Could he have been depressed? Well, there certainly was enough going on in the business to depress anyone. But even if he was, he never let on about it to me. That was his style. A very private person."

CHAPTER 39

"My sister doesn't want to have anything more to do with you. She wants you off the case," Captain Klinger told me, later that day, when we met, after my appointment with the CPA, Irving Balter.

We were in the cocktail lounge off the lobby of the Marriott Hotel in Woodland Hills. Klinger was working on a Jack Daniels and water. I was nursing my usual club soda.

Thinking back to my telephone conversation with Margaret Corrington the night before last, I wasn't surprised.

"I knew she was pissed at me," I said.

"Pissed is putting it mildly. Margaret called you every name in the book. Some of the kinder ones were, 'incompetent, couldn't investigate a dog's death, he's lost it' – you get the idea."

"What do you think?" I asked the Captain.

"I think my sister is crazy. The whole thing's crazy. And the sooner I get rid of it, the happier I'll be. Anyway, you told me you've finished your investigation, so Margaret wanting you off the case doesn't affect anything at this point, now does it?"

"No, it doesn't."

Klinger continued. "The only thing I see different, is that instead of the two of us meeting with her tomorrow night, I'll handle it myself. I just need all the facts from you."

I took out my note pad, and began.

"Captain, I do not know why your sister keeps insisting her husband was a homicide victim. In my book, she's absolutely wrong. Everything points to what the Department originally ruled. Death by suicide. Donald Corrington took his own life."

"I never had any doubts," Klinger said.

Now, I began listing the key points of my investigation.

"First, and as you already know, Corrington had an advanced case of pancreatic cancer. I met with his physician, Dr. Watlow, who told me that Donald knew the cancer was terminal."

"For a lot of people, that in itself might be enough to commit suicide. Watlow feels Donald was one of those people. That he decided the suffering through to the end, and having those around him also suffer, wasn't the way to go. Better to end it on his own terms."

"Second, I met with Corrington's lawyer, Elliott Goodrich, and with his accountant, Irving Balter. They both told me Corrington Imports was having severe financial problems."

"Profits were down, and the banks were questioning the worth of the company's inventory that served as collateral for loans."

Klinger said, "Wouldn't be the first time a business man decided to end it, when his company was going down the tubes."

"Right," I agreed, and then continued.

"Third, and this is more a hunch than a hard fact, but I feel pretty certain about it. Donald Corrington was in a depressed state. Goodrich, who was close to Corrington, agrees with me about this."

"That makes three of us – Dr. Watlow, Elliott Goodrich and me – all in agreement that Donald Corrington was depressed – probably a combination of business troubles and his terminal pancreatic cancer. Doesn't take much to conclude that suicide was his next step."

"Fourth, and switching subjects a bit, I don't see any way to tie George Palermo into this as Donald's killer. Yes, I do believe Palermo was dealing in illegally importing stuff and selling it through the Individual Desires division. But there's nothing I could find to support the idea that he killed Donald Corrington. Again – I repeat -- it was suicide."

Klinger interrupted.

"The last time we met, we…discussed the…possibility that…Margaret may have been involved with Palermo in…killing Donald. Based on what you just said, that's out the window now, right?"

"Absolutely," I assured the Captain.

Klinger nodded, relieved at my assurances about his sister.

Then he asked another question.

"What about those memos Margaret found? The ones where Palermo was demanding his money back, and threatening Donald if he didn't get it?"

"Turns out, that the wrong Palermo was writing those memos."

"The *wrong* Palermo? What do you mean?"

"George Palermo had a brother...Michael. And I've met with him. Michael is the Palermo who counts...meaning he put up the investment capital, and he calls the shots. George was just an on-the-scene order taker and observer for Michael."

"But George wrote those memos to Donald."

"Yes, he did. But Michael didn't know about them, until Margaret showed them to him. Michael Palermo did not want his investment capital back. It looks like George Palermo was just blowing hot air when he wrote to Donald Corrington. Just a dumb brother making like he was a smart businessman."

I closed my note pad and told Klinger, "I'll put all this in a written report for you. It'll be ready for your meeting tomorrow night with Margaret."

Klinger shook his head.

"Not a meeting I'm looking forward to."

I asked, "How are you going to handle it?"

"I'm going to tell Margaret to forget this whole bizarre idea of hers. That her homicide claim is ridiculous. The Department thinks so. I think so. And now, after you've gone over everything, you think so, too."

"And that if she wants to continue to make a fool of herself, by going public with her claim, I can't stop her, but the Department will burn her, hard, with its rebuttal."

Klinger sighed, and then continued.

"I don't know where Margaret is coming from. And I really don't care. But it's got to end."

Klinger sighed again.

"You know, this is like she used to act, when she was a teenager. It had to be her way. When something was going on, what she decided was the way it had to be. What she decided was right. What everyone else decided was wrong. She was a regular pain in the ass."

Klinger was silent for a moment. Then he raised his glass.

"Will, it was good to work with you again. You were a hell of a cop. And you're still first class as an investigator."

I raised my glass of club soda.

"I'll drink to that," I said.

And I did.

CHAPTER 40

Not sure why.

Maybe it was sitting in the cocktail lounge at the Marriott with Klinger.

Or maybe it was my raising that glass of club soda in a toast.

But when I left Klinger, I felt a need to attend an AA meeting.

I didn't get these urges often, so when I did, I paid attention.

I found a meeting in a church, on Topanga, just south of Sherman Way. The meeting was well attended – about thirty people. Several of the attendees took chips for achieving days, weeks or months of sobriety. Others got up and shared their experiences and thoughts.

I didn't say anything. It was good enough for me to just be there. To satisfy my need.

At the end, I stayed on for a few minutes, to be polite, as people came up to greet me, since I was a new attendee. But then I left.

The church parking lot was crowded with cars, but there were no people. Everyone was still inside.

I walked toward my car, pulling out my keys.

There was a loud sound, and at first, I thought it was a car, backfiring on nearby Topanga.

I turned in the direction of the sound, curious to see if I could spot the car.

As I did, I heard the sound again. Then it was immediately followed by another sound, which happened to be the shattering of my car's front windshield.

It finally registered on me.

Someone was shooting at me!

I dropped to the ground, next to my car, thinking about getting inside, to the glove compartment, where I kept my Glock 19 and ammo.

It was quiet, and I wondered if the shooter might be moving in on me, to try again at closer range. No sense waiting. Have to get to my weapon. Now.

Staying low, I circled around the back of my car and up to the passenger side front door. I slipped the key into the lock and opened the door, slowly.

Damn!

The interior light went on.

I slammed the door shut.

What now?

I listened. No sound. No slight scraping of leather on asphalt, to indicate that someone was approaching.

Couldn't be certain of anything, though. Someone might be

getting in closer, maybe wearing sneakers, which would be a lot quieter. And if that were the case, then I was fast becoming an easy target.

I needed to take a chance with that interior light.

I opened the door again. The light went on. I stayed low, reached my hand in, and pushed the button to the glove compartment. The door opened and I grabbed my weapon.

Now, I raised myself up a bit and started to scan the parking lot. Nothing. No sign of anyone moving.

Suddenly, the search became impossible, as the people from the AA meeting starting coming out of the church and into the parking lot.

Couldn't spot anyone now, I realized.

I went back to my car, picked up my car phone and called the West Valley Division.

CHAPTER 41

"So far," Detective Phil Gleason told me, about two hours later, "we haven't found that second slug."

He and I were standing inside the yellow police crime scene tape which cordoned off most of the parking lot.

Other detectives and uniforms from the West Valley Division were fanned out through the lot and the surrounding streets, looking for whatever they could find – possible witnesses, physical evidence.

Captain Klinger, having heard about the shooting on his police scanner, also was there, standing with Will and Gleason, observing.

Back in the church, the AA meeting attendees were being questioned by the police. Although they were inside when the shooting took place, they were being asked if they had seen anything, or anyone suspicious in the vicinity of the parking lot or church, when they first came to the meeting.

"We figure," Gleason went on, "that since it doesn't look like the bullet hit any other car here in the lot, it probably traveled across the street and into the wall of one of the buildings on the other side. I've got uniforms over there, now, checking. We should know something pretty soon."

Gleason looked with concern at Will.

"You okay?"

I nodded.

"I guess so. Only, I'm getting damned tired of being shot at." I was thinking back to my shoot-out a few days ago, with the Shane brothers at the ATM machine in Calabasas.

Gleason had the same thought. He asked, "You think tonight might be the Shane's? Getting back at you?"

"Anything's possible."

"I'll contact Deputy Tony Vargas." Gleason said. "Ask him to check them out. But do you really think they would be stupid enough to do this? I mean, they'd be the first ones you'd think about. Wouldn't they realize that?"

"From what Vargas told me," I said, "no one in that family is a threat to do well on the I.Q. charts."

"Any other candidates?" Gleason asked.

I thought for a moment.

"Remember I talked to you about Michael Palermo? You get to see him yet?"

"No."

"It's a long shot," I said, "But if Palermo's a candidate for the Hahn killing, maybe he can be nominated for this one, too. He knows I've figured out the importing scam. I as much as told him so, when we had our meeting."

"We'll see him tomorrow," Gleason said. "Any other ideas? Any perps from the past? Guys you put away, who've been holding a grudge until they got out? Like now?"

"Can't think of anyone. But I'll check that out."

I had a question for Gleason.

"What about the bullet you dug out of my car seat?"

"A .38 S&W. Standard. I already sent it down to Ballistics. We should know something by about noon tomorrow."

Another detective called Gleason away, leaving Klinger and me alone. We stared at each other. I had a question that I didn't want to ask, although I knew that I had to.

I could see that Klinger was going through the same process.

Finally, I asked it.

"When the case was closed on Donald Corrington's suicide, what happened to the .38 S&W he used?"

Klinger answered, reluctantly.

"It…was returned to Margaret. She promised to get a license for it. And she did. I processed the application for her."

Klinger shook his head several times.

"Damn it, Will. I know Margaret is screwed up about her homicide claim on Donald. And that she's very, very pissed at you. But I can't believe that she'd try and kill you. No matter how pissed off she might be."

"Look. I don't think so, either. But I have to ask."

Klinger nodded. He knew what he had to do, under the circumstances.

Flimsy as the possibility was, weak as her motive might be, the fact that Margaret Corrington was angry with me, and the fact that she had a weapon of the same make and caliber as that used in tonight's shooting, could not be ignored.

"Okay," he said. "I'll turn her weapon over to Ballistics in the morning, to do a comparison with the bullet from your car seat."

CHAPTER 42

"Will you all please calm down?" I said to Lu, Rose and Melanie, near midnight that same evening. I'd just arrived home, after leaving the crime scene at the church.

While still there, I'd told Detective Gleason my concern about the safety of my family. The question being – if someone is shooting at me, is my family safe? Or might that "someone" decide to go after them?

Gleason ordered a patrol officer to pick up Rose and Melanie at Rose's apartment and to bring them to Lu, at our condo. And he said he'd keep that cruiser parked outside our unit, until I got there.

That's when I called Lu, to tell her what was happening. And I asked her to call and explain to Rose and Melanie why a police officer was going to be picking them up very shortly.

Now that I'd arrived home, all three of them wanted answers to the question of what was going on.

"First off," I started, "I'm fine. Not hit by anything. Okay? But there is someone out there, who means to do me harm. We all need to be alert to this fact."

I addressed Rose and Melanie.

"Until we figure things out, you two are staying here. And Lu, you too. No offices tomorrow. And the police are going to keep a black and white outside."

"You mean I don't have to go to school?" Melanie asked.

"Don't look so happy about it," Rose said. "You have your books, so you will study here. Just like you are in school."

"Is all this really necessary, Will?" Lu asked calmly.

"Yes. Just can't take a chance. Until we know what's going on."

"Any idea who shot at you?" she asked. "Do the police know anything?"

"No idea," I said.

CHAPTER 43

The next morning, I had to answer the protests from Lu and Rose.

What were they protesting?

"Why can you go to your office, and I can't go to mine?" Lu asked.

"And me to mine?" Rose pitched in.

I turned to Melanie.

"How about you? You want to go to school? Or stay here today?"

"With Rose checking on me, it's like this *is* school," Melanie answered. "So either place is okay with me."

"One smart young lady, don't you think?" I asked Lu and Rose, as I pointed at Melanie.

"No, Will," Lu protested, "You don't avoid answering by talking about Melanie. Rose and I want answers."

I became serious.

"Look, I am going to be very careful when I leave here. And I'm only going to one place – my office. The door will be locked, and I've got two weapons. In other words, I'll be safe. You two, on the other hand, are definitely going to be safer, staying here, rather than being anywhere else."

They didn't try and argue with my logic, except for a warning from Rose.

"Listen, if you are in the office, you better approve those client invoices that need to go out. I left the file on your desk. And it better be done, whenever I do get back to the office. Or you won't be safe there, no matter how many guns you have."

"You have my word, Rose," I said.

"Your word I don't want. It's your signature, on each invoice, that I want."

I didn't try to answer. From past experience, I already knew I'd eventually lose the discussion. I never win with Rose.

....

A half hour later. I was in my office. Front door locked. My weapon on my desk, primed and ready.

After settling in, I called Sheriff's Deputy Tony Vargas. I knew that Gleason was calling Vargas last night, to check on the possible involvement of the Shane family in the shooting directed at me.

Vargas was ready with the information.

"Like I told Gleason, the shooter was not a Shane."

"All members accounted for?" I asked. "The brothers I had my run-in with? Or any other eligible Shane's?"

"Everyone," Vargas said. "Seems yesterday was the parent's 35th wedding anniversary. Would you believe it? That those scumbags actually observe that shit? I thought decent people celebrated wedding anniversaries, while people like the Shane's only remembered the dates they got out of prison. Anyway, the whole family had a party last night at the Topanga Roadside. Know the place?"

"A dump." I said.

"And that makes it a perfect setting for the Shane family's party," Vargas said.

He continued, "I know the owner. He may run a dump, but he's honest. At least with me. And he told me all the Shane's were there from about seven o'clock on."

"So scratch them," I said. "They're not as dumb as I thought they might be."

"At least, not last night," Vargas agreed. "Got any other suspects?"

"Gleason's working on it. And I'm checking people I put away, who might want to even things. Some long termers might be getting out around now."

After I finished with Vargas, I started going through my files, checking for convicts who might be holding a grudge, and more to the point, be in a position to do something about it.

I also went through the file of invoices that Rose wanted me to, so that she could get them out.

All morning, I'd let the phone calls go through to our answering machine, while I monitored them. None important enough to pick up. They could all wait until tomorrow, while I continued my search for more convicts to add to my list of possible shooters.

Another call started coming in. It was Captain Klinger. I picked up, and as soon as he spoke, I could hear the relief in his voice.

"The bullets don't match, Will. Margaret's .38 is not the weapon used in last night's shooting."

"That's good news, Captain."

"Yes, that's good news," Klinger said. "Of course, Margaret hit the roof when she found out why I wanted her gun. What I was testing it for."

Klinger laughed.

"She is not talking to me right now. Maybe she will again, in five or so years."

"We take our blessings where we can get them."

"I'll remember that," Klinger said. Then he switched subjects. "Any word from Vargas, about the Shane's?"

"They're out of it. All accounted for, at a family anniversary celebration last night."

"And Palermo? Gleason see him?"

"He said he was going to see him today, but I haven't heard anything yet."

After Klinger's call, I finished going through my files, looking for more ex-cons. Ended up with six possibilities. All very doubtful, but I'd give Gleason the list. You never know…

The phone rang again, and as before, I let it ring through to the answering machine. It was Detective Waldo Watson. I picked up.

"Waldo, what's up?"

"I thought you'd like to know that Eugene Catlin is dead. His body was discovered about an hour ago. He was in his car, out at Chatsworth Park South, in Chatsworth, at the west end of Devonshire."

"What happened?"

"Looks like suicide. Pending the coroner's report, of course. The guy put a gun in his mouth."

"Damn!" I said. "Makinowsky pushed him too hard!"

Then I told Wilson, "You know, after you called me, I went and saw Carl. Talked to him. And he promised he would ease off."

"Maybe he did and maybe he didn't," Wilson said. "Catlin was already pretty far gone, emotionally, when I called you. Too far gone, it turns out. Too bad. He was a nice enough guy. But I guess, when someone who's lived all his life in a laboratory, gets the kind of pressure he was under – well – you never can tell what might happen."

A thought started forming in my mind as I tried to recall something that kept eluding me.

"You still there?" Wilson asked, when I was silent.

I asked myself – what was it Wilson said, the last time we talked?

Then, I remembered, and I said to Wilson, "Waldo, when we talked last time, didn't you tell me that Catlin was mad at me? That he blamed me for his problems? Because I found out about his affair with Maria Fletcher?"

"Words to that effect." Wilson confirmed.

Now, I also remembered how Catlin had glared at me, when I waved at him in the parking lot at Floragenics.

So, I thought to myself, it just might be possible, given the guy's state of mind...

I asked Wilson, "Did Catlin shoot himself with an S&W .38?"

"How'd you know that?" Wilson asked, surprised.

"A hunch. Just a hunch," I answered. "Listen, Waldo, tell whoever is handling the investigation in the Northridge Division to get the weapon over to Detective Phil Gleason in West Valley, and to have Ballistics check it against the .38 bullet fired at me last night. I think Catlin might have been the shooter, when I came out of that AA meeting."

After the call with Wilson, I sat at my desk, thought about Catlin, and I gave out a major league sigh.

I felt guilty.

Yeah, I know that, logically, his death wasn't my fault. But I couldn't shake the guilt. Because I was the one who discovered that Catlin was having his affair with Maria Fletcher.

"The dumb, poor bastard," I said aloud.

I pushed aside my file of ex-con suspected shooters. No need for the list now. We had our shooter, I was certain.

Time to go home. And to tell Rose and Melanie to go to theirs.

Then the phone rang again. I let it go through to the answering machine.

"This is Carl Makinowsky, and I would like to talk with Will Jonas."

Makinowsky sounded tired, tense.

I picked up.

"Hello, Carl."

"Oh, you're there."

"On my way out, actually."

Makinowsky said, "Eugene Catlin...is dead. He...he shot himself."

I was in no mood to play babysitter.

"Carl, I told you, that you were pushing him too hard."

"I...I know."

I didn't say anything. I just wanted to go home.

"I...I'd like to meet with you," Makinowsky said.

"Not tonight, Carl."

"Then tomorrow morning. First thing. At 9:30?"

"At 9:30," I confirmed.

CHAPTER 44

The next morning, before my 9:30 meeting with Carl Makinowsky, I called Phil Gleason at West Valley Division.

"You were right," Gleason answered my question. "Ballistics found a match between Eugene Catlin's weapon and the .38 caliber bullet from your car seat. Evidently, Catlin was the person who shot at you, in the parking lot."

Although I had pretty much suspected this last night, it still was good to get confirmation. No need anymore, to be looking over my shoulder for an unknown shooter.

I asked Gleason another question.

"Did you meet with Michael Palermo? And how did that go?"

"Saw him yesterday afternoon. And you were right about him. He's smooth as a baby's ass."

"Anything there?"

"Could be. We're checking out his alibi for his whereabouts the morning of Hahn's killing. Palermo says he was at home, exercising. He lives alone, so there's not much to confirm. And we're starting to question him about the importing activities at

Hahn and Corrington. We'll just have to see what develops."

It was a few minutes after 9:30 when I turned into the Floragenics parking lot in Northridge, and steered my car into a reserved-for-visitors space.

When I got out of the car and walked toward the lobby entrance, I passed a section of spaces reserved for company executives. Included was a space –empty -- with Eugene Catlin's name painted on the curb. I couldn't help wondering how many Floragenics executives were already maneuvering to get that space.

When I came in to Makinowsky's office, it looked to me like the man had not slept well the night before.

"I feel like shit" Makinowsky said. "I never expected anything like this to happen."

He looked at me, and I got the feeling that he wanted some comforting words from me – something like, "It's okay, Carl. Not your fault."

But it *was* his fault. And I wasn't going to let him off the hook so easily.

"If you want some sort of dispensation, Carl, You're not going to get it from me. I warned you to ease up on Catlin. Remember?"

Carl looked at me. For a second, I thought we were going to get into a shouting match. But then, he took a deep breath.

"I've decided to take care of Catlin's family."

"Now that's a good idea, Carl."

"Yeah. Catlin didn't have much of an estate built up yet. He would have been a rich man, when we went public in a couple of years, what with his stock options."

Makinowsky looked at a file on his desk.

"Right now, his wife and three children aren't left with much. Even his life insurance isn't worth diddly, since he committed suicide."

"I'm putting Mrs. Catlin on staff. She won't have to work here, just do a few things at home. She'll get a good salary, all the medical and insurance benefits, and enough stock options so that whenever we do go public, she'll never have to worry, financially."

I was impressed. And I said so.

"That's terrific, Carl. *You're* being terrific."

Makinowsky gave a small smile.

"Thanks for saying so," he told me. "I...I needed to hear something like that."

After some more, "feel good" small talk, I left Carl. On the way back to my car, I laughed to myself.

Hey, I thought, I should have been a psychologist. Look how I made Carl feel. If being a private investigator ever bores me...

CHAPTER 45

After leaving Floragenics, I was driving south on Canoga Avenue toward my office in Woodland Hills, when I was hit by a "mind trick" feeling.

What's a mind trick feeling?

It's something that happens to me once in a while, when I sense that my subconscious is trying to break through. Trying to give me information that will help solve some problem connected with an investigation I'm working.

When I get one of these mind trick feelings, I do two things.

First, I think about what I've been doing the last few days, who I've been talking to, what we were discussing, stuff like that.

If no productive information comes up, then I do the second thing.

I drop the whole exercise, knowing from experience that it will be useless to *actively* look for the information. In time, whatever is trying to get through will work its way to the conscious part of my mind. Either in a few days, or sometimes, in a few hours.

In keeping with the first part of the exercise, I thought back to the people I'd met with.

They included Margaret Corrington, Captain Klinger, George Palermo, Eugene Catlin, Elliott Goodrich, Hal Watlow, Irving Balter, detectives Phil Gleason and Waldo Wilson, Mary Chase, Jim Karp. And of course, this morning, Carl Makinowsky.

I reviewed my meetings with each of them. Nothing useful. No light bulbs flashing.

So I went to the second part of my routine when faced with a mind tricks situation. I backed off from the whole exercise, for the time being.

By now, I was in my office, and I called Phil Gleason at West Valley. I had a favor to ask.

After I connected with Gleason, we spent a couple of minutes going over the ballistics report, tying Catlin to the shooting at the AA meeting. Then, I started to talk about the real reason I'd called him.

"Listen, Phil, now that you've established that Catlin was the shooter..."

"Actually," Gleason interrupted, "we can't establish that. Yes, it's Catlin's gun. But there is no way, specifically, to put Catlin in that church parking lot, shooting at you. Obviously, since he's dead, we can't grind him on it. And we can't find any witness, or any other evidence, that places him there. We can only conclude that everything *points* to his being in the parking lot and shooting at you."

Gleason didn't realize it, but being the cautious cop that he was, he'd just given me an opening for the favor I wanted to ask.

I said, "Phil, so you're never going to be able to specifically put Catlin in that parking lot, right?"

"Right. Not going to happen. I just wanted to be clear on the record with you."

"And I appreciate it. Because it ties in with a favor that I want to ask."

"What's that?"

"Can you bury your report on Catlin? Close the case and forget it? The guy's dead. You can't prosecute him. So can you close the file, and keep this one out of the media?"

"What's up, Will?" Gleason asked. "What's going on here?"

"Something pretty simple. But important. I'm trying to protect Catlin's wife and three young kids from having to suffer more than what they are going through, already. Look, his wife knows that her husband cheated on her. She knows he tried to shoot me. She is painfully aware that he left her with no means of support. And that he committed suicide."

"That's one hell of a lot for her to handle. And for her kids to handle, too, as they are growing up."

"So, can we possibly avoid having all of this splashed as 'Breaking News' on television? And in the Times and Daily News, as well?"

"Can you give her a break, by closing the file now?"

"That's all I'm asking."

Gleason was silent. I didn't say anything, figuring he was

deciding what he wanted to do. Finally, he spoke.

"Hey, Will – when you were on the Job, you didn't have a reputation as a 'soft cop.'"

"Well, if this makes me soft, I can live with the label. I'm just trying to help Catlin's wife and kids. That's all I'm doing."

Another long pause, until Gleason spoke again.

"Okay, pending my captain's approval – and I don't think that will be a problem – we can close this one, quietly."

"Filed and forgotten?" I asked.

"Filed and forgotten," Gleason confirmed.

I hung up. The agreement I'd just reached with Gleason eased a bit of the guilt I was feeling about Catlin's suicide. I was grateful for that.

I thought about Catlin. Although the man had tried to kill me, I didn't feel any anger toward him.

Only sadness, that a nice man, someone who had played by the rules most of his life, had gone so far astray, so quickly, and had paid such a terrible price for it.

Well, I thought, at least Makinowsky is being decent about things. More than decent. By providing for Catlin's family, financially. Otherwise, they would have next to nothing.

Then, suddenly, there it was again!

The mind trick!

Chipping away at my brain. Something trying to get through. Some bit of information.

What the hell could it be?

Again, I reviewed the events of the past few days, looking for some connection that would draw the information to the surface.

Nothing.

Drop it, I advised myself. It'll come.

Rose came into my office, with a thick file.

"I already did the client invoices," I protested.

"Yes," Rose said, "but these are the checks we need to pay our vendors – gas, electric, telephone, things like that."

"And you can't handle these?" I asked her. "What do I pay you for?"

"Not to forge your name on checks," Rose said. "You need to sign these."

She put the file on my desk, and then lectured me.

"Will, I know you don't like the paperwork in running a business. But you need to do this. You need to keep up, about how the company is doing. It is important."

"You're right," I admitted.

And so I sat down and spent the next hour going through the paperwork, signing the checks, and in the process, getting a good picture on how the Agency was doing.

Pretty well, thank you.

To the point where I needed to ask Charlie Black – again – when he planned to retire from the LAPD, and join me. We had enough business, to make it financially okay for both of us.

I closed the vendor payment file and called Rose on the intercom to pick it up.

Now, there was only one file folder on my desk. It contained the paperwork that Mary Chase had put together for me on Corrington Imports, the first time I went there.

I wondered if Mary might want any of the material back, so I opened the file and began checking. There was a Corrington Imports organization chart, the company brochure, Donald Corrington's personnel file, a life insurance policy on Corrington, some product literature, and the latest quarterly profit and loss statement.

Nothing that Mary would need back, I decided. I was sure she had copies of all of the items in the folder.

I started to close the file, when the mind trick hit me again.

And this time, it was stronger. Very strong. Close to the surface.

I sensed it was connected to something I'd just seen in the Corrington file.

I sat quietly for a moment. I thought to myself, I probably should, as usual, just turn my mind away, and wait for whatever is going to surface.

But the information was almost there! I could feel it. I knew it.

I started going through all of the material in the file, top to bottom.

And then I found it!

The information stared back at me.

The mind trick was completed.

I read the information again. Checked the dates.

Next, I made a quick call to Elliott Goodrich – Donald Corrington's lawyer – and asked him a question.

And then I called Captain Klinger.

When he answered, I said, "We need to meet at Margaret's house. Tonight."

"Why?"

"Because I know why your sister's been claiming her husband was murdered."

CHAPTER 46

"Neither one of you is welcome here. I don't know why you came, and I'd like you to leave."

Margaret Corrington stared at Captain Klinger and me, as she blocked the entrance to her home.

"Margaret," Klinger said, his voice taking on a hard edged, official tone, "We have to talk. And damn it, sister or not, if you would rather do this at the station, that's the way it will be."

Margaret hesitated, then let us in. She walked toward the living room, not looking back, seemingly not caring if we followed.

In the living room, she sat down in one of the wingback chairs flanking the sofa. She looked at her brother, then at me, but she said nothing.

I broke the silence.

"Margaret, I know why you've been claiming your husband was a homicide victim. But you might as well give it up, because it's not going to work."

Margaret sat, rigid, not moving, staring back at me, saying

nothing.

But Klinger was just the opposite. Impatient to know more.

"What are you talking about, Will?" he asked.

I answered, "Captain, both of us, ever since this investigation began, could not understand how Margaret came up with this out-of-left-field claim that Donald was murdered, rather than his death being a suicide. We couldn't figure out what the dickens gave her the reason – the motive – for making such a claim. You agree?"

"Yes," Klinger answered.

"Well, guess what? Margaret *did* have a motive. Hell – she had three million motives."

"Three million...motives? What's that supposed to mean?" Klinger asked.

"Three million –dollars that is – is the payout amount of the life insurance policy Donald Corrington had on himself. Of course, as Elliott Goodrich told Margaret, when she asked him about it, there was no way to collect. Because Donald had committed suicide within two years of when the policy first was issued. And the policy does not pay off, in a suicide situation before the two-year mark."

I looked at Margaret.

"Margaret, hope you're not going to deny what I've just said. I checked with Elliott and he told me you were very insistent when talking to him – trying to figure out a way for that insurance policy to pay off."

Margaret continued to be silent, but her body was much tenser now, giving the lie to her calm exterior.

"So," I continued, "The question facing Margaret was, what could be done, in order to get that payoff? And here is where Margaret got really clever, thanks to the timely death of...would you believe it...George Palermo."

"Her inspiration? Why not claim that George Palermo had killed her husband? After all, neither Donald nor George could dispute that claim. They were both dead."

"Good idea. But it did have one major problem. Motive. Why would George Palermo even *want* to kill Donald Corrington?"

I looked over at Margaret. What I was saying was beginning to have an effect on her. Her body language gave her away. There was just a bit more of a sag to it, a sort of drawing inward.

I continued.

"Well, Margaret is one clever person. We know that. So it shouldn't surprise us to learn that she found a way to establish a motive for George killing Donald."

"And that was...?" Klinger asked impatiently.

"Enter that exchange of supposed memos between George and Donald, in which Palermo demanded the return of his money, and Donald told him the company could not afford to pay him back. Memos that grew increasingly angry in tone, leading up to the last one from Palermo, which was clearly threatening."

"You just said – 'supposed memos,'" Klinger pointed out. "Are you saying those memos are forgeries?"

"Yes, I am. As I've told you before, I met with Michael

Palermo, and by all accounts, he had all the brains between the two brothers. He put up the investment capital to buy into Corrington. He told me that, until Margaret showed him those memos, he had not seen them. And he was sure George would never write memos like those. It was the sort of negotiating that only he would do, on behalf of their investment company."

Klinger posed another question for Will.

"But why wait until after the official police investigation had been completed and the suicide ruling was handed down, to then claim it was a homicide? Wouldn't it have been easier to make this claim right from the start?"

"Of course," I agreed, "but not everything can be manipulated. And no matter how nimble Margaret's mind is, she couldn't get around certain timing factors."

"You see, George Palermo didn't die until *after* the LAPD ruled Donald Corrington's the death a suicide and closed the case. About three days after, in fact."

"If you go back and check your memory, Captain, I bet that's just about the time Margaret came to you with her homicide claim. I figure – that when George took his plunge down that ravine on Mulholland, Margaret saw the possibilities for claiming that he killed Donald. All she needed was some physical proof. Enter the memos. Easy enough to put together."

I looked at Margaret. She was definitely on the downside in the battle to keep her composure. But she made an effort.

"Why would I do such a foolish thing?" she said defiantly.

"After all, I'm already rich, without that insurance money. I've inherited Corrington Imports."

"What you've inherited is a company in trouble, according to both the accountant and the lawyer for the company," I said. "Even if the company is sold or liquidated, the proceeds will be thin. Not near enough, I bet, to even keep you in this house."

There was a long silence which was finally broken by Klinger. His tone was so heated, his manner so tightly wound, that Will thought Klinger might physically assault his sister.

"Margaret," Klinger began, "you are beyond me. I cannot figure you out. To even think about something like this! It is beyond my comprehension. Beyond my understanding. And you know what? I don't even want to try."

"George..." Margaret began.

"Don't say a word!" Klinger shouted at his sister. "Not one goddamn word!"

Again, silence, until Klinger continued.

"I could throw the book at you," he warned. "Intent to defraud. Forgery of evidence. And a lot more if I put my mind to it."

Margaret's last vestige of control disappeared. She sagged in her chair and began to cry.

Klinger stared at his sister. He didn't say anything. Torn between his anger and his family ties, he just kept looking at Margaret.

I decided to leave. This painful scene between family

members was not something to be witnessed by an outsider, I decided.

I waited in front of the house for Klinger. After a few minutes, he came out. Calmer now. More in control. I spoke to him.

"I've been thinking about it, Captain, and you don't have to press any charges, you know. She never did make an actual claim to the insurance company. And what the hell, even though those memos were forgeries, they weren't used in any new police investigation of Donald's death. So, technically, you could say there's no possibility of any charge of tampering with the evidence."

Klinger managed a slight smile.

"You should have been a lawyer, Will. That's the most hair-splitting summation possible of this situation."

I knew how uncomfortable Klinger was, with what his sister had done. Now, this by-the-book police captain was troubled by allowing such behavior to go unpunished. But I felt no purpose would be served by bringing charges against Margaret Corrington, and I tried to convince the Captain of this.

"Look, Captain, I know how you feel. You want to do something. But nothing's going to be accomplished if you do try and bring charges against your sister. For sure, you'll be publicly embarrassed. And so will the Department. And with it all, Margaret will still probably get off with only a slap on the wrist. If even that."

Klinger took his time answering, and when he did, he was resigned.

"You're right, of course. I'll…have to live with it. With doing nothing. But…"

Klinger looked at me, and nodded slightly. Then he lowered his head, and looking at the ground, he walked slowly toward his car.

I followed, keeping some distance between us. There wasn't anything more I could say to the man.

Want To Read Another Will Jonas Mystery?

We have attached an excerpt from MANIFESTO/YOU
REMEMBER – YOU DIE.   The book is available as an e-book on
Kindle and as a soft cover printed book on Amazon and other
outlets.

....

PROLOG…1973

They're dead," he said.   "They killed them."

Sadness and anger were intermingled in his voice.

"My three sons.   My wife.

"What can I do?

"What can I do now?   For our family?"

THE YEAR….2002

CHAPTER ONE

Until seven years ago, I was a homicide detective with the Los
Angeles Police Department.   Then, after my thirty on the Job, I
retired and opened my agency, Will Jonas Investigations.

That's thirty-seven years of dealing with this thing called –
"Crime" – and the people who generate it.   Plenty of odd cases in
that mix.   And now, as I drove on Winnetka, toward the Northridge
LAPD Station on Devonshire in the San Fernando Valley, it

looked like I was about to get involved in another odd one.

Someone had come to the Station and predicted the upcoming death – to be more precise – the murder –of a high level public official. Possibly one of the 15 members of the Los Angeles City Council, he claimed. Although he thought the victim might not be on the Council – and instead, be a career civil servant, or even a California state elected official or bureaucrat.

Now, whatever you think about these officials, when someone says one of them is going to be killed – you have to pay attention, right? You have to get involved. And that's what I was about to do, after getting a phone call from Charlie Black, my former partner in Homicide and still with the LAPD.

Charlie said that Captain Klinger, head of the Northridge Station, wanted to talk to me about the person who was making the prediction.

A word about Captain Klinger.

When I was still on the Job, Klinger and I did not get along. The Captain was a by-the-book operator. I am not.

Charlie and I, as a team, also were not. Our view was, what will it take to get this obviously guilty slob into the prison system for a long time? And if a few rules got bent along the way…

Can you see the conflict here?

I arrived at the Station, parked in back, walked around to the front entrance, and went in. Charlie was waiting for me.

When we were partners, Charlie always played the "good cop," while I was the "bad" one. Easy enough to see why. Charlie was 5 feet 9 inches, and weighed a well-rounded – and I do mean, well-rounded – 195 pounds.

I'm six feet four inches, weigh 210, and at age 58, I'm still in pretty good shape.

What Charlie lacks in buff, though, he makes up in brains. One of the smartest people I know.

"Ready for this one?" Charlie greeted me.

"Who's going to die?"

"That's for you to find out."

Charlie nodded toward the back of the station.

"Come on. Klinger's waiting for us."

I followed Charlie to the double doors of a small conference room. I knew the room. We used to hold press conferences in it.

Klinger was waiting, sitting at the head of the table. He stood, and we shook hands.

"Will," Klinger said, "Thank you for coming in, on such short notice."

His voice was friendly, no sign of the usual tension he and I used to feel toward each other. So I played it the same way.

ABOUT THE AUTHOR

After careers as a broadcast journalist and then a public relations counselor, Saul Warshaw, at age 86, is now happily enjoying his third career as a mystery writer. Five of his novels have been published. Each features Will Jonas, a private investigator and former homicide detective with the Los Angeles Police Department. Saul and his wife, both native New Yorkers, are longtime residents of Los Angeles. If you would like to write Saul, please do so at:

Saul1warshaw@gmail.com

www.ingramcontent.com/pod-product-compliance
Lightning Source LLC
Chambersburg PA
CBHW030133060726

47499CB00014B/142